Sam's

Elegy: *n.* a song of mourning, a p
ous, pensive or reflective mood. *example*: Gray's *Elegy Written in a Country Churchyard.*
Sam: *m.* proper name, usually dim. Samuel: not uncommon among private detectives.

As he lingers in a Sussex country churchyard before climbing the tower to unblock a water spout, odd job man Sam Bevan has no idea he will soon be sent flying earthwards.

Is it an accident, or a failed murder attempt? And why is Sam suddenly being offered some very odd jobs?

Sam's Elegy introduces the not-so-sleepy village of Miston, where a symbolic skull, wild jealousies, threatening mail, an apparent suicide and an almost certain murder interrupt Sam's 'pensive and reflective' rural life.

At the heart of *Sam's Elegy* lies a crime darker perhaps than murder itself. But the tale twists along with much humour, as Sam copes with the vicar's beautiful, unpredictable wife Dora, with young Josie who cheerfully leads him into dangers galore, with Dr Janine Quibbley who might be too clever for her own safety, and with the manipulations of Francis Wyatt, a curiously laid-back policeman. Also on hand, to help or to hinder, is Sam's dog, Eddie.

TERRY JAMES

Sam's Elegy

Elegy: *n.* a song of mourning; a poem of serious, pensive or reflective mood. *example*: Gray's *Elegy Written in a Country Churchyard.*

Sam: *m.* proper name, usually dim. Samuel: not uncommon among private detectives.

THE CRIME CLUB
An Imprint of HarperCollins *Publishers*

First published in Great Britain in 1993
by The Crime Club, an imprint of
HarperCollins Publishers, 77–85 Fulham Palace Road,
Hammersmith, London W6 8JB

9 8 7 6 5 4 3 2 1

A catalogue record for this book is
available from the British Library

ISBN 0 00 232440 7

Photoset in Linotron Baskerville by
Rowland Phototypesetting Ltd
Bury St Edmunds, Suffolk
Printed and bound in Great Britain by
HarperCollins Book Manufacturing, Glasgow

To Jennie

CHAPTER 1

High Views and Low Intentions

Stained glass windows, seen from the outside of a church, can be puzzling. Patterns of darkness, veined with lead. No pictures. No story. Trying to imagine the view from within is as fanciful as trying to guess what goes on inside an unfamiliar house.

The practical answer is to go into the church. Some are still left unlocked. Gaining entry to a house belonging to strangers is not so simple. If you aren't a burglar an invitation is required, and even then it's best to be wary. You might find yourself straying further than expected into those strangers' lives. What started as a mild curiosity might lead to trouble.

As an odd job man I've had access to houses familiar and unfamiliar. I've listened to tales of woe and confusion from many an inmate, but I would always draw the line when more than a surface involvement was on offer.

Recently it turned out that this careful detachment of mine was not built to last.

Late on a sunny mid-May morning I was waiting outside St Olaf's, our village church. The waterspout which jutted from the north-west corner of the bell tower was blocked up, probably with dead leaves from last autumn. After a series of recent downpours, rain had gathered deep enough inside the parapet to seep through the lead roofing. This was discovered early on a Sunday when bellringers set to work and received an impromptu shower—a fate which in turn received the blessing of those villagers who preferred a peaceful lie-in to Holy Communion.

My job was to clear the blockage because the vicar wasn't up to it. Not that he was old and doddery. The Reverend

('Call-me-Steve') Philpot, was a tall, super-fit thirty-two-year-old who turned out with great effect for the local football, cricket, and tennis teams. My world of sport was restricted to an occasional—generally boozy—game of darts, but unlike 'Call-me-Steve', I didn't suffer from vertigo. Apparently there had been times when he went dizzy just getting up into a pulpit. That's some occupational hazard! It was Mrs ('Call-me-Dora') Philpot who told me this, while I was up a rickety stepladder papering and painting their bedroom ceiling. Even though her name seemed a little old-fashioned, I found it easier to call her Dora than to call him Steve. I also wished I could call her—(as a random example)—*my Darling*.

I wouldn't have missed it for the world, but decorating in the vicarage had been both backbreaking and heartbreaking. Quite often, though the marital bed was covered in a dustsheet, lovely Dora would lie on it and chatter away to me. Once she even closed her eyes and drifted off into a brief snooze. This gave me precious moments in which to gaze down at her soft brown curls, her rosebud lips, her ever-so-slightly plump cheeks. On that occasion she was wearing a cotton jogging suit, the top of which was snowy white with two black stripes which curved beguilingly down from her shoulders. The sight was so hypnotic I nearly fell off my ladder. For safety's sake I forced myself back to the non-drip emulsion.

It was on a Tuesday some weeks later, waiting for Dora's husband, that I diverted myself from unsettling memories by staring at the exterior gloom of the stained glass windows, trying to recall what they represented. This wasn't easy, since I had been inside the church on very few occasions. I was about to give up and take a look inside when the Revd himself appeared, jogging through the churchyard in tennis kit. He mopped his brow with a wristband, saying: 'Sorry I'm late, Sam, but Dora refused to let me beat her in straight sets.'

I wished he hadn't said her name.

My obsession with the vicar's wife was, of course, 'terribly bad form', but I couldn't help it. Dora was not only a delight to my eyes. Even when she was talking about herself she made me feel that I was the centre of her warm attention, that it was only my presence which could have triggered what she had to say. Also, she was a very fine cook. Cakes, biscuits, pies both sweet and savoury; such were the luxuries I'd received when working for her and which I was missing since I'd finished at the vicarage.

'Sam? Are you all right?'

'Eh? Oh. Sorry, Vicar.'

'You seemed to go into a daze. If you've got cold feet, I of all people wouldn't blame you.'

I put on a feeble smile and said, 'I think I'm still half asleep. I'll be all right once I'm up top. There should be a cool breeze.'

There was no evidence for this. The day was getting warmer by the minute, and not even the tallest trees were showing movement in their upper branches. I was simply throwing out the sort of daft remark one makes to the husband of a woman one is crazy about.

Fortunately the vicar's mind was firmly on the task I was helping him avoid. He gave me a comradely slap on the shoulder, saying, 'Good chap! I'll unlock the tower for you.' And into the church he jogged, a man who would never walk if he could run. I followed at a shambling pace, pausing inside to grab a quick reminder of the stained glass. Mostly I saw respectful but dull representations of Gospel scenes, but there was one striking side window in memory of a militaristic bishop of the early fourteenth century. Would he nowadays have stuck to tennis, football and so on? With this flippant thought, I progressed to the rear of the nave and found my employer of the day wrestling with a large, rusty key.

'Careful, or you'll snap it.'

'The damned thing's always stiff, however much I oil the works. I would leave it unlocked, but there's a risk of children climbing the tower and falling.'

He moved aside, and I had a try. After several easings to and fro the lock slipped fully open.

'Is that the only key?' I asked.

'Yes. It's ancient. I tried to get a duplicate made, but the ironmonger laughed at me. Made some crack about their firm not being *that* old and established!'

'You ought to fit a new lock.'

He looked shocked. 'This one's a piece of village history.'

'If the key snaps, you'll have to break down the old door itself. What price tradition then?'

He stroked his baby-smooth chin, pretending to weigh the options, but it was obvious he wouldn't budge. With a shrug, I opened the tower door and went in, muttering that I would file the bolt down later, to make the old lock easier. He relaxed for a moment and followed me. 'That would be grand,' he said, flashing a rare non-professional smile.

The inside of the bell tower was new and interesting to me. I had a good gaze up and around while receiving instructions on how to reach the roof. The structure was fitted out with a series of three lofts, each attainable by a built-in ladder from the floor below. The first two lofts had a sizeable section cut away for the bell ropes to go though. These holes were fenced off by, as far as I could see, not very sturdy guard rails. At least the floor of the uppermost loft had a metal grid over its centre section, allowing again for the ropes to pass through, but also for anyone tending the bells not to have to lean across a high-level void.

The vicar ended up by saying, 'I hope I'm giving you the right information, Sam. I have it all on the word of Mr Ainsly.' This Mr Ainsly was the seventy-nine-year-old, very part-time Caretaker. With a sigh, the Revd added, 'I look after three parish churches, and I've never seen the view from the top of any of them.'

'Ah, but you can put your mind to much higher things!'

It wasn't much of a joke, and the Revd, in a daze of his own, didn't seem to hear it. I left him to his reverie and went to fetch a few odds and ends from my van. This coincided with the return of the divine Mrs Philpot. One of her tennis-playing friends had given her a lift to the vicarage, which was—slightly confusingly—next-door-but-one to the church. Exactly next-door was a new bungalow, built on what used to be the orchard section of the vicarage garden. The occupant was something to do with the nearby university.

As her friend's car drove off, Dora spotted me. I was standing, gawping like an idiot, with a plastic rubbish bag in one hand and a shovel and long-handled brush in the other. She gave a wave and headed my way.

'All ready for the big climb, Sam?'

'Yes. Just came to fetch my parachute,' I said, raising the rubbish bag.

A faint, nervous smile flashed across her face as she put a hand lightly on my arm. 'Please don't take any risks. I'd hate you to be hurt.'

She might have been saying this in a spirit of neighbourly politeness, but her unblinking grey-green eyes stared so beseechingly into mine that I was tempted to tell her there and then that I loved her. Instead, I put on a mature and sensible voice and said, 'I'll be very careful. Don't worry.'

'You'd better be.' She dropped her hand away, letting the tips of her fingers stroke my forearm in the process. As if it was an afterthought, she added, 'Oh, and if Steve tries to be "brave" and follow you up part of the way, tell him not to be idiotic.'

'OK, but will he listen?'

'If you're forceful enough. I'll be along soon to keep an eye on him. You can tell him that!' Looking a lot more at ease, she wished me luck and walked towards the vicarage.

Back in the church, I went straight to the bell tower, but the Revd was nowhere to be seen. In a moment of panic I thought he might have already tried the climb himself. Dropping my bag, brush and shovel at the base level, I rushed up and around each loft in turn, until I reached the top. Not a vertiginous vicar in sight! After a brief pause to catch my breath I went back down. Peering through into the main church, I finally saw him. He must have been in a side room before. Now he was kneeling, close to the altar, presumably in prayer. He had changed out of his tennis clothes. This suggested a certain seriousness in what he was up to, so it didn't seem right to interrupt just to say I was getting on with *my* job and that his wife would soon be there to stop him being idiotic. I re-entered the tower, collected up my cleaning gear and started a more leisurely climb.

It was no great surprise to find that the hatch to the roof wouldn't open without having a shoulder put to it. This was a difficult feat to perform at the top of a ladder, but the risk and effort were worth it. Once I had scrambled out on to the leads I was treated to a genuine mind-blower of a view. During two years of living in the village I had enjoyed looking at the local Downs from many angles, but the exclusivity of that morning's panorama gave it a wonderful, extra edge. There I was, alone on 'my' tower, lording it over the interweaving green slopes as they basked in the spring sunlight. I also had a master-spy's vantage point over the village itself, but nothing gossip-worthy seemed to be happening.

Turning to the wooded hillside west of the church, I was surprised to see a human figure who had actually spotted me. It was a man, and he was waving. How friendly, I thought, and waved back. Let no one say that Sam Bevan, Lord of the Tower, was ungracious. The man on the hillside waved again. I squinted hard and came up with an unexpected identification. It appeared to be Mr Ainsly, the aged part-time caretaker. But if he could walk up hills, why couldn't he climb towers? I didn't think this seriously, but I did wonder why he was still waving. Perhaps his old eyes weren't up to seeing my first response, so I waved back again. Then I got down to work.

As I'd suspected, there was a layer of sodden, dead vegetable matter up against the inner edge of the parapet. The waterspout was thoroughly choked up, and it was surprising a blockage hadn't occurred months ago. Perhaps it had taken the fierceness of the recent storms to move the muck around. I kept poking through the spout with the handle of my brush until most of the leftover rain was drained off. Then came the truly messy part, bagging the stuff, though thankfully there were no waterlogged birds' nests to cope with. Some fifteen minutes later I was tying up a plastic sack half full of horrible, leafy gunge. Most of any new rainfall would be spouted out over the churchyard. However, it struck me as worthwhile to do the job completely, which meant popping down to the van to see if I had the wherewithal to seal two cracks I had found in the lead roofing.

Leaving my gear on the roof, I climbed down through the hatch. I paused for a moment to look at the bells. None of them were spectacularly big, but I wouldn't have liked to pass through that loft while the bellringers were in action.

Feeling an unnecessary sense of relief, I backed my way down the next ladder, but before my feet had touched the boards of the loft below, I was grabbed around the legs. I tried to kick myself free, but in the split-second panic of it all I lost my grip. The next thing I knew, I was tumbling sideways off the ladder, towards the hole in the loft floor.

As my shoulder hit it, the guard rail broke like matchwood.

CHAPTER 2

Quasimodo Lives!

An extract from the not quite bestselling booklet, *Gruesome Legends of East Sussex*:

> The village of Miston, lying west of the road which runs from the county town of Lewes to the port of Newhaven, is perhaps the least legend-bound of the villages in the vicinity of the River Ouse. Even the late Saxon church of St Olaf's is noted only for its square tower added in the 13th-century, not for any dark, graveyard activities.
>
> However, Miston does have one tale of yore & gore.

It concerns one Sydney Piggens, landlord of the Broken Harold Inn at the time of the Regency, who had a series of dogs, all called Boney. These dogs were each (in sequence) ill-treated to a lethal degree, so that their owner could boast, 'Never a day passes but that I make Boney wish he were never born.' This was all in revenge against Napoleon Bonaparte, whose navy shot off Bosun Piggens's left leg at the Battle of Trafalgar.

Even after the original Boney's final defeat at Waterloo, Piggens morosely and viciously continued his old habits . . . until the night he disappeared. His current dog—and all the other village dogs!—disappeared too, though only for the space of a few hours.

Next morning a search party discovered Piggens's wooden leg on the edge of the Downs. It was thoroughly scarred with tooth marks, and the earth for some yards around was stained dark red. No other remnant of the vicious landlord was ever found! Not the smallest bone!

The problem was, what should be done about the 'murderers'? The idea of putting down twenty to thirty animals was hotly debated, especially since some nervous villagers claimed to espy a brutal glint in the dogs' eyes.

In the end, kindness, lethargy—and business sense—prevailed. Piggens's more rational nephew became the new landlord of the Broken Harold and he ran a good tourist item in being able to point out that the dog snoozing by the fire 'is reckon'd to 'ave ate my uncle Syd—oo well deserv'd eatin', I might add!'

I have a dog called Eddie. Also, I'm no stranger to the Broken Harold Inn, though its local nickname is the One-in-the-Eye. But I managed to avoid becoming the second gruesome legend of the village of Miston, splattered all over the stony floor of the 'square tower added in the thirteenth century'.

My escape was a desperate homage to Charles Laughton in *The Hunchback of Notre Dame*. As I fell through the guard rail, I grabbed the nearest bellrope, hoping my grip would be firm enough to prevent a straight slide down. 'Hold tight, Sammy!' I yelled to myself, but having successfully 'stabilized' my position, a new problem arose.

The bellrope, acting as a bellrope should, moved down a couple of feet and rang the bell. Then it jerked double the distance up the other way as the bell did its counter-swing. I was whipped up with it, which was bad for the nerves. I clung on tighter than ever, till the next lowering swing, when I transferred to the adjacent rope. In such a way, I worked along the row, ringing out an improvised peal over the neighbourhood. By then I was about six feet above the ground, and, since the lower end of each rope was tethered to a board on the wall of the tower, I had no choice but to jump. I closed my eyes, took a deep breath . . . and heard a scream. Dora Philpot was staring up, wild-eyed, as I launched myself into the uncluttered air. I landed quite springily for a twelve-stone thirty-six-year-old, but still with enough force to make the soles of my feet sting. As I hopped about, cursing in a respectfully low voice, my spirits were lifted by words of comfort and concern. 'Darling! Stay there. Don't move.'

I was about to utter a casual, 'Don't worry, I'll survive,' when the penny dropped. She was still staring up, calling to her husband, whose ghostly face peered over the edge from which I'd fallen. From which he'd pushed me? All of a sudden I was shaken by the deeper implications of what had happened. And to make matters worse, I came under a new attack.

'What on earth possessed you to play games with the bells? You may have ruined Steve's hearing! And you promised not to let him go climbing up there! Come and help me fetch him down.'

All this was yelled while she virtually dragged me across to the first ladder. I wasn't very enthusiastic about climbing back up the tower. Suppose the Revd *had* been trying to murder me! Would he be ready for a second crack? And what had been his motive? Jealousy, I supposed, if the man was a mind-reader, though it hardly seemed fair, the way the woman of my dreams was treating me at that moment.

When we reached the second loft it was pretty clear her husband was unfit for any murder attempts. He lay face down, moaning quietly into the woodwormed planks. There was evidence in a corner that he had thrown up comprehensively, and on the whitewashed wall near the third ladder there were bloodstains. I checked and saw that the nails on both of his hands were in a gory state. Had he tried desperately to cling to the wall? This could mean that when I came down the ladder he had grabbed me for his own safety's sake, not intending homicide. Moved by his pathetic appearance, I decided to give him the benefit of the doubt.

'Don't just stand there, Sam!'

Dora wasn't about to give me the benefit of anything. With a sigh, I lent a hand. It took us twenty minutes of coaxing to get Steve down to solid ground. Dora led him off to the vicarage after muttering a cold thank-you. I watched them for a moment or two, bitterly debating whether to leave the mending of the roof cracks to Mr Ainsly, the seventy-nine-year-old hill-climber. Finally, in a mood of martyrdom, I collected a tube of sealant from the van and went back up. Although there were no bogeymen lying in wait, all the fun of being on the tower had gone. I worked as fast as I could, trying not to think beyond the fact that I would soon be off to the One-in-the-Eye for a well deserved pick-me-up.

The garden gate gave a ghost of a squeak as I called in at my house on the way to the pub. That was enough to send Eddie the Dog into his battering act against the inside of the front door. Then he recognized my footsteps on the path and switched to a noisy but welcoming bark. I let him out and was more pleased than usual to be slobbered over. The love shown by this brindle-coated cross between alsatian, labrador and goodness-knows-what-else didn't, for once, seem a poor substitute for human affection. As we went on our way, I didn't even kick him for nearly tripping me up every other minute.

According to a mock scroll framed and hung inside its low front door, the Broken Harold Inn dated, at least in what was now the public bar, from 1650. This always surprised me. It was only one year after Charles the First had lost his head, leaving those miserable Puritans in charge. Surely they didn't approve of pubs? But maybe the first landlord got away with it by hoisting a sign of an even earlier king getting his come-uppance. The inn sign Eddie and I passed under was of a much later date, possibly Victorian, but it still showed poor King Harold with the fatally embedded arrow. The artist had gone to town with the spurting blood, and his work was best not looked at closely on a full or queasy stomach. After my adventures in the church tower, I pointedly ignored it.

The pub clientele mostly fell into two groups; regular locals who clustered together in the tiny public bar, and car-borne visitors—from Lewes, Brighton or beyond—who heaved together in the lounge/dining-room or spilled out into the garden. I had become accepted as a local after my first year's solid attendance. This speedy admission into the clique came of my having done occasional jobs for nearly all the regulars. It was also justified historically because I inherited my house from an aunt who had lived in Miston all her adult life.

Present on the day of my fall from the loft and from Dora's favour were Alfred and Albert, both in their sixties and both nearly blind. They sat, bolt upright, at the small round table nearest the fireplace. Sometimes they wore heavy-framed dark glasses, but perversely on that sunny day their eyes were vacantly visible, and both men sported thick overcoats with upturned collars.

'I bet it's the handyman,' said Albert.

'What's so clever about that?' said Alfred. 'You can hear his dog.'

'I wasn't tryin' to be clever. But since he's here he can do a spot of fetchin' and carryin'.'

This meant a spot of buyin' too, which I only resented when business was bad. Just then I was quite flush, though it was going to be an embarrassment getting payment for the church tower job. Shrugging this thought off, I collected Albert and Alfred's empty glasses and went to the bar. Sitting there was Ron Woodhouse, a semi-layabout in my own age-group. He owned a garage and filling station on a corner where the main access route to the village led off the Lewes–Newhaven road. Barely looking up from an oily copy of the *Sun* he murmured, 'Those old boys are psychic. Their glasses were two-thirds full a minute before you came in the door.'

'Us old boys aren't deaf!' said Alfred—or was it Albert? There were embarrassing occasions when I couldn't tell them apart.

'No,' said Ron in a firmer voice, 'and there's some who reckon you're not so blind as all that.'

'Take it easy!' I said. 'I'm here to recover from a heavy morning's work.'

'You've come to the wrong place. It'll take an hour to get served,' Ron muttered, gazing with a curiously blank expression at the creased photograph of a naked girl. I leaned over the bar and got a sidelong view of the crush in the next room. All the staff were serving at a frantic pace, but one of them caught sight of me and decided to escape from the main chaos. Her name was Josie and she was the great-niece of Mr Ainsly, the church caretaker.

'I didn't know your old uncle was one for hill walking, Josie.'

She passed me the first of the pints, saying, 'He's always sneaking off up the Downs. Dad reckons he meets a woman up there.'

'At seventy-nine years of age?'

'Who knows how old she is?'

'I meant Mr Ainsly—and him a religious man too.'

Ron butted in. 'Those holy ones are always over-sexed.'

'Never mind sex. Where's our beer?' called Albert (or

Alfred). I gestured for Josie to include Ron in the round and ferried the first two refills over.

'I saw him on the hillside when I was up the top of the church tower,' I said, returning to the bar. 'There was no woman in sight.'

'P'raps she was hiding in the bushes,' Josie said, straight-faced. She had pulled the remaining pints, and took a tenner from my hand. I received my change without further comment, though she gave a groan before diving back into the fray next door.

'So what were you doing up the tower, young man?' Ron asked. When I first moved to Sussex and got called 'young man' I thought it was a compliment to my youthful looks. I soon realized it was a frequently used local irony. The older you were, the more you were likely to be called it.

'Clearing out the guttering.'

'Oh yeah.' Ron grinned suggestively.

At this point Albert turned to Alfred—a sip of beer had recharged my powers of identification—and murmured, 'Remember?'

'About what?' snapped the other.

'About the handyman havin' a soft spot for the vicar's missus.'

'He was always cock-a-hoop doing that decorating for her.' And they both went into fits of bronchial laughter.

'Watch it!' I said. 'Or those are the last pints you get from me.' To back me up Eddie the Dog gave a low growl, and a flicker of dismay crossed the near-sightless faces.

'Must be True Love if you can't stand a leg-pull,' said Ron. I frowned and lifted my glass. He tapped the naked girl in his paper. 'I knew she reminded me of someone.' Before I could drink any more my hand started shaking uncontrollably. By the time I'd put my glass back down on the bar a third of the drink was spilt.

'Bloody hell, mate! Calm down. None of us meant anything.' Ron reached a hand to my shoulder.

'We can feel you shakin' from here,' said Alfred, and Albert backed him up. On top of all this, Eddie started jumping up and whining. And so I blurted out part of what had happened.

'I . . . I nearly had a bad accident. I tripped and fell from the second-to-top loft in the bell tower. If I hadn't grabbed hold of the ropes . . .'

'No wonder you're all of a jitter,' Ron said. 'It's what they call delayed shock.'

I didn't know who 'they' were, but I felt that he had hit the nail on the head—and from that moment of realization my shakes eased away. I held an almost steady hand up at eye-level and said, 'Ron, you're in the wrong business. You should be a psychoanalyst.'

He laughed. 'I'm a shrink and sawbones rolled into one —only it's usually for motor engines.' Then he leaned across the bar and yelled, 'Josie, there's an emergency down this way!'

Once again Josie extracted herself from the mêlée. 'You're a thirsty lot!'

'Too true, but this time Sam spilt half his before he got started. We reckon the bar's uneven.'

'More likely you've been playing some daft game!' She looked unmoved but topped my glass up all the same. It was only what happened next that genuinely surprised the girl . . . and me!

'The lad needs a Scotch as well,' called Albert, to which Alfred added, 'A double! But put it on the slate as a single from each of us.'

Josie stretched across the bar and planted a firm kiss on my cheek. 'Happy Birthday,' she said, before slipping back and setting up the whisky. I told her I wasn't celebrating anything. 'Never mind,' she said and was gone again.

I turned to the old boys, raised my glass and said, 'Cheers. But I promise I won't go falling down bell towers every day.'

'You might not be so lucky next time,' said Alfred darkly, adding more cheerfully, 'I heard a peal of bells. Didn't sound so bad as the Sunday lot.'

Albert said, 'But did you hear that smacker Josie gave him?'

'Yeah,' added Ron. 'She fancies you for sure.'

'No, she doesn't. Anyway, she's only nineteen. And there's her boyfriend.'

'Darren'll kill himself on his motorbike soon enough,' Ron said with a macabre laugh. I knew better. If I was foolish enough to try anything on with Josie the boyfriend would be more likely to kill me first. Besides, I was too busy, feeling broken-hearted over the cruel treatment I'd received from my one true love.

Two hours and too many drinks later Ron and I were outside, blinking at the daylight, when old Mr Ainsly came across the oblong of grass which just about passed for a village green. He waved a walking stick at me and said, 'A lot of use *you* were!'

'Eh?'

'I wanted you to come down from that tower and see what I'd found up on the hill.'

'I was in the middle of your job, clearing out the water-spout. You ought to have known that.'

Grudgingly he muttered, 'Vicar did say something about it. I'm too old for that sort of thing.'

'Never mind the waterspout,' Ron said. 'What did you find, you old fool?'

'Don't see why I should tell a couple of drunks.'

''Cos there's no one else around,' Ron retorted, 'and you came rushing over bursting to tell someone!'

'As a matter of fact, I'm on my way to the pub to tell our Josie. It might be to do with her young man.' He walked past us, but a few steps on he turned and announced with a gesture towards the Downs, 'I found a motorcycle—half way up there—bang in the middle of an elderflower bush!'

CHAPTER 3

Myths and Machines

Motorcycles have never featured largely in my life. I was unstable, even on a pushbike. However, I am always willing to admire a skill in others, and Josie's boyfriend Darren was one of those bikers so perfectly wedded to their machines that they become a modern version of the centaur. Perhaps he was constantly endangering life, but there was something magnificently balletic about the way he tilted and curved his way through the local lanes.

The reason I mention Darren is that the bike we pulled from the elderflower bush half an hour later was confirmed by Josie to be his. She had half-heartedly joined her great-uncle, Ron, Eddie the Dog and myself on the expedition, but now she flew into a panic. 'Darren hasn't been around for four days. Something's happened to him. I know it!'

'Calm down, girl,' Mr Ainsly muttered. 'It's only a bike we've found. Not a cadaver.'

'Thanks a million, Uncle Jack! I was only thinking he's in danger. Now you're suggesting he's dead.' And she stomped away across the hillside.

'That's never what I said,' the old man spluttered in frustration, but it was too late. Ron stayed with him, examining the machine, while Eddie and I went after Josie.

She was leaning back against a rickety stile. Tears were slowly running down her cheeks, but she made no attempt to wipe them away. Eddie nuzzled her leg, got no response, and wandered off to examine some rabbit holes. I bided my time before saying, 'It must be a practical joke of some sort, Josie. Don't get too upset. If someone really had it in for Darren, they wouldn't have done something so daft.'

'Where's the joke, exactly?' she asked with a combined sneer and sniff.

I shrugged. 'It's not every day you get motorbikes being dumped half way up a Sussex Down.'

'True enough, but it doesn't make me laugh. Got a tissue on you?'

I found a disintegrating Kleenex deep in my coat pocket. She took and used it without comment. When the mopping up was over, I asked, 'Better?'

'Not much. But thanks for trying.' She turned and leant over the stile only to recoil immediately. 'Yuk! Someone's chosen a nice spot to throw up their dinner.' Facing me again, she said, 'We had a big bust-up Friday lunch-time.'

'You and Darren.'

'Who else! He reckoned he was earning enough now for me to stop working at the pub.'

'You mean he wanted to marry you?'

'P'raps. But first we'd live together in a flat he'd found in Brighton. I was to stay at home and keep house. He'd be the breadwinner.' She gave another of her sneer/sniffs. 'I told him to stuff the idea!'

'You don't like Brighton?'

'Not much, and I fancy being a prisoner in some bloody flat even less.'

Before she could tell me more about their row, Ron yelled across to us, 'Found the key!'

Josie pulled a face. 'Darren always hides his spare in the bottom of the pannier. I told him the bike would get nicked one day.' There was a blast of engine noise as Ron set off on a brief ride along a rough hill path. Somehow he managed a skidding turn and headed back towards a terrified Mr Ainsly who sought safety by tumbling back into the elderflower bush. A furious and very unreligious response came from the bush, but this outburst was oddly cut short. By the time I got close, a contrite Ron was off the bike and helping his victim up. Mr Ainsly hardly seemed to hear the apologies being offered. He was much more interested in an object he was clutching while being helped to his feet. Josie was also back with the group and exclaimed, 'That's Darren's crash helmet!' The object was indeed a crash helmet, but something was stuffed into it and held in position by a patch of oil-cloth which was taped to the edges of the helmet. As Mr Ainsly started loosening the tape, a sick presentiment made me rush towards Josie and spin her around before the contents could be revealed.

'Sodding hell!' Ron's brief words seemed to echo off the hillside. The next sound was a clunk of something hitting the ground. By this time Josie had broken free and pushed past me. She screamed. I followed after her and saw Eddie sniffing at a human skull lying on the path.

Before Josie could take off into full-scale hysterics, Ron held her firmly by the shoulders and said, 'Whoever it is, love, it ain't your boyfriend! Look at the colour of the thing. It's ancient! And small!'

We all—even Josie—took a calmer look at the skull. It was medium-brownish and seemed to have a sheen of varnish. Eddie became aware of the group stare and backed off furtively. This provoked Mr Ainsly to a bizarre notion. 'Suppose it's nearly a couple of hundred years old! They never did find any of the bones of that landlord the dogs was supposed to have ate.'

'They didn't have crash helmets in Nelson's time,' Ron muttered.

The old man was reasonably confused. 'You're the one who said the skull is ancient.'

Before they could get into another argument, I interrupted, 'Calm down, both of you. Even if the Landlord Piggens story is true, that skull is too clean. And it looks like the lower jaw is wired on.'

'None of you gives a toss about Darren, do you?' Josie snatched the crash helmet from her uncle's hands. 'And don't anyone dare tell me it's a joke! Even if nothing's happened to Darren yet, some bastard's set this up as a warning or a curse or something!'

Ron and I shared the task of wheeling the motorbike down to the village, and I was glad there were two of us to heave it over the crumbling wall by the gate at the bottom of the slope. If a single person was responsible for taking the bike on its upward trip he must have been pretty strong. This made a group caper seem more likely. Darren's courtship of Josie had put more than one local nose out of joint.

Once we were into the lane, Ron turned to Josie and asked for the crash helmet. 'I'm not pushing this bloody thing any further.'

Josie shook her head. 'I'll ride it back to his mum's.' With a grimace, she donned the 'cursed' helmet and moments later the bike was roaring down the lane. Eddie gave futile chase before rejoining the rest of us as we walked slowly and silently in a similar direction. Mr Ainsly, who was carrying the skull, suddenly stopped at the gate of the bungalow beside the church.

'Professor Quibbley would know all about how to date this skull.'

Ron snorted. 'Who's Professor Wotsit when he's at home?'

'Shush,' Mr Ainsly replied. 'She's a lady. A high-up at the university. She moved in two and a bit weeks ago.' Without further discussion he turned and walked along a neat gravel path to the Professor's front door. I had not yet clapped eyes on Dora Philpot's new next-door neighbour, but nosiness was outweighed by my unease at hovering near the vicarage. I called for Eddie to walk on with me. The stupid animal had followed Mr Ainsly and totally ignored my shout.

Ron grinned. 'Come on, Sam. We might as well all see what this lady Professor has to offer.'

We joined Mr Ainsly as he was ringing the bell for the second time. He whispered, 'I heard movements inside, so she's definitely at home.'

'Maybe she's busy doing a bit of private tuition,' Ron suggested with a wink.

'If you can only make lewd suggestions, why don't you bugger off to that garage of yours?'

It was during this non-whispered request that the door opened. Somehow Mr Ainsly managed to go red-faced and then quite pale in quick succession. The Professor, whose height in slippers could only have been an inch or two over five foot, was swamped in a distinctly male dressing-gown. Her hair was hidden under a floral plastic cap, and her face was caked in a dark green cream except in the immediate areas around her mouth, ears and eyes. All in all, she looked like a pygmy martian, though the accent was lowland Scottish.

'Good God! A delegation! Just what I needed in mid-facial. Well? What's the petition in aid of?'

Mr Ainsly squirmed a bit as he murmured, 'I can't apologize enough, Professor . . .'

'No, you can't. But the flattery helps a little. As it happens, I'm merely *Doctor* Quibbley. And before you describe your aches and pains, that's as in Doctor of Philosophy.'

Mr Ainsly was too dumbstruck to describe anything. Taking over, Ron said, 'The old feller has a skull he'd like you to date.'

She looked down at the skull and sighed. 'I have occasionally gone out with older men . . . but no one quite this decrepit.'

Ron also fell silent, and through slightly gritted teeth I spoke my turn. 'We want to find out the approximate age of the skull. Mr Ainsly thinks you're an expert. But, since it's unofficial, perhaps we shouldn't be wasting your time.'

Gazing out of the green facial mask, Dr Quibbley's eyes were disconcerting. Towards the other two they had flashed in playful irony. On to me she turned a disappointed look, suggesting that I'd gone and spoilt the fun. In no mood to feel bad about it, I gave a shrug. She turned back to Mr Ainsly and said, 'I'm not the expert you need. I'm a historian, not a palæontologist. However, I'm also subject to base curiosity.' She took the skull from Mr Ainsly, turned it over several times and held it up to the light. During this operation, with the large sleeves of the dressing-gown flopping about, she started to resemble Mickey Mouse as the Sorcerer's Apprentice.

'Don't quote me in court, but I would say . . . ten years old at the most.'

'What!!!' This last came from all three of us unbelieving males.

'Sorry, gentlemen. It's in much too good condition to be older than that. Even the best plastic shows wear and tear with the passage of time.'

'Plastic!!!' The trio sang out again.

Dr Quibbley handed the skull back to Mr Ainsly, pointing out a very faint ridge over the top of the cranium. 'That's where they joined the two halves of the mould, but I admit it's almost invisible. The weight is what really gives it away.'

Ron stepped in and took it from the old man. He weighed it in his palm, burst out laughing, and tossed it to me. It seemed quite light, though I'd not handled enough genuine skulls in my time to make a fair comparison. Instead of admitting this, I found myself eager to explain to Dr Quibbley that this was the only time I had actually held the thing, but she spoke first. 'I must go in before I start laughing. It's strictly forbidden with this so-called beauty treatment. Goodbye.' The door was firmly shut before any of us could speak again.

Mr Ainsly reclaimed the skull from me and we moved on our way down to the centre of the village. Our mood had turned into one of humorous disappointment. Even the old man was seeing the joke by then. It was only when we parted company by the Miston Stores that I noticed Eddie the Dog had gone missing. I felt much too tired to go searching for him. He would have to find his own way home.

CHAPTER 4

The Most Visited Man in Miston

Late in the afternoon I retreated to my bed too worn out, emotionally and physically, to do more than kick off my shoes and crawl under the top blanket. The sleep I fell into was shallow and uneasy, but in no way was I prepared for an intruder. Normally, Eddie would have been barking his head off, but Eddie wasn't there. The first thing I (barely) registered was a creak of the bedroom door. Then a hand firmly grasped my shoulder and I surfaced fast in a cold, cold sweat.

'I got to talk to you. Urgent. There's a job I want you to do.' I turned my head and focused initially on a hand holding a wad of ten- and twenty-pound notes.

'How did you get in, Darren?'

'Through the back window. Didn't want anyone seeing me. You ought to fix the catch some time.'

'Handymen are like doctors.'

'Eh?'

'Never look after their own health.'

He grunted and stood aside for me to escape from the bed. I made a move to draw back the curtains but he called out, 'Leave them shut!'

Darren was a well-built six-footer in his early twenties. I was a slightly flabby five-foot-niner in my mid-thirties. However, I'd been messed around enough for one day. I marched towards him, grabbed the collar of his leather jacket and dragged him out on to the landing. There I threatened, 'Either walk out of my house, or I'll throw you out.'

He moved half way down the stairs before turning and pleading, 'Have a heart, Mr Bevan! It's dead serious.' And as a last throw, 'Josie swore you'd be the best one to help me.'

'Wait there,' I muttered, and went to reclaim my shoes. Then I joined him on the stairs, saying, 'Let's go down to the back room.'

This room—which was my workshop and tool store—contained the window by which Darren had forced an entry. I rattled my way through a few boxes and drawers before finding the replacement catch I'd bought three months back. Grabbing up a screwdriver, I stood on a chair by the window.

'You're going to fix that now?'

'Talk to me while I'm doing it,' I said as I set to removing the broken catch. 'Who's got it in for you, Darren?'

'That's what I want you to find out for me.'

'Me?'

'Yeah. You're perfect for it. You work all over the place. In and out of houses, all round the area. I want to hire you . . . like a sort of detective.'

'Don't be daft.'

'Here's a hundred and fifty quid down. You'll get another hundred when you bring me the name.'

I spent a silent half-minute concentrating on the loosening of a rusted screw. When it yielded at last, I turned to look Darren in the face. 'How can you throw around that sort of money? I didn't know dispatch riders were that well off.'

'I do a milk round as well. Anyway, what's two hundred and fifty quid these days?'

'A quarter of a grand—which is still a lot to the likes of me.'

He shrugged. 'Want me to offer you less?'

'Forget it altogether. I've got safer jobs to do, thanks all the same. If I was to discover who hates your guts, they wouldn't like me too much, either.'

'They needn't know. You'd be mending their window catch and say, "What d'you think of that bastard Darren Glover? I can't stand him myself!" '

'Very subtle.'

'You'll think of something cleverer. Josie says you can tease secrets from folks. Thanks for bringing my bike down the hill, by the way. I should never've left it outside the pub, but I had to shove off for a few days in a hurry.'

'Not by bike—obviously.'

'No. In someone's car. Anyway, I was only just back when up rides Josie. Looking a treat.'

Each time he mentioned Josie there was a slight catch in his voice. In contrast to a bulky frame, his face, already quite thin and drawn, seemed to contract further. I said, 'You two haven't made it up, have you?' He gave a miserable shake of the head. Taking pity, I went on, 'If I was to do this asking around for you, I'd need to know what I was looking for.' He said nothing. 'Basically, I'd need a list of candidates. Any husbands whose wives you've been seeing on your milk round. That sort of thing.'

He glared at me. 'I love Josie, and don't you forget it!'

'OK, tell me who else loves her.' This provoked a fiercer glare. 'I'm not suggesting she's two-timing you, but Josie's a good-looking girl. There could be a passionate rival out there. That skull turned out to be plastic, but it's the thought that counts. Is stuffing a death's head inside a helmet some sort of jealous biker's ritual?'

'What happened can't be to do with Josie. Any of the lads would know I'd kill 'em!'

I shrugged. 'Fine, but this is getting to be like playing darts in a blindfold. Are you serious about finding your hate-merchant?'

He pulled a scrawled-over sheet of notepaper from his inside pocket. 'Here's where I live when I'm not at my mum's. I wrote it ready . . . in case you took the job. Get us another bit of paper and I'll jot down some names. But never let anyone see them. Try and memorize them or something.'

But for the skull and bike business this would have seemed melodramatic. I was back to not wanting the job, but all the same, I hunted through the mess of my workbench for a notepad. Just as one came to hand, the doorbell rang. Darren swore under his breath, immediately pushed up the back window, and climbed out, murmuring, 'I'll phone you later, OK? And thanks for not chucking me out.' In a melancholic mood, I watched and waited till he'd scrambled through the hedge at the bottom the garden. By then the doorbell was ringing for the third time, accompanied by a familiar bark.

'This creature must have sneaked into my house while I was ruining your and your companions' prehistoric fantasies.'

I stared at the speaker for a silent moment. She had dark, wavy hair, slightly flecked with grey, which framed a pixi-ish, pleasantly smiling face. Eddie the Creature licked her hand and then threw me a glance to say, 'This is my new friend. Watch it!'

I politely asked Dr Quibbley, 'Would you like to come in?'

'I'm only delivering your dog back.'

'Yes, but . . . I could make you a cup of tea for your trouble.'

'Another time, maybe. I'm sure it would be pleasant to talk to you away from a doorstep. Right now, I'm off to London, to make a fool of myself on television.'

'Which side? I'll watch.'

The smile broadened. 'You'd like to see me make a fool of myself? OK. It's Channel Four. Eight-thirty. I'll be the one hiding under the table.' She gave Eddie a stroke on the nose and headed for the street. The daft dog followed her till she turned him back at the gate, saying, 'No, no. You live here. It says so on your collar.' Eddie, slightly hanging his head, came and stood by his supposed master, and the two of us watched Dr Q. get into a mud-spattered Metro and drive off. The car must have reached forty in half a second, and she managed a gangster film skid-and-screech as she took the nearest corner.

*

It is a rare evening when I don't even poke my head round the door of the pub, but inane banter with Alfred and Albert was not what I fancied that night. Also, I had had enough of Ron's company for one day, and I wasn't that keen to see Josie until I'd had another word with Darren.

As a result, by eight-thirty, after an epic clear-up in a kitchen whose disgusting existence I'd been ignoring for about a week, I was sitting in front of the TV, tucking into a poached egg on cheese-on-toast and sipping a glass of dubious homemade ale given me by a grateful client. Suddenly there was Dr Quibbley on the screen, which sent Eddie into a total state of confusion. It was a discussion programme about the imminent auction of an entire archive of seventeenth-century papers and books. These had resided in a Norfolk castle, which was also up for sale. The castle had to stay put, but the archive was almost certainly headed for the States. Dr Janine Quibbley was representing a last-minute rescue committee, but apparently she was up against academic rivalries as well as the sheer need for cash. She clearly and bitterly stated the degree to which the cause was lost unless haggling over which university got the goods was shelved for the time being. At one point, a male (and genuine) professor attempted to give her a patronizing pat on the head for her brave, 'but perhaps slightly mishandled efforts'. Dr Quibbley's response was fast and I didn't get it all, but the professor was left puce and spluttering, looking for all the world as though he'd been kicked in the balls. Eddie barked encouragement, and I was tempted to shout at the set, like I do when I'm watching football. Then the bloody doorbell rang.

You can't always get what you imagine you want, and, if you do once in a while, there's the chance it will come as a complete and disconcerting surprise. Thus, on a beautiful evening filled with the scents of lilac and cut grass I opened my front door to find Dora Philpot on the step, and my heart, contrary to all projections, fell.

'I know this isn't much of a way to make amends. In fact, it's so inadequate I wish I'd never brought it at all.'

She held out a large round tin with a picture of Canterbury Cathedral on the lid. I accepted it with a mumbled thank-you. Easing off the lid, I discovered an iced sponge cake. Iced sponge is one of the few cakes I cannot stand, a quirk which Dora had discovered during my decorating visits. The high emotions of the day must have wiped that fact from her memory. I didn't think it polite to remind her.

'How have I got back in your good books?'

'Steve told me what had really happened. He's racked with guilt . . . and so am I.' She looked well on it. A slight flush in the face made her look even more gorgeously healthy than usual. She stood all fresh in a crisp, white and blue striped blouse and a tight denim skirt, and my initial dismay evaporated. To make things even better, she asked, 'Can I come in for a minute?'

'Yes, please. I mean, please do.' I stood aside for her to pass. 'Er . . . the front room's the least untidy, which isn't saying much.'

'I'm sure it's fine.' We went in and found Eddie still glued to the television. 'Good heavens! It's our next-door neighbour. How on earth did she get on the box?'

'It's a special programme about a campaign to save some ancient library.'

Dora stared at the set for a few moments. Then she said crisply, 'I expect it would all be above my head. Are you a fan of Dr Quibbley?'

'I never met her till today.'

'Steve seemed to take to her. They've had a chat over the hedge.'

'She's been wiping the floor with the men in this discussion.'

'Hm. Should I leave you to watch and admire?'

'No, no. I'll turn it off.' I went towards the set, but Eddie gave a loud growl. I merely lowered the volume, telling Dora, 'By accident my dog spent the afternoon with her. They obviously hit it off in a big way. Let's go to the kitchen.' She went out first, and as I turned to pull the door after me I saw the TV screen filled with a lingering, big close-up of Dr Quibbley. Someone in the studio control room was definitely a fan.

As if trying to give the impression of being very together, Dora deliberately made sure the latch of the kitchen door had clicked home. She then sat straight-backed at the table. I was still clutching the tin she'd brought and feebly asked, 'Can I offer you some of your cake?'

'Have you any brandy? I've had one hell of a day. So have you, of course.' I set the cake tin down and opened my humble booze cupboard. Deep in the recesses I found a half-bottle of Martell. 'I drink it neat,' she added as I hunted out a suitable glass.

'Say when.' I poured at least a treble before she made a sound. After handing her the drink I recapped the bottle.

'Aren't you joining me?' she asked, almost in the aggressive tone she'd used back in the bell tower.

'No, thanks. I just had a beer.' This was me being perverse. Her mood swing had sent my spirits tumbling again and I was dying for a drink.

She stared at me with a frown before taking three quick sips. Then she put the glass down and burst into tears. For the second time in one day I was faced with a weeping woman. Josie had not minded being left for a while to get on with it. Dora was different. On getting no immediate move from me she slumped forward. Her forehead audibly bumped on to the table. I blurted out, 'Dora, love! Please don't!' and quickly moved a chair close to hers. As I sat down she twisted around and, still sobbing, buried her face in my shoulder. This was an alarming situation on (at least) two counts. First, I wasn't at all sure how to deal with her. Secondly, I wasn't sure how to deal with myself. Her face was only inches away from mine. My arms were around her, and her arms were around me. The temptation to make manœuvres towards a kiss was unbearable. As a distraction, I stroked her hair. The sobbing eased off, and she turned her face slightly to mine. As a further distraction, I stroked her damp cheek.

She turned her face even further, looked up at me with

big eyes and rosebud lips, and whispered, 'Do you love me, Sam?' I merely brushed my lips against hers, but she moved a hand behind my head, pressing our faces together, and the kiss became all too committed. I don't want to suggest that I didn't enjoy it—but at the same time my mind was already flashing forward to problems that might follow in its wake. After all, adultery is tricky in any circumstance, but especially so with the wife of a churchman . . . a potentially murderous churchman. Her words 'He's racked with guilt' came back to me as a suddenly ambiguous presentation. Was he feeling guilty because he had tried to kill me on purpose, or because he had nearly killed me by accident? These were difficult questions to put when engaged in an increasingly passionate kiss. By this time, my hand had completed an unopposed wander over the front of her blouse and was undoing a button or two. Then the bloody telephone began to ring.

'Leave it,' she murmured, barely removing her lips from mine.

'I've been expecting an important call.'

'More important than this?' She started to kiss me again before I could answer. The phone continued to ring and I could also hear Eddie barking in frustration at discovering that he'd been shut in the front room. With her clear encouragement my hand was now inside the blouse, but the cacophony of dog and telephone ruined my concentration.

I disengaged with a quick apology and rushed into the hall, picking up the receiver in time to be told by an impersonal voice that the caller had cleared the line. I too cleared the line, banging the receiver down hard on its wall bracket. I'd missed Darren's call—if it was him—and I'd probably lost my chance with Dora as well. Before confronting my emotional fate I turned off the television and released Eddie into the back garden.

Back in the kitchen, Dora was standing by the window, sipping her brandy. I flicked a glance at the bottle. She had helped herself to a handsome refill. I went and stood by her. She immediately moved a couple of feet away. When she turned to face me, revealing no more tears, I decided to play it as if I was cynically relieved. With a shrug I said, 'I suppose it's just as well we were interrupted.'

'Is it?' Her voice was neutral.

'Unrequited love is more my style. I've got used to that in recent years . . . since my own marriage ground to an end.'

'Mine hasn't got long to go,' she said softly. She put her glass, still quite full, on the draining-board and moved close to me again. 'The doctor came this afternoon and gave Steve a very powerful sedative. He was sleeping when I left the house and he'll probably sleep through till morning. That's what happened after the last major panic attack.'

'Shouldn't you be with him, in case he wakes earlier than expected?'

'No. He'll be calm when he wakes. My nerves are still shattered. I need you.' She put her arms loosely around my neck and we gazed into each other's eyes for a few moments. Then we kissed for the third time. Previously, I had hardly noticed the brandy. Now the borrowed taste—in league with stirred emotions—made me feel sympathetically woozy. Both of us wavered and stumbled, but we still managed to make it upstairs to the bedroom.

The telephone stayed quiet, and the front doorbell wasn't to ring for another three hours.

CHAPTER 5

The Most Visited Man: II

Dora didn't climb out through the back window, but she left by the back door. I had assured her that my next-door neighbours on both sides were 'weekend villagers' and so we walked hand-in-hand down the garden. After I'd helped her through the gap previously used by Darren, she leaned across the hedge for one last kiss. Then she said in an urgent whisper, 'We must talk things over tomorrow. But let's meet away from Miston.'

'Where? And when? I'm booked for a job which will take till mid-afternoon.'

'Say eight o'clock in the evening. By the entrance to Brighton Pavilion. Can you make it?'

'If my van doesn't break down. How about you?'

'Don't worry. I'll manage. It's important. We've a few lives to sort out. Good night, dear Sam.' She went off along the footpath which ran from a dead end behind next-door's garden to an alley which connected with Church Lane about fifty yards from the vicarage.

I lingered by the hedge. My head was buzzing with many things that hadn't been discussed. Was this the beginning of a secret affair? Would it stretch into an affair at all? Might we even go public, and if so, how violently jealous would the Revd turn out to be? Considering that he might have sent me hurtling down the bell tower on purpose when I merely longed for his wife, what chance would I stand after this visit? Though I knew I might as well postpone any major anxieties until I saw Dora again, unease (and a measure of guilt) reined back the joy I wished I could feel. When I finally turned towards the house I almost stumbled over Eddie. He was standing dead still, like a statue of a dog, except that his eyes glinted as they moved in the moonlight.

'What are you looking at?' I asked.

'Whorrorf,' he said.

'Hm! Let's get indoors.' He followed me to the door but turned to give a loud bark just as we were going to enter. I spun round and caught a glimpse of a dark shape moving beyond the hedge. Was it a person, or was it a bush shuddering in the breeze? Since Dora was well on her way home, I decided against being a bold investigator.

Twenty minutes later, almost on the stroke of midnight, the doorbell rang. I was dozing in an armchair. Eddie was soundly asleep across my feet and barely stirred when I stood up. It was Josie, and she came straight into the house. 'I've got to get a new job. That bastard Koerner is always buggering off, leaving me to do most of the clearing up. He and his bloody missus hardly lift a finger.' Tony Koerner was landlord of the pub. His wife was a cheerless woman called Marianne.

'Perhaps they get worn out, counting the profits. I pay them a fortune just on my own.'

'Yeah, your lot should go on a beer strike.' By the time she was saying this, Josie had advanced to the kitchen where she started to fill my kettle. 'I'm dying for a coffee. Hope you've got some.'

'Only instant. Um . . . don't take it the wrong way . . . but why are you here?'

'To check if you've heard from Darren tonight? He said he'd phone. I saw him after he hired you.'

I frowned at this. 'He hasn't absolutely hired me yet. I sort of said I'd think about it.'

'But he left you some cash in advance.'

'Hang on a minute.' I slipped across the hall to the back room. In the middle of my chaotic workbench I found Darren's £150. It was folded inside the sheet of notepaper on which he had written his alternative address. He must have put it there while I was hunting for the pad on which he didn't list his possible enemies. I checked the address—somewhere in Brighton—before putting the paper into a back pocket of my jeans. For caution's sake I hid his money in a secret compartment which I'd built underneath the workbench. Unless Darren did get in touch it wasn't a fee I'd be likely to earn.

Josie had made two black coffees and was opening up Dora's cake tin. She frowned at the sight of the icing. 'Can't stand very sweet things. You're lucky Darren didn't see it. He'd have woofed it down. Did you find the cash?'

'Yes. But I'll probably give it back to him. I don't really want to go snooping on people.'

She was not impressed by this excuse. 'Can't you understand how scared he is? He looks tough, but most of it's just show.'

I did recall Darren's sudden vulnerability when I'd been about to throw him out of the house. Josie, with her spikey fair hair and her slim but sinewy body, looked far tougher. I had seen her shifting beer kegs about with ease. She could probably beat either of us in a fair fight. Thinking of the pub, I said, 'Why not take on the job yourself? You've got more chance of picking up information than me. The One-in-the-Eye's a hive of intrigue and gossip.'

'Bird-brain! No one's going to tell me direct, are they? They know I'm his girlfriend. Well, used to be.' There was no wild emotion this time, just a cool determination to help out her former young man.

'He told me he loves you.'

'Wants to lock me away. That's not the same thing. But please help him, Sam. I'll pass on anything I do hear. You can go and check it out.' She handed me a mug of coffee and gave me a pat on the cheek. 'We'll make a great partnership. Specially since you don't fancy me.'

This notion didn't seem completely logical to me, or relevant, but I didn't bother to argue the point. Instead, I threw up an operational problem. 'Suppose you discover a suspect I've never done work for? How can I question them?'

'You ask if there's anything they want doing anyway. Tell them your most recent job's been hijacked by someone called Darren Glover who's a real cowboy. Test their reactions.'

'Yeah, if they believe a word of it! If Darren hadn't been so neurotic, I'd already have his list of possibles. The phone went once tonight. Whoever it was rang off before I could answer.'

'You should've been sitting by it.'

'My phone's in the hall. I don't sit out there . . even if I'm hoping the love of my life will call.'

Josie cocked her head. 'Not even for the vicar's wife, you mean?' I said nothing, though I was wondering if Dora had been seen at my door? Was the scandal already going round the village? Josie squashed that worry and put another one in its place. 'You're wasting your time there, Sam. If she's sweet on anyone, it's Gordon Summing.'

'Who the hell is Gordon Summing?'

'The dairy owner. Darren's been doing a milk round for him. Bit of a smooth bugger. More a London businessman than a real farmer.' She paused and stared at me. 'You're really upset, aren't you?' I didn't answer. 'My mum says Mrs Philpot is just a tea-party tease. Anyway, I can't believe the way blokes go misty at the mention of her name. Dora!' She gave a dry chuckle. 'Mind you, a few of the locals have been switching their fancy lately. I wonder how darling Dora feels about the Midget Brain-Box.'

'Dr Quibbley? Has she been to the pub? I never clapped eyes on her till today.'

'She had lunch there once. But she's been seen around. What did you think?'

I shrugged. 'She seemed nice enough.'

'But your loyalty's unshaken?'

'Sure, rock solid!' I said, forcing a smile. It hardly made sense that Dora would think of the other woman as some sort of rival, but once again Josie's little burst of gossip didn't help my peace of mind. In self-defence I moved the discussion back to Darren and his worries, giving a promise that with Josie's help I would try to uncover his ill-wisher as long as it didn't get in the way of my normal work. She exclaimed once again that we would make a great team, shook my hand in formal settlement of the deal and left the house. As I watched the departure of my fourth visitor, I felt thoroughly depressed and exhausted. But the disruptions of that day and night weren't over.

This time Eddie was up and barking. Somehow I had undressed, fumbled my way into a pair of pyjamas and stumbled up to bed. It wasn't so easy to fall into a restful sleep, but I had almost made it when some idiot started rattling my letter-box. With a groan, I switched on the bedside light and reached for my multi-function watch. It told me the date and that it was Wednesday. After three attempts I managed to change the mode to ordinary time. By then it was nearly quarter past one on a Wednesday morning, and the dog downstairs was still noisily doing his duty. He only eased off when I joined him in the hall and told him to belt up. As I approached the front door, the letter-box opened wide. With a chill, I recognized the voice which came through the flap, though it had taken on a slurred quality which wouldn't have been fitting for a Sunday sermon.

'Sam . . . Sam . . . I know'slate . . . but . . . I mus'talk t'you.'

A sozzled vicar was all I needed, but my embattled conscience said, 'You owe him a hearing, at least.' I unchained the door and let 'Call-me-Steve' across the threshold. He staggered a bit, but I couldn't smell any booze on him. I guided him into the front room, saying, 'Shall I make you a coffee?'

'No, no. I . . . tooksome . . . verystrongpills.' And, as soon as he sat down, his very strong pills sent him off into a profound slumber. I fetched a rug from the airing cupboard and slung it over him.

Back in my bed, I found sleep as elusive as before. In spite of having Eddie the Great Bodyguard to protect me, I was scared. I couldn't help feeling that my latest caller already knew what had occurred between me and his wife. But fear wears itself down in time. When I finally did slip from consciousness, it was with a stoic suspicion that I might not surface again, except perhaps to acknowledge a death blow from my uninvited guest.

CHAPTER 6

A Risk Of Over-employment

I was caught up in a complicated dream. The first part found me in my garden digging with a heavy spade in the middle of the lawn. Almost immediately the spade hit something hard, and I began to feel afraid. Even so, I knelt down and cleared away the earth to find a cake tin with a picture of St Olaf's Church, Miston, on its lid. As I pulled the tin from the ground it revealed itself to be much deeper than the average cake or biscuit container. I opened it to find a mass of human hair within. Tresses of various lengths and colours, some curly, some straight, some wavy, had been dumped together, like sweepings from a hairdresser's floor. In disgust, I threw this disparate bundle of human debris up in the air and a sharp breeze spread it all over the garden, draping plants and bushes.

Instantly I was transported to my bedroom, where I lay down and drifted into a dream-within-the-dream. There I was also in my bedroom, but I was not alone. Dora stood by the bed, getting dressed and chatting cheerily. Suddenly she pulled a blonde wig from her bag, fitted it over her curly brown hair, winked at me and walked out of the room without another word. I came to the painful conclusion that she was leaving me for good. In desperation, I yelled her name again and again, until my shouts awoke me from the inner dream . . . to find her husband standing beside my bed!

With a fixed smile, he whispered, 'Do you know that half the men in Miston call out Dora's name in their sleep? But I'm putting them out of their agony one by one.' To prove his generosity, he brought a cricket bat from behind his back, raised it high and began to bring it down fast towards my head.

I woke up from the main dream in a sweat, trembling from head to toe, and there, across the room, was Steve Philpot stooping in full reality. It took a moment to remember that I'd let him into the house during the small hours. There was no sign of a cricket bat. Instead, he was staring downwards with great concentration. The full light of morning spilled through a divide in the curtains and made a pool beside his feet. As I sat up, he spoke without moving his gaze. 'Extraordinary. This rug is an exact replica of one my grandmother used to have.'

'It *is* the one *my* grandmother used to have. My aunt, her daughter, inherited it, and it got passed on to me with the house.'

He straightened up and murmured, 'I wish I had a place to escape to, somewhere I could call my own. If I left the church I would be homeless, you know. I could never afford to buy a house.'

I noticed in this little speech his constant use of 'I', not 'we'. Had Dora actually gone back and told him their marriage was over? Edgily, I asked, 'Are you going to tell me what brought you here?'

'First I've got to explain what I was trying to do yesterday morning.' He fell into a brief silence, maybe to clear his thoughts. When he started up again his voice was trembling. 'The reason I attempted to climb the tower was to prove how desperately I needed your help.'

Unsure that I wanted to hear any more, I mumbled, 'I was already doing the job you asked me to do, Steve. I didn't need any extra convincing.'

'I don't mean the church roof. I'm talking about a completely different job. One that will either save or destroy me.' He gave a convincing shudder as he added, 'As it was, I nearly killed you.'

'So I noticed. Er . . . why did you push me over the edge?'

'Blind terror! Having climbed that far I was grabbing at you for safety. All I could think of was my need to be led down. But you fell!' He shook his head and moaned, 'I'll never forgive myself.'

'Don't be daft, Vicar! It's bad enough having regrets over disasters that did happen.' So far, except in my dream, he had been consistently grim-faced. Now, at this piece of cracker-barrel wisdom, his solemnity went into a brief eclipse. We smiled at each other, and then I found myself starting to blush. Whether or not it would lead to disaster, something had definitely happened in that very room. It made me behave like a guilty idiot and say, 'By the way, does Mrs Philpot have any idea where you are?'

'Dora didn't come back last night—at least, not before I came out. When did I arrive here?'

'Just after one o'clock. But is that so very late? Couldn't she have been with a friend?' I asked bluffly. At the same time I was wondering, what bloody friend? When Dora left I'd been sure she was heading for home. He overrode the spoken questions.

'Can I ask you the favour I intended to ask at the top of the tower? Have I convinced you how genuine my desperation is?' I gave a nod and waited for an anguished request to leave his wife alone. If only he had skipped the proof-by-personal-risk bit and asked me straight out the day before, I could have told him he was suffering from a jealous delusion. (Then Dora and I would certainly have just remained friends.) Now I was preparing to lie in much the same fashion, but after a slow, deep breath he threw me by asking, 'Will you act as a sort of marriage counsellor for me and Dora?'

'Me? Why me?' Was the man being extremely sneaky, or was I not a suspect? Whatever the case, he ignored my reaction.

'Our marriage is going through a bad patch. I need to find out why I've driven her away from me. If it's something I've done, perhaps I can change my ways. You must find out if she wants to be won back.' He turned his face away for a moment, murmuring, 'I'll insist on paying for your services, of course.'

'Ridiculous!' I said. 'If I help at all it'll be as a friend. But why not talk to her yourself?'

'Because . . . I'm afraid of losing control.' Reading my face he quickly added, 'I don't mean I'd hit her. I've never done such a thing. But, you see, I'm often so heavy-handed in my own private life.'

'I was no marital genius myself.'

'I know you are divorced but, if it's not too painful to call on, your experience might help us. The thing is, Dora loves to talk to you. She so enjoyed your company when you redecorated the vicarage. She said it was a wonderful antidote to her parish socializing. She could relax and unburden herself to you more than to anyone else in Miston.'

'We've never discussed anything serious.' This was true, until very lately. And out it came: 'Until she popped round early yesterday evening.'

'She was here? What did she say? Why didn't you tell me before?'

'I've hardly had a chance. You've controlled the conversation.' His response was a moody silence. 'Dora called by to apologize for being rude to me in the bell tower. She thought I'd enticed you into climbing beyond your limit. So she really tore into me.' He still didn't speak. 'When she discovered what really happened she was extremely sorry.' He still didn't speak, and I was getting fed up. 'Look—here I am, actually trying to be helpful, and you clam up on me!'

He finally, darkly spoke. 'Did she say anything about her lover?'

'Not at all. What lover?' I nervously plumped my pillows and suddenly I became aware of a perfume around me. Dora's perfume! Earlier the two pillows had lain side by side. Hers had now become partially uncovered again. I leapt out of bed, pulling sheet and blankets right up. 'Let's go downstairs. I can hardly believe Dora has a lover, but you'd better tell me about it over a cup of tea.'

Icily he said, 'I don't need tea! And it's obvious you

would simply line up on her side. I shall go.' This was the first good news of the day, though he proceeded to walk very slowly past the bed. To stretch my nerves further he was breathing heavily, but the scent didn't seem to catch his attention.

A few minutes later I watched from the bedroom window as he shuffled down the road. He looked quite unlike the tall, fair, super-fit athlete of even a day ago. I felt a mixture of relief, guilt and pity. I was also a mass of tangled suspicions. Had he actually come to my house because he expected to find his wife there? Did Dora have a lover for whom I was perhaps being used as a blind? Had her husband's pathetic request for a marital go-between been genuine, or a trick to flush out a confession?

If this last notion was the case, what he didn't know was that he'd been damn close to getting one!

The rest of the morning I was safely wrapped away from traumas and temptations. I spent it repointing a garden wall for a sweet old lady called Mrs Leigh-Harcourt. She brought me regular refreshments and even tolerated Eddie as he occasionally went on the rampage through the shrubbery. Her own dog had died earlier in the year. I worked so fast that the job was all but finished by lunch-time. Mrs L.-H. offered to feed me, and it was difficult to refuse without being rude. As a trade-off, I wondered whether she would be kind enough to entertain Eddie while I nipped away for another 'appointment'. She was only too delighted. Five minutes later I was in the pub.

It was one of those occasions when, almost immediately after you've heard a name for the first time, the flesh and blood version puts in an appearance. Josie came through from serving in the lounge bar to say, 'Gordon Summing's asked me to see if you'll leave the Public for a few minutes and have a drink with him.'

'I don't know the man.'

'Don't worry. I've put a word in for you.'

I doubted if she'd done me a great favour, but I decided

to have a look at this gentleman anyway. Leaving my barely started pint under the limited gaze of Alfred and Albert, I slipped around the outside of the building and entered the lounge. As usual, it was crowded but Josie pointed me in the right direction. Seated at a window table was a soberly dressed gent in, maybe, his early forties. He had a modest but even tan and dark brown hair with just the right feathering of white-grey at the temples. As he studied a menu through gold-rimmed half-specs, Tony Koerner, landlord of the Broken Harold stood in attendance. (Lunch orders were normally given over the bar.) Koerner turned towards me with false bonhomie. 'A rare treat, Sam, to see you on this side of the house.' Then, quickly looking me up and down, 'I didn't realize it was so dusty out.'

'I'll wear a suit next time I'm clearing your drains, Tone.'

He either laughed or cleared his throat before Summing broke things up by handing him the menu. 'I'll order later, Tony, but might you slip this hard-working fellow a pint of the best?'

'As you wish, Gordon.'

I said, 'A half will do, there's a pint sitting waiting next door.'

For a fraction of a second Summing looked miffed at this limiting of his generosity. Then he nodded Koerner on his way before standing to greet me formally. 'You come highly recommended,' he said with a firm handshake.

'Recommended as what?'

'A man of many talents.'

'I'm just the product of a long list of night school classes.'

'And why not? Though I think that you are overplaying the modesty.'

Josie brought my drink across. She irritated me by ruffling my hair and saying, 'He's older than he looks, Mr Summing. Mature and reliable.' Turning away from him she gave me a wink and went back to the bar.

Gordon Summing's gaze followed her briefly. 'If only she would lose her "Queen of the Coven" look . . .' He turned to me. 'But I should watch my tongue. You might be the new man in her life.' I sipped my beer. 'No comment? You'd be a big improvement on the unlamented Darren.'

'Darren's OK.'

'You think so? I had to roll my sleeves up and do a milk round on account of his absence this morning.'

'Is that what you're offering me? The chance of a milk round?'

He impersonated a guffaw, showing at least two gold fillings in the process. 'There's a back-up lad for that sort of thing, only I couldn't get hold of him today.' He lit a cigarette, cast a glance at the neighbouring tables, and leant towards me. 'I have a block of dilapidated cow sheds on a farm I've just bought, further down the valley and towards the river. The foundations are sound, as far as I can tell, and I would like to use roughly the same lay-out for weather-proofed storage buildings. The first stage, obviously, is to get some plans drawn up ' He leant back, and I thoughtfully sipped my beer. With a faint sigh he said, 'I can see you're totally riveted.'

'I do odd jobs around the village, Mr Summing. This sounds a bit out of my range.'

'Come off it, Sam. I happen to know you trained as an architect.' He paused to see how I reacted to this last personal detail. I sipped more of my beer. 'This project would be a doddle for you, even if you've been out of practice for a few years.'

I emptied my glass and stood up, saying, 'Why don't you use someone who's in practice?'

He also stood up, almost looking as though he might grab my arm to prevent me leaving. 'The obvious answer to that one is that you'd be cheaper.' I smiled. 'The other reason is practical. I want someone who'll concentrate on the job for the short time it will take, not have it as one fiddly item among the big stuff.'

This did sound sensible, but I said, 'I have a few regular clients of my own. What if a local emergency crops up?'

'No problem. As long as it's quickly done.' He passed me a card. 'Let me know by the weekend.' Instead of a formal farewell he sat down again and looked out of the window. As I left the crowded lounge, I slipped his card into the back pocket of my jeans alongside Darren's note from the night before.

When I was out in the forecourt of the pub I heard a stage 'Pssst!' Josie (she must have been standing on the toilet seat) poked her head through the exterior fanlight of the ladies.

'Are you going to do Darren's job?'

'It wasn't on offer.'

'Eh?'

'Listen, Josie. Have I ever told you what job I used to do when I lived in London?'

'No. What did you do?'

'Never mind. I didn't think I had.' Before she could ask again we were interrupted by the muffled voice of Tony Koerner's wife, Marianne.

'Josie, you've been locked in there for hours. Get a move on or you'll get the sack!'

Josie muttered a curse and bobbed out of sight. I went back into the public bar, trying to remember who, apart from Dora Philpot, I'd told about my former career.

CHAPTER 7

Wrong Time, Wrong Place

I was late for my rendezvous, but only by a couple of minutes. Dora wasn't waiting for me, and I assumed she had also been held up. For such a vital meeting she would hardly have travelled all the way into Brighton and not bothered to hang around. My problem had been finding somewhere to park. Even at seven-forty there was no space anywhere near the Pavilion. In the end I left my van on the edge of the Kemp Town district and half-walked, half-ran back to the entrance of the Prince Regent's seaside extravaganza.

By half past eight I was feeling apprehensive. I knew the Pavilion building well enough. There was only one way in for the public and that was now closed, so Dora couldn't be waiting just inside. But suppose, in her emotional state, she thought a different door was the entrance? The trouble was, if I went off to explore this possibility, she would probably arrive in the right spot and assume I'd lost patience.

I stayed put.

Dora still didn't turn up, but Dr Quibbley did, heading in the vague direction of the seafront, closely followed by a group of serious-looking young people. 'I don't often do the academic courier bit,' she said, pulling an exaggerated frown. 'These fine folk all hail from Hungary . . . I think.'

'That is absolutely correct. We come from Hungary, just as Dr Quibbley thinks,' said a girl with rosy cheeks, and the whole group laughed in unison.

Dr Q. turned to me with a puzzled shrug. 'I'm glad something's cheered them up. But do you realize, Sam Bevan, we're meeting on yet another doorstep, albeit of a more grand variety?'

'So we are.' I flushed slightly, having suddenly caught sight of Dora some fifty yards away.

'Come to tea tomorrow. Four o'clock, and walk straight in at the back door. It's about time we broke the formalities.'

'Er . . . yes, I agree. Thanks.'

To my relief she marched her Hungarian troops off on a route which would avoid an embarrassing crossing of paths with her neighbour from the vicarage. But to my almost immediate disappointment, the approaching woman when seen in close-up didn't look like Dora in the slightest.

At ten o'clock I was on my way back to the van. Ever since a futile teenage experience (waiting three hours for a girl on what turned out to be the wrong railway platform) I've stuck to a strict sixty-minute hanging-about-limit, and that only in extreme cases of emotional expectation. This time I had dutifully waited till nine, mooched off to the nearest pub and neurotically idled my way down a pint, gone back to the meeting place, found only a couple of teenage lovers who told me quite quickly to 'piss off', returned to the pub and had a pointless half, returned to the meeting place which was now totally deserted, returned to the pub and had an even more futile alcohol-free lager, returned to the meeting place, found a policeman and policewoman in deep conference, and gave up all hope.

My mood as I retreated was dark and brooding. From the moment Josie first mentioned the name of Gordon Summing, I'd suspected that the prospects of my illicit romance were doomed. The vicar's bizarre visit had not helped, nor had the meeting with Summing himself. And now I'd been stood up, left obsessively wondering where the hell had Dora got to? Was she with the dairy owner? Or had she touchingly made it up with her husband? I was feeling manipulated, and it struck me that the person who might have some inside information—at least about the Summing person—was Darren. I dragged his sheet of notepaper from my pocket and checked the address. The street name wasn't familiar, but when I reached my van I was able to consult a Brighton map book.

It happened that Darren's flat was only a block from where I was parked. I locked the van again and walked on, soon finding myself outside the house. At the kerb side stood a couple of motorbikes and one of them looked like it could be Darren's. Since there were no names to suggest who lived in which flat, I pressed the bottom bell. It brought to the door a bleary-eyed youth. 'Sorry. I'm looking for Darren Glover.'

'Oh yeah?'

'He told me I could find him here. This is his writing.' I held out the now crumpled notepaper.

The boy sniffed. 'I'll believe you. Top floor. Tell him to get his bell fixed.'

'I didn't know which one to try. It might be working.' I pressed the top bell and heard a distant ring. 'Sorry,' I said again and started the climb. It was a three-storey, narrow building, which meant the stairs were steep. By the time I reached the top I was puffing like an old man. Only a day and a half had passed since I was going up and down the bell tower but I felt considerably less fit. Darren hadn't responded to the bell, so I knocked on the door. No answer. I knocked again, more loudly. At the third attempt a muffled yell from the middle floor told me to shut my racket! I did so, because at the third attempt the door slipped open of its own accord. The Yale lock must not have clicked home. I entered, quietly calling out Darren's name. The place was in near darkness, and when I tried the switch nearest the door nothing happened. Even though I'd given up smoking soon after my move from London, I still carried a lighter. I flicked it alight, moved further into the lobby and spotted an open box on the wall. Inside was the electricity meter. The master switch was up and off, which seemed curious and possibly sinister. I should have got the hell out of there but caution was overridden by bloody-mindedness, a touch of Dutch courage and a measure of concern for my 'client'. As I pulled the master switch down, nearly all the lights came on at once.

The front hall and stairwell of the house appeared not to have been decorated for several decades, and not swept for at least a year. Darren's flat was a complete contrast. There were new, fitted carpets, the walls had recently been painted, and the furniture, though sparse, was expensive. Much of the main room, a spacious bedsitter, was taken up with items of new electronic equipment, some still in their boxes, and in the part furthest from the door stood a double bedstead with brass fittings. So this was where Josie would have felt herself a prisoner.

Moving on to the bathroom, I had to hold my breath as soon as its door was open. An unpleasant, acrid smell was mingling with the odours of aftershave, talc and other stuff, but there was no sign of anybody. I closed the door and went into the kitchen, where I found a tin with a picture of Winchester Cathedral on its lid. A slight coincidence, but enough to bring on a sharp attack of paranoid jealousy. With shaking fingers I opened the tin and found only a packet of chocolate digestive biscuits. There weren't even any crumbs to suggest the former presence of a homemade cake. I cursed Josie for corrupting my image of Dora, cursed myself for letting my suspicions run riot, and decided I didn't want to snoop any more. I wasn't at all sure what was going on, but as a last gesture I called out quite clearly, 'Darren! This is Sam Bevan. Do you want to come out of hiding and have a chat?'

No one burst forth from a fitted cupboard. The only response came from the fridge which perversely turned itself off, leaving the flat in a dull silence.

I retreated to the outer landing, pushing up the electricity master switch *en route*. I also pulled the flat's front door firmly after me, making sure it was locked this time. The stairwell was pitch dark by then and I pressed in a decrepit time-switch before starting my careful descent. I was half way down the top flight of stairs when the light went out. I paused, wondering whether to resort to my lighter or to feel my way carefully down to the next landing. At that moment I heard a muffled metallic click and the creaking of floorboards from somewhere above. Instinctively, I turned my head, which was by then level with the topmost landing, and saw a thin strip of light beneath the lower edge of Darren's door.

My bloody-mindedness, Dutch courage and client-concern were completely exhausted. At the risk of breaking my neck, I moved quietly but quickly on down the stairs. Even when I was back out in the street I didn't hang around. I went straight to my van and drove straight out of town. The notion that I could have been bashed over the head—or worse—at any time during my wander round the flat made the decision for me. I was going to return to the more conventional activities of a village odd job man.

CHAPTER 8

Transparent Disputations

Eddie the Fickle barely managed a tail-wag when I turned up at Mrs Leigh-Harcourt's house next morning. After the garden wall repairs were done, my dog had been invited to stay on. Thinking I was destined for an evening of secret romance, I had gratefully accepted the offer on his behalf. There had been no messages from Dora since my return to the village, and now, with Eddie coolly padding off into Mrs L.-H.'s kitchen, I felt doubly rejected. 'He hasn't quite finished his breakfast,' said the old lady, slightly embarrassed. 'We slept late after both of us were woken in the small hours. They were having such a barney over the wall.'

'Noisy neighbours?'

'Ones who ought to know better. I'm not religious myself, but I wouldn't be surprised if someone complained to the Bishop. The wife was absolutely shouting her head off at one point.'

My previous day's work had been out at the front. I'd forgotten that Mrs Leigh-Harcourt's rear garden partly backed on to that of the vicarage. When we followed Eddie through, I looked from the kitchen window diagonally across to Dora's house. 'With the two gardens it's a fair distance for a voice to carry. Did they have the window open?'

'Oh no! They were *in* their garden. At least, she was. He was in that old shed. The row seemed to be to do with him refusing to go indoors.'

'This was after midnight?'

'About one-thirty. Wasn't it, Edward?' I looked around, thinking someone else must have joined us, but she was addressing the breakfasting hound. Eddie looked up at her and gave a friendly bark. Then he finally came and nuzzled the side of my leg. 'There!' said Mrs Leigh-Harcourt, relaxing. 'I knew he'd be glad to see you.' A little later, when Eddie and I had said our thank-yous and were leaving by the front door, she confided, 'Whenever I've met Mrs Philpot, she's struck me as very kind and considerate . . . but only because it served some hidden purpose.' I made a neutral response and went on my way. Less than two days ago I would have leapt to Dora's defence.

There were no jobs lined up that day. I had my tea invitation from Dr Quibbley, but several hours needed to be killed beforehand. In the normal way I would have sneaked along to the One-in-the-Eye at opening time, but I didn't want to be lurching drunk by mid-afternoon. The only distraction to hand was my van, which had stalled several times for no obvious reason on my return trip from Brighton. Eddie and I got aboard and I drove haltingly down to Ron Woodhouse's garage. Ron didn't look overworked either. He was dozing in a deckchair at the edge of the forecourt when we hiccupped to a halt. As Eddie and I got out, Ron struggled to his feet with a grin. 'Good to see you, mate. Last night our pals with white sticks reckoned you were a goner.'

'What d'you mean?' Albert and Alfred in their near-blindness sometimes appeared to possess psychic powers. For a chilly moment I thought they had sensed the danger I had risked at Darren's flat. Ron immediately scotched that notion.

'They were worried that you'd taken the pledge. P'rhaps because of that fall of yours.'

'I came straight to the pub after I fell.'

'Not that same night, though.'

'I was drinking there yesterday lunch-time.'

'Not last night, though. Albert and Alfred think anyone who doesn't come to the pub twice a day has given up the game.'

'I had things to do, but I'll have a pint at lunch-time.

And I'll be back there this evening, unless my tea with Dr Quibbley runs into overtime.'

Ron gave me a look of disbelief. 'The green-faced dwarfette? You can't fancy her!'

'You don't know the woman. I've met her since. And it's nothing to do with fancying her, anyway. She's very interesting. I saw her on the telly, reducing some smart-ass male professor to a gibbering idiot.'

'So what'll she do to you, my friend? Or does she like a bit of rough? I hear they sometimes do, these clever females.'

'Piss off, will you!' My work kept me reasonably fit, but I was no muscleman. 'I think she's looking for some contact with the village, that's all. Meantime, any chance you can find out why this van is suffering from mechanical asthma?'

Ron took my keys and moved the van into the garage workshop. There he left the motor running, got out and opened up the bonnet. After a cursory look and listen he muttered, 'Dear-oh-dear-oh-dear! Tell you what, I'll give you a fiver for the tyres.'

'Twenty quid, and it's a deal.'

He grunted, and started connecting the vehicle up to an electronic box of tricks which always left me baffled. My odd job skills were wide-ranging but did not include motor repairs. I went and sat in Ron's deckchair while he got on with it. Beside the chair was a copy of the previous day's local evening paper. The front page featured an arsonist caught 'flaming-red-handed' in the storeroom of a sports shop. The youth in question had failed to qualify for an athletics team even though he had spent a fortune on the best gear. Unrepentantly, he reckoned he 'knew where to put the blame!' I concluded (not for the first time that week) that sport didn't always lead to a balanced and healthy mind. Feeling a little smug, I flipped through the inner pages till my eye fell on a photograph of Dr Quibbley. She looked fetching in a beret and a light-coloured raincoat with its collar up. The associated article read:

WILL DOCTOR JAN TAKE
LIBRARY DOWN THE BRAIN DRAIN?

It is reported that local university high-flyer, Dr Janice Quibbley, 41, fierce defender of Britain's right to retain the contents of the Heatherstone Castle Library has been 'head-hunted' by an American college.

Heatherstone, near King's Lynn in Norfolk, is owned by Sussex millionaire businessman Rudolph Wescott, who has decided to sell the castle in order to concentrate on South Coast interests. 'Heatherstone is a nice ancient pile, but I'm intending to create employment opportunities in my own back yard. Sale of the castle library to the highest bidder—from America or Japan—will help transform the lives of youngsters in Sussex.' On hearing that Dr Quibbley herself is to be exported, Mr Wescott said, 'I always felt there was an underlying hypocrisy in the opposition to my plans. These academics fly to and fro across the Atlantic whenever they like, and then make a fuss at the movement of books and papers they can check on micro-film.'

Experts say that the Heatherstone Library could fetch upwards of £1.2m.

When Ron came from re-tuning the engine I waved the paper at him. 'Did you read this? About Janine Quibbley —except they get it wrong and call her Janice.'

'Nah,' he said, wiping his hands on a rag. 'I hardly ever read the stories. I look at the pictures.'

'There's a good photo of her. I'm surprised you didn't spot it.' He took the paper out of my hands.

'That isn't anything like the woman we met.'

'She doesn't wear a face-pack all the time.'

'Mm. Not bad for forty-one. Looks like one of those women in the French Resistance.' After reading further he added, 'Good job you aren't after her, Sam. You'd have to emigrate. This Wescott character sounds a bit of a wanker. Why doesn't he just admit he wants a load of ready money, like the rest of us?'

'How much do I owe you?'

'Didn't mean that. But since you mention it and since I can't be bothered to put it through the books, you can buy me a proper lunch.'

'Tony Koerner won't let you in the posh bar looking like that.'

'So I'll wash and change. Ralph should be here to take over in five minutes. You can mind the forecourt till then.'

I stood up as he handed me the key to the till. Serving petrol was something I'd done for him one or two times before. Before he moved off, I said casually, 'If you don't want that paper any more I'll have it.' He hit me on the head with it and then stuffed it in at the open neck of my shirt.

'There. Right next to your heart. But remember, you need a visa to go to the States.'

'Do us a favour! I'm off women altogether at the moment, especially if they live in Miston.'

'So why were you seen the night before last, letting young Josie out of your house at half-midnight?'

'She was worried about Darren.'

Having been surprised into confirming the story, I expected Ron to press for more details. Instead, he said, 'Darren's not around. Anyway she's s'posed to have given him the push, you lucky lad!' And he set out for his house up behind the garage, muttering, 'I dunno. It's not bloody fair. Why do they all call on you? What about the rest of us unattached fellers?'

He didn't turn back for an answer, and I was left to wonder who had been keeping an eye on my house late at night. Quite soon I was diverted from this new bout of futile worry. Eddie had wandered to the far side of the main road and had to be called back when there was a lull in the traffic. Then three cars in quick succession stopped for petrol.

When Ron and I entered the dining area of the pub there was no sign of Gordon Summing. Tony Koerner was his usual charmless self, stepping back and regarding our comparatively tidy clothes with a smirk.

'If it wasn't for the dog I'd think you were two other blokes, but really I think you ought to leave Fido in the van if you want to eat, Sam.'

'OK, as long as you ban your own animal.' The landlord's dog, an overweight corgi, was wandering between the tables. Instead of pressing the point, Koerner turned and walked over to an unfortunate bunch of diners who looked embarrassed when asked if the meal was to their liking. Eddie followed Ron to a table while I went in search of a menu and some drinks. Immediately I ran into Josie who came from behind the bar and led me to a quiet corner.

'Have you heard from Darren yet?'

'No.' I kept quiet about my visit to his flat. 'What about you?'

'Not a word. Why weren't you in here last night?'

'I went somewhere else—to see a friend, OK?'

She didn't look satisfied, but the landlord's wife, Marianne Koerner, didn't give her a chance to say so. She swept past, muttering, 'Josie, get back to work, or else.'

Josie glared after her and murmured, 'I'm going to kill that woman!'

'Can you get us a couple of pints first?'

'All right, since it's you, me old partner! But we must have a chat later.' She went back behind the bar, saying, 'I was going to come round your house after closing, but I was too wiped out.'

'Just as well. You were seen the first time.'

'Who cares?' she said, but her eyes showed surprise and a hint of worry. When the drinks had been served and paid for, she asked, 'So who would have been watching your house that late?'

'I'm not sure.' It was odd that Ron hadn't pulled my leg about it the very first lunch-time after Josie's visit. She was called away to the other bar before the matter could be discussed further. I tucked a menu under my arm and took the drinks to the table where Ron stirred from a doze.

'Sorry, mate. I was up early, fishing. It's left me knackered. That reminds me . . .' He brought from his pocket an oblong piece of celluloid about the size of a post-card. 'I found this on the riverbank.'

I held the transparency up to the light and could just about make out that it was divided into many small sections with (possibly naked) bodies (probably) getting up to no good. 'What you need is a micro-fiche viewer like they have in libraries and bookshops.'

'OK. Why don't we pop into Lewes after lunch? Ralph is manning the pumps for the rest of the day.'

'As long as we don't get arrested. Whatever's on that sheet ain't as innocent as a catalogue of books.'

Ron gave a dirty chuckle and took the celluloid sheet from me. 'I'll mind it. You're already having enough fun. I saw you and Josie in a huddle before the dragon-lady came and broke it up.'

'We were just chatting. But who told you she was at my house? Why didn't you get on to me about it this time yesterday?'

'I never heard about it till late afternoon, from your new chum, Gordon Summing! I was up at the dairy doing a call-out repair on a depot wagon. When I went into the office, he said, 'You're a pal of Sam Bevan's, aren't you? How serious is it between him and that barmaid at the Broken Harold?' I looked dead surprised, so he said how he'd been out to dinner in the village and parked near your house, and when he was just about to turn the key and drive off home, who should come skipping out through your garden gate but . . . !' And he nodded unsubtly across the room.

'When I first met the guy he made a crack about me being her new boyfriend. I refused to respond.'

Ron grinned. 'I told him you must've decided to try out Albert and Alfred's advice.'

'What advice?'

'To switch your affections from you-know-who. But I said I thought the lovely lady of Church Lane would always be your true love. Smoothy Gordon didn't seem to see the funny side of this. He ended the discussion sharpish.'

Ron attended to his drink and the menu while I uneasily considered Summing's curiosity. How had he known he was parked near my house? And did this extreme reaction to the mention of Dora mean he was another dangerously jealous man? That hardly seemed fair when there was a potentially violent husband on the loose.

'Can you run to a T-bone steak?'

'What? Oh, sure, anything you want. Unless you fancy eating somewhere else. After all, we are going on into Lewes.'

'Yeah, but we're here now,' Ron insisted. 'I'll have it well done, with chips and forget the salad. Ta very much!' He handed me the menu. I decided I could just about face a bowl of soup and went back over to the bar where Marianne Koerner took my order. As she wrote it down with unsmiling concentration I wondered if there was anything I could say which would make her go easier on Josie.

'That's £14.45.' No 'please', and certainly no 'sir'. I paid up, relieved that I hadn't opened my mouth. This woman was clearly in a bad mood. She didn't even change her manner at the approach of the man I least wanted to see. Instead, she handed over my numbered ticket and went off into the kitchen without wasting another word.

Gordon Summing gave me an apparently friendly pat on the arm. 'Good day, Sam. Does this mean you've taken a liking to our side of the pub?'

'Not for long at these prices.'

'Is the food cheaper in the public bar?'

'Since I usually stick to a sandwich, yes.'

'Accept my job offer and such considerations won't worry you for a while. Perhaps I should have been more specific about remuneration. Do you have a minute?' I looked across to where Ron was awake and watching us. He raised his glass in our direction. This seemed to discourage Summing. 'Since Mr Woodhouse awaits you, we'll leave it. But ring me any time.' He moved off to his window table and was immediately attended by Tony Koerner.

We were out of the pub in less than an hour, but not without incident. While I switched to coffee after my soup, Ron put away two more pints and a double Scotch. He then brought out the transparency and dangled it before the face of a bearded gent at the next table. 'You look like a librarian. Could we borrow your whateveritscalled to look at our dirty pictures?' The man totally ignored Ron who (to my great relief) took this for a reasonable refusal.

As we stepped into the car park, a stranger blocked Ron's path and said in a wheezy, whispering voice, 'You have something of mine.' This man was not young, and he didn't look well. Cropped grey hair came down in the ghost of a fringe along the top of a sallow, sucked-in face. His striped suit hung loose, seeming to cover a painfully skinny frame. But because he looked like a man in close personal negotiations with the Grim Reaper, I couldn't help feeling that he was a dangerous character. Ron was too tanked up to notice anything of this. Without a word he pushed past the stranger and went to straight to his car. We had left my van at the garage.

'Do you think I should drive?' I suggested, catching him up. I was prepared for an argument, but he tossed me the keys. Unfortunately, as he walked around to the passenger's side his way was blocked again. I clenched my teeth, fists and anything else that was clenchable. Fights weren't my scene, but I knew how to get tense. In the spirit of the occasion Eddie gave a long low growl, but unlike me, he moved up close behind Ron.

The stranger repeated his initial remark, and Ron calmly said, 'Are you telling me you've lost something?' The man nodded. 'Well, suppose I was to hand whatever it is in at the local cop-shop, would you go and claim it?'

'That's none of your business.' The man's voice sounded even more like gas escaping from a metal pipe.

'But it is. You see that man over in his garden, the guy

in the blue shirt? That's our rural bobby, tending his nasturtiums. Let's go and check it out with him. Ask him if I ought to hand anything over to you without proof of your ownership.'

The man looked across at the stooping figure, then back at Ron. He took a slow inward breath before saying, 'I could leave you standing there a dead man and even your chum the other side of the car wouldn't be sure anything had happened . . . but I'll bide my time.' He turned and walked away.

Ron looked at me, winked and asked, 'By the way, who is that bloke digging the police house garden?'

I didn't have a clue. It wasn't the local constable, but I wasn't sure Ron had pulled off such a great trick.

By the time we entered the library Ron had completely sobered up. His speedy power of recovery still managed to surprise me, though I felt his internal organs might eventually and drastically pay the price. For the moment he was clear-headedly approaching the micro-fiche viewer. I hung back a little, ready to distract any member of the public or staff who might try to look over his shoulder. Luckily, the place was almost empty of borrowers. The only visible librarian was shelving a trolley full of books three stacks away. As I waited, the quietness became an exaggeration of what a library should be like. All I could hear was the hum of a distant extractor fan, the occasional wheel squeak from the librarian's trolley, and Ron's breathing. Suddenly there was a violent scraping of a chair as Ron got up, turned towards me, and stood there silent and white-faced.

'Not a great turn-on?' I asked softly. He shook his head. I moved past him and sat down. The viewer had gone out of focus. I turned a nob, leaned in to have a close look, and wished I hadn't. The smaller sections of the transparency did indeed contain photographs (possibly film or video stills) of sexual acts, and in each case at least one of the participants was a child. Mostly they were girls—usually South-East Asian in appearance—but as I moved the scanner in a hypnotic daze of disgust I discovered a handful of boys among the victims. They could only be described as victims. The photos were technically very clear, and wherever the child was smiling, the eyes showed fear. Mostly though, the faces were bled of expression, courtesy of drugs or some other brutality. Whatever the background circumstances, each photo brazenly sported a clear code number in its top left corner. This piece of celluloid was indeed a catalogue, though whether for larger scale photographs or for videos it was not clear. And it became unlikely that I would find out. Just as I was switching off the machine and removing the offending sheet, a hand reached in and snatched it from me. The man from the pub car park! When I tried to get up, he lowered his free hand and found a pressure point which kept me pinned down in agony. The wheezing voice asked, 'If I was to give you a piece of advice what would it be, Sonny Jim?'

'Don't move?'

He increased the pressure and I groaned, but my groan was not allowed a hearing, because he had simultaneously pushed my face against his waistcoat. The cloth smelled of dry-cleaning fluid. Bending down he whispered, 'What I would advise is a big attack of amnesia!'

I was suddenly released, and by the time I had rubbed my neck and breathed in some non-chemical air, the man had disappeared. At this I was greatly relieved, but didn't feel good at all when I realized that Ron had disappeared as well.

CHAPTER 9

Tea with Menaces

Remembering the stranger's car park boast—that he could kill someone without a close bystander knowing—I searched the nearest bookstacks dreading to find one dead (but possibly still upright) garage owner. Not a sign. I went out to the street. Not a sign. I didn't feel well myself, and I sat down on a step. Within moments I felt a tap on the shoulder.

'Sorry I walked out on you, mate. I was dying for a drink of water.'

'You what!'

'I trespassed in the staff area. A nice girl took pity on me. Said I looked very ill. Not surprising. Those bleeding photos turned my stomach. So how are you feeling?' He sat beside me.

'Fucking lucky to be alive, is how I feel, mate!' I rubbed my neck again but the discomfort persisted. 'I was sneaked up on—while you were getting water and sympathy!' After hearing the full sorry tale Ron did his best to apologize, but I grumbled on. 'What the hell's going on round these parts, anyway? In a single week I could have been murdered twice! I think I'll move back to London. It's safer!'

Ron stood up, turned and pulled me to my feet. 'Come on. The least I can do is treat you to a few pints. There must be an all-day pub nearby.'

'I don't feel like a drink. Let's just get back to Miston.'

'If you insist. I don't blame you for feeling rough.'

We went around the corner to our parking place on Lewes High Street. Eddie, locked in the car, saw us and started to bark. At the same time, my attacker came out of an alley and walked away from us up the hill. We didn't give chase but checked out where he might have been. The alleyway, signposted as Ladd's Court, became a narrow tunnel between and under two shops before it emerged into a wider, open area. A quintet of early seventeenth-century buildings gave on to this courtyard. The furthest and best kept one sported a solicitor's brass plaque beside its door. The rest seemed to be private houses, two giving straight on to the court, while the others had tiny, overgrown gardens. There was barely a sign of life, except for two young women chatting over a photocopier on the solicitor's ground floor. Somewhere a telephone purred to itself.

'Shall we tell the police?' I asked.

Ron pulled a face. 'No witnesses. No remaining evidence. No point.'

My determination not to look towards the vicarage was nearly successful. I had walked around the church side of Dr Quibbley's bungalow and found the kitchen door wide open. Since I was shuffling along, eyes downcast, I spotted splinters of glass on the mat. One pane in the door had been thoroughly smashed. I retreated a couple of paces, wondering if the break-in had been witnessed, and threw a glance up at the next house. A curtain twitched as whoever was watching me withdrew deep into shadow. No offer of help seemed likely, so I cautiously entered the bungalow alone, expecting to find Dr Quibbley bound and gagged—or worse! I discovered her in a small, office-like room. She sat glumly at an antique desk but appeared to be physically unharmed. An answering machine was playing back its messages. She gestured me towards the room's only other chair. For a minute or so the recorded calls were nothing but beeps and silences. Finally, there came a welcome burst of Scottish humanity: 'Jan, dear, this is Mum. Can you ring me soon? I've been hearing rumours about you going to America!'

Dr Q. reset the machine and stared at it for a moment. Then she turned to stare blankly at me. Slightly embarrassed, I said, 'I'm Sam Bevan. You invited me for tea.' She slowly nodded. 'And as the local odd job man, perhaps I could temporarily board up your back door.'

'Could you?'

'Sure. And unless you want a specialist glazier, I could finish the job off tomorrow with reinforced glass—much harder to break in. Have you called the law yet?'

'I was the one who broke in. I left my keys here when I went to work.' She shook her head. 'But someone else might be tempted to follow my example. Could you check the other doors and windows while I put the kettle on? Those silent phone calls worry me.'

'Lots of people still don't like leaving messages on machines. Me, for instance.'

'I think it was the same person ringing again and again.' She got up and left the room. I eased myself into the space beyond the desk and found a shut and locked double-glazed window. Similar fixtures were to be found in the other rooms, and the front door had locks strong enough to deter anyone except a super-pro . . . or a mad axeman. I joined her in the kitchen where she was sweeping up the last of the glass. 'Sorry. I should have done this before you had to walk through it.' The kettle came to the boil and I took over the tea-making. 'What a useless hostess I am! By the way, where's your friendly dog?'

'Sleeping off a late lunch.'

'Perhaps it's just as well. I wouldn't have wanted him to cut a paw.' Her kitchen was efficiently laid out, everything easy to find. A great deal of expensive and advanced hardware lined one wall. She saw me looking and said, 'I haven't a clue how half these labour-saving wonders work. I took this place furnished and fitted. My landlord's a particle physicist, earning a fortune at a "defence" establishment in Texas. He got signed up just after this dream-house of his was finished.'

'I think I saw him a few times, hanging around while it was being built. So you don't have much furniture of your own?'

'Only my desk and typing chair and a few thousand books, though some of them still have to be fetched . . . from the flat I used to share . . . with my ex-fiancé. Shall we have this tea before it stews?'

We transferred to the sitting-room, armed each with a plate of biscuits and a mug. The particle physicist certainly knew about comfortable chairs. The one I chose had a built-in leg rest and gave me the sensation of floating in mid-air. 'Oh God! Can I borrow this? I don't have anything to sit on that doesn't give me backache.'

Dr Quibbley smiled and relaxed a little. 'I dropped off

in one last night. Probably would have slept there till morning if it wasn't for the racket in next-door's garden.'

'Oh?'

'For some reason our poor vicar was wanting to spend the night in their shed. But before he could get his sleeping-bag spread out, Mrs Vicar came screeching at him to come indoors. He eventually gave in, but on the condition she would leave him alone in his study.' Dr Quibbley gave me a mischievous look. 'I live outside the world of village gossip. Perhaps you can fill me in on the background here.'

'I've always thought they were a happy couple.'

'You think such a thing exists?'

'Occasionally. My late marriage had its brief moments of contentment.'

'And then?'

'Rosemary opted for brief moments of contentment with someone else. A fellow journalist.'

'A fellow journalist of yours?'

'No, she was a journalist. Still is.'

'Locally?'

'In London. I moved down here a couple of years ago. My aunt died and left me her house. A shame, but it couldn't have been more timely. Meant my ex-missus could keep the flat and buy me out gradually.'

'Very civilized.'

'There was a fair bit of blood-letting before that. But now we get on OK, mainly because we hardly ever see each other.'

Dr Quibbley sipped her tea before asking, 'What were you in those days? I can't help feeling you're in a sort of exile here, pretending to be an odd job man. Just like you pretend to have very little interest in the doings of my next door neighbours.'

'I used to be an architect, but I'm not in exile. I like it here. I feel settled. As for the Reverend Philpot . . . and Dora . . .'

She smiled. 'As for Dora?'

The world's most comfortable chair couldn't hold me

back. I felt the need to be on my feet as I launched into a speech for the defence. 'All of a sudden half the village seems to have got it in for her, but it's not really fair. The vicar's a pretty weird character. Dangerous to himself and others. Two days ago he accidentally knocked me off a high gallery in the church tower. If I hadn't swung down on the bell ropes I'd be dead—or heading for life in a wheelchair!'

'You're sure it was an accident?'

I shrugged. 'He says he grabbed at me in panic, because he has terrible vertigo.'

'Why was he up there at all, with vertigo?'

'He claimed it was to show how desperate he was to ask me a favour. But he never got his request out . . . not until he turned up at my house later.' Dr Quibbley waited patiently. I was unable to stop the story half way. 'He asked me to act as an amateur marriage guidance counsellor for them.'

'That *is* weird, if, as you say, they're a happy couple.'

I sat down again, saying, 'OK, so they aren't. But he doesn't want to lose her.'

'I suppose losing a wife must be painful and very embarrassing if you're a man of the cloth. But do you know why he asked you in particular?'

'Dora used to talk to me a lot when I was decorating the vicarage. He hoped I could find out why she had fallen out of love with him. To give him a chance to put it right.'

'But supposing you had personal reasons for not wanting them to make it up?'

'Why should I?'

'Some men still find an English Rose irresistible.' I failed to respond. 'So it wasn't Mrs Philpot you were waiting for outside the Brighton Pavilion? When you couldn't wait to get rid of me and my Hungarians?'

'Sorry if it looked like that.' I glanced at my watch. 'Shouldn't you have phoned your mother? She sounded quite anxious.'

'She always sounds anxious. But I'll call her later. She plays poker in the afternoons. And wins, more often than not.' She got up and took my empty cup. 'Would you like something stronger than tea? I fancy a gin and tonic.'

'Thanks. Unless you've some Scotch.'

'I should certainly hope so,' she said, heightening her accent. As she went through to the kitchen, I heard a motor-bike pulling up in the lane. The bungalow had a small lobby inside the front door. There was a clatter of the letter-box, and my mind jumped through a quick series of associations. Special delivery—dispatch rider—Darren! Again, I leapt from my luxury chair. Through a window I saw a leathered and helmeted figure striding back towards the lane. I banged on the glass. The biker turned for a split second, but the helmet visor completely blacked out his face. I rushed into the lobby and tried to open the front door. A mortice lock made this impossible, and there was no key to hand. I ran through the living-room, through the kitchen (almost crashing into my startled hostess), and out and around the building, reaching the front garden path just as the rider was back astride his bike and revving his engine. When I waved and shouted, 'Darren! Wait a minute, who-ever you are!' he tossed his masked head back—in laughter? —and roared away. Within moments he was turning the corner out of the lane.

Strong drinks were needed. When Dr Quibbley opened the specially delivered envelope, out fell a single sheet of paper which had been singed around the edges. In the centre of the sheet, painted in sludgy red letters by means of a child's stencilling set was the stark message:

EMIGRATE OR ELSE

CHAPTER 10

Riverside Blues

I drove my revitalized van into Lewes to fetch two panes of strengthened glass, arriving back at the Quibbley bunga-low by the middle of Friday morning. As I was unloading my stuff, the old caretaker, Mr Ainsly, came from the church. He was his usual portentous self as he confided, 'The vicar's not at all in the best of health. He's leaving us for a few days—maybe even for longer—to go on a rest cure.'

'I could do with one of them,' I muttered.

'If you were suffering like Reverend Philpot you wouldn't be so flip! He may look like a strong young man, but every so often he's subject to nervous collapse.'

'No kidding!'

'If you don't want to believe me . . . !'

'I do, I do. So they're going today?'

'Today or tomorrow, depending on how fit he is to travel. Mrs Philpot will have to do the driving, of course. She's a brick.'

Since kind remarks about Dora had become rare, I patted him warmly on the shoulder. 'If you see them before they go, give them my best wishes.' A flash of mistrust crossed his face. Then he must have decided I was being sincere because he promised to pass on the message. I went back to work with mixed emotions. Life would be less of a turmoil with Dora out of the village, but I still longed to know where I stood. Was I right to suspect that her visit to my house had only been a wild spin-off from her marriage crisis? That it had hardly been anything to do with me?

An hour later, Dr Quibbley's back door was re-glazed and more secure. She was still out at the university, so I locked up with her spare keys. As I finished packing away my tools, I heard a voice softly calling, 'Sam! We must talk!' Dora's face peered between two trellises. I was shocked by the extreme pallor of her cheeks. 'I'm sorry I stood you up. There's no time to explain right now, but will you give me a second chance?'

'Is it worth it? Your husband came to see me the other night. An hour and a half after you left.' She gave a nervous glance behind her. 'He passed out on my sofa, but when he came to in the morning he asked me to help save your marriage.'

'Oh hell!'

'Since you and I "got on" so well, I was to find out how he can win you back from your lover—whoever that might be.'

'You know.'

'Do I? Since he never accused me directly, I wasn't sure at all.'

She gave a defiant stare. 'Meet me in half an hour. By the Garden Centre.'

'Which one?' There were two of these overblown nurseries close to the village.

'The one just south of Woodhouse's Garage.' I suppressed a smile. This would be a secret meeting almost under the nose of Ron, King of the Gossips. She went on to be more specific. 'There's a lane beyond the Centre's entrance, leading towards the river. Half way down it you'll find an abandoned car. I'll see you there.' And she disappeared, leaving me still in a muddle. I was pleased to be back in contact but I was also wondering who she usually met at this out of the way location.

There was no sign of proprietor Woodhouse as I drove past the garage. My meeting might remain private as long as I didn't go and spill the beans myself. Leaving the pub the night before, Ron had quizzed me about an earlier slip of the tongue:

'Listen, mate. There's something that's been niggling me. Back in Lewes you said you could've been murdered twice. Once would have been by the geezer at the Library. Who was the other failed killer?'

'I wasn't being serious.'

'Oh no? I bet you were thinking of Steve Philpot.'

'Don't be daft.'

'That accident of yours, falling down the tower—I got the feeling at the time you weren't telling all. So . . . is our vicar a raving, jealous maniac?'

'It was an accident. But he was involved.'

'I knew it! I knew it. But don't worry. Your secret's safe with me.'

Well, either it was or it wasn't. And at least I hadn't told him anything like as much as I'd confided to Dr Quibbley.

I parked my van in the Garden Centre car park rather than take it right down to the meeting place. After checking to see if Dora had done the same—she hadn't—I walked a short distance along the main road and looked down the dirt lane. The dumped car was just visible amid a mass of nettles. I was already on edge, and my nerves were jangled further by a sudden burst of sirens, distant but getting nearer. I ducked away from the road and went warily along the lane. The car was an old beetle-style Volkswagen, so completely rusted that there was no evidence of its former colour. Since Dora couldn't be hiding in the nettles, I walked on as far as a tubular steel gate. Wheel tracks ran from the lane into an open field but soon forked left and right. Beyond that, the field rose as a grassy bank which I guessed would fall away to the river. This area was new to me, though it was near where Ron did his fishing. The strip of obscene celluloid must have been found not far away, and yet it was hard to imagine my very urban attacker losing it in such a spot. As I stood and pondered this oddity, the existence of the river was confirmed. A yacht's mast-head slowly bobbed along, just visible above the bank.

'Sam! Sam Bevan!' In shirt-sleeves but wearing heavy cord trousers and strong leather boots, Gordon Summing came striding across the southern section of the field. He could see me because the hedge by the gate dipped below shoulder level. Halting some twenty yards off he called, 'Have you come to size up the job?'

'Sorry?'

Summing gestured behind him with his walking stick. In the near distance stood a line of ruined outbuildings. 'A sad sight, I know, but the foundations are surprisingly sound. Come across and have a proper look.' Without waiting for a response he turned and headed straight towards the collapsing cow sheds. With as little enthusiasm as possible, I ambled through the gate and plodded across the uneven pasture. When I finally caught up with him, Summing put on an air of amused concern. 'You're unfit. You should change your lifestyle, Sam. Too much time spent in the public bar of the Broken Harold Inn.'

'Profound advice. Must make a note of it.'

Summing snorted and gave the nearest timber upright a push. A sizeable section of wall crashed over. He laughed excessively. 'Never mind! All this junk will have to go before you can work your wonders.'

'I'm still not clear what wonders you want. Why did they put cow sheds all the way down here in the first place?'

'Look over there.' He pointed to another ruin some fifty yards back towards the road. 'That was the farmhouse. Completely gutted by fire thirty years ago. The farmer died getting his family out.'

A dark edge to his voice made me ask, 'Was he a friend of yours?'

'No. Not at all. I was a schoolboy, nowhere near here.' That was the limit of his personal revelation, except that he went on to say, 'But I was the one who persuaded the widow that the land had gone to waste for long enough. She'd been keeping it as a futile memorial.' Summing jumped up on some uncluttered concrete. 'What I want is a couple of sturdy storehouses that won't go flying up to Lewes next time there's a hurricane.' There was a steady wind coming up from the sea that morning, but it didn't altogether block off another siren echoing from further inland. Summing didn't seem to notice it. 'What I want here are structures that you enter from the top, by means of an exterior staircase or something. That way the walls can be proofed up to a level of, say, three metres—in case of flooding from the river.'

'How often has the Ouse burst its banks?'

'Weather patterns are dramatically changing the world over.' He looked at his watch. 'I'm nearly late for a meeting. Come and see me with your decision tomorrow.'

'Easier just to phone you.'

'That would be inconsiderate. If it's "no", I want the chance to argue you out of it face to face.' He raised his unneeded walking stick in a brusque gesture of farewell (or dismissal) and paced away. With uncanny timing, a Range-Rover came through from the next field along. It moved in a shallow arc, paused to pick the Boss up, and headed for a gateway to the main road. I walked back towards the dirt lane, resentfully determined to phone in my refusal, or else not even bother. Dora still hadn't showed and I waited another ten minutes only. My mood did not improve as I asked myself, where was she this time? Had she phoned Summing to let him know where I would be? And, even if that encounter was a complete coincidence, what were these bloody storehouses going to be used for anyway, out in the middle of nowhere?

The CLOSED sign was up at the garage as I drove back, so Ron would already be installed at the pub. His assistant, Ralph, didn't always turn up on time, but that never distracted Ron from his daily habits. I needed a drink myself, but I went to my house first to liberate Eddie. As I let myself into the hall, I received a curious sort of reception from the moody creature. He came and licked my hand, but there was a shifty look in his eyes. I squatted down and said in a soft voice, 'OK, what have you been up to, boy?'

'Orrrh!'

'Yeah? Go on. Show me.'

He hesitated before leading me into the kitchen where a chewed-up, soggy envelope lay on the floor beside his food bowl. I picked it up with a measure of distaste, followed by a rush of emotional anxiety. The contents were damp but not destroyed.

My dearest Sam,

I've let you down again, I was about to leave the house when Steve went into what almost looked like an epileptic fit. Thank God, he came out of it quickly, but he pleaded with me to stay near. Now at least he's dozed off, so I'm hoping I can manage a quick dash to your letter-box before we go away.

Did you know we are going away? Heaven knows how long for, because Steve's breakdown has become so extreme, I shall write again, but I want you to know how much the other night meant to me. I wasn't able to face going straight home. I walked for miles and miles in the dark—and when I did get back Steve wasn't in the house. I was praying that he had left me, but I suppose I didn't deserve such luck.

As far as I am concerned, *you* are my lover—until you tell me otherwise. Obviously, from your remark across the garden wall, you think there is someone else—but that is based on a delusion of Steve's. The horrible coincidence that he decided to come to you for help is going to make it even harder for me to choose the right moment to tell him the truth. But that's my problem, not yours.

I know how unreliable I must seem, but please be patient. You can see that the mess I'm in will take a bit of getting out of!

You mean so much to me!

All my love,

Dora.

I read this through three times before hiding it in the secret compartment under my workbench. After that, I still needed a drink, but, in defiance of all the possible complications, I felt a lot happier. Full of smiles I waltzed into the One-in-the-Eye's public bar to find only Albert and Alfred. It was Eddie who sensed the mood of the place before I did. He immediately lay down in a shrinking pose as I slipped on to a stool. Looking across at the white-sticked double act I said, 'Good day to you too, gents.'

In response, I received a harmonized grunt. Then Albert said, 'There's no reason he should know.'

'Fair enough,' Alfred replied. 'But why does he have to be so bleedin' cheerful about it.'

'Because he doesn't know, you silly old bugger!'

According to tradition, it was now my turn. 'OK, I give in. Apart from all the usual things, what is it I don't know?'

Albert took a long sip from his pint. And Alfred said, 'Ron Woodhouse has had it.'

I only half took this in, because I was leaning across the bar looking for the possibility of being served. There was no sign of Josie. Albert finished drinking and said with a slight catch in his throat, 'He's a goner.'

Remembering that they had recently applied this term to me I said, 'Come off it! He won't be long. He hasn't missed a drinking session in all the time I've lived in the village.'

The two of them fell silent as Tony Koerner came through. While automatically pulling a pint for me, he murmured, 'What can I say, Sam? Ron and I had our occasional differences, but it's a tragic thing!' Albert and Alfred muttered a grim chorus of agreement. I started to bring out some money but Koerner raised a hand. 'No, no. This one's on the house. I'm sometimes a bit off-hand to you gentlemen, but you're the backbone of our clientele. That's the truth.'

I forced a 'Thanks, Tony,' and wished with a passion that I could be anywhere else. In my head I was no longer ignoring the obvious, in fact, I was desperate to know the full details, and yet I wished I didn't have to learn them here. This was extremely perverse, of course. Ron himself had relished many a calamity in this very bar and at my first swig of beer I knew I was slighting his memory as a pub gossip. Koerner was back in the other bar, so I went and sat at the table with Alfred and Albert. Before I could ask anything, Albert kicked off the routine with which they would be informing all the other regulars as the lunch-time session progressed.

'Young Ralph turned up early to take his turn at the petrol pumps . . .'

'. . . but not early enough!'

CHAPTER 11

Original Weapons

By two-thirty I was weaving along the middle of the church lane, that is until Eddie barked me clear of an oncoming car. The driver—not a local—slowed down and swore at the two of us. I responded with a shakily aimed punch which glanced off the rear coachwork as he drove away. My knuckles ached.

Having tottered on to the vicarage, I surveyed an empty drive. Was Dora out shopping for their journey? All the better. I would confront her husband before she returned. Straight talking might even shock him out of his state of nervous collapse. After ringing the doorbell, I started to practise my speech aloud:

'Steve, I've come to say you've got it wrong about who Dora's lover is. It is me, Sam Bevan! And she loves me, Sam Bevan, in return. And in case you're wondering why I'm telling you this . . . this is why I'm telling you. I now know I must not risk any more delay in this world. The sudden death of a good friend has convinced me there's no time to lose. That's why I'm telling you how things stand, even though you're ill, which I'm extremely sorry about, by the way!'

I mumbled on a bit before it dawned on me that no one had come to the vicarage door. I rang the bell again, but was shouted at from nearby before I could restart my declaration.

'Forget it, Sam! They've been gone these two hours.'

I lurched around to see Dr Quibbley beyond a low privet hedge. Eddie gave a gleeful bark and bounded off in her direction. I successfully followed his leap into her garden, but momentum took me on to trip over the bloody animal as he turned and looked back in amazement. With a groan

I rolled on to my back, looked up at Dr Q., and said, 'I'm pissed.'

'Och well, come in and have a coffee. Or be sick. Or both.' She offered a hand and pulled me up with remarkable strength for such a small person. I was made to spin round so she could brush off twigs and grass. 'You must have been sober this morning. My kitchen door is in great shape.'

'Thanks. But I saw Dora just after I'd finished the job, across the back fence.'

'And did she break your heart, or have you been out celebrating?'

'We were supposed to meet later—away from here, and then she couldn't make it, but that was all explained in a letter she left at my house. I need to see her badly. A good mate of mine's been found dead in his car . . . with a hosepipe to the exhaust.'

'No! That's awful.'

'So I need to see Dora—and to tell her husband that life's too short. I need to see her.'

'So you've said.'

'To force the issue . . . to take her away with me . . . not just because I'm drunk . . .'

She took my arm. 'Absolutely not, but they aren't there, all the same.' Eddie raced ahead as she led me into the bungalow. She left the front door only on its Yale lock, a detail which I pointed out with a drunkard's insistence. 'Never mind. I'll make sure to double lock it when you're not here to defend me.'

'Are you glad I'm here? We haven't known each other long, but we're good friends, aren't we?'

'I hope so. I need a good friend.' And she left me in one of the super-comfortable chairs. In spite of my relaxed position, I was fighting off the urge to throw up over the expensive carpet. It seemed reckless of her to abandon me in this condition, but soon she was back with a plastic bucket. 'Here! In case the worst comes to the worst.' I hugged the bucket to me, feeling socially safer though no less nauseous. Coffee didn't help much. Half a sip made my stomach shudder. She took the cup away. 'What do you usually take when you're in this state?'

'Water, maybe.'

She returned to the kitchen and I could hear her every action amplified through alcoholic distortion. And then I could hear a motorbike in the far distance. I could hear it coming down the lane. I could hear it stop. I could hear the rider walking down the path—by which time I had dragged myself to just inside the front door. As that day's special delivery edged through the letter-box I pulled the door open to confront the leathered and helmeted bike-boy. Although he had height and probably strength on his side, I took him by surprise. He staggered and fell backwards on to the flagstones. I launched myself on top of him and yelled, 'Who sent you?'

He laughed as he struggled to get up. 'Get off me, you fucking prat! I'll knock the shit out of you if you don't!' I ignored the threat and tried to force his visor up, wanting at least to get a look at his face. In immediate response, he grabbed my wrists and drove my upper body away from his. My especially weak condition, if not my age, seemed to be siding with him until I suddenly spewed with a tremendous force. Vomit swamped his helmet and the top of his jacket. Even though his vision was impaired, I wasn't fit to take advantage. Luckily, Dr Quibbley and Eddie hurried to the rescue. She was carrying what looked like an ancient club and clobbered the biker's legs while Eddie circled his sprawled body, barking and growling by turns. Above the racket the sudden loser yelled, 'What's going on? I can't see a thing!'

'Take your helmet off then, before I bloody well knock it off!'

'Who's that? How many of you are there?'

'Just the three. Now—off with the helmet!'

'Hang on!' he cried out. My dizzying nausea had faded, and I watched keenly as he revealed his face. It wasn't Darren. But I had a notion I'd seen him before. He, on the other hand, was not concerned with looking at us. 'Fucking hell! My jacket's ruined!'

An unmoved Dr Quibbley stood over him, club at the ready. 'Who are you delivering for?'

'You wouldn't really use that, would you, love?'

She slammed it against his shoulder. The crunching contact even made me flinch. He rolled over, clasping his arm and moaning, but he still didn't reveal anything. While she was helping me up again, he got to his feet unaided, grabbed his dripping helmet, and hopped off at remarkable speed. Eddie followed, barking away, but it was not long before the bike's roar was fading into the distance. Dr Quibbley let drop her club and stood with hands on hips. 'Damn it all! I should have had another go at his shins!'

'Don't worry. I've remembered where I saw him before. I know where he lives.'

'How does that help?'

'If I stake the place out I might discover the connection you're after—without them knowing. Then I could be your star witness in court.'

Eddie, back from the lane, worked off his frustration on the discarded club until Dr Quibbley took it from him. 'I'll get you something else to chew. This is almost an antique.'

The dog moved over to me, looking up in a plaintive fashion. I shrugged at him. 'It's a valuable antique she just happens to whack people with.'

'As a matter of fact, it's my old hockey stick, but I keep it around in case of burglars. That's the first time I've ever hit anyone with it . . . apart from the odd schoolgirl.'

Around sunset, we were crouched in the back of my van, spying on the house which contained Darren's Brighton flat. I was sure the vomited-over delivery boy was also the youth who had grudgingly let me in several nights before.

His second message—or rather, the second message devised by his employer—had read:

TRAVEL IS GOOD FOR YOUR HEALTH
STAYING PUT IS VERY BAD

It was printed as before, using a child's stencil set, though not so neatly. Several of the letters were smudged, the red ink giving a slight hint of bleeding. The recipient was so angry she had nearly torn up the 'evidence'. I'd called out, 'Dr Quibbley, you mustn't!' She had thrust it at me, saying fiercely, 'You look after it, then, till I've calmed down. And since I call you by your first name, isn't it about time you returned the bloody compliment?' Holding the piece of paper and feeling slightly foolish, I'd said, 'Tell me where you filed away the first one, . . . Janine. I'll put this one with it.'

The back of my van was certainly not a place for formality, nor was it a place to relax. I had put tape over the rear windows, leaving a couple of spy holes. In the resulting privacy we were left to many agonized shifts of position and the occasional fit of cramp.

My recognition of the bike-boy was confirmed when he emerged from the house. Not surprisingly, he had changed his entire get-up, though he still paused to sniff at himself before hobbling around the corner. He was alone, but perhaps was on his way to meet the source of the stencilled messages. We clattered out of the van like a couple of true amateurs, with Janine going ahead while I locked the rear doors. By the time I rounded the bend neither of them was in sight. I rushed on, only to be grabbed from a domestic porch just before I reached the pub on the next corner.

'It's OK. He's gone for a drink.'

'So what do we do?'

She opened her shoulder-bag and pulled out a headscarf and a pair of shades When her 'disguise' was complete she said, 'Pretty bleedin' good, don'tcha think?'

'Passable, but why are you talking like an Australian?'

'That's my Brighton accent, you bastard!'

If a Brighton accent is a second cousin to Cockney, she was talking like a fifth cousin three times removed. I said, 'At least it isn't North of the Border, but I shouldn't try any long sentences.'

'No problem. You can do the talking.'

'Eh?'

'No one would recognize you as the pale and sickly figure of this afternoon. And you wouldn't want me to go into an unknown, maybe dangerous pub all on my own, would you?'

I gave a sigh. 'Pity you didn't bring your hockey stick.'

'You didn't bring your dog.'

'I know what he's like in the back of the van!' Also, Eddie was not a great help in an argument, except as a noise-maker. I turned up the collar of my clean shirt—I too had changed my clothes—and in we went, in among a crowd of about a hundred people, of whom at least sixty seemed to be queuing for a drink. If the bike-boy was intending to have a secret meeting, in many ways he couldn't have chosen a better place. It took several minutes before we caught sight of him at all. He was playing pool with some other lads. There were also a trio of girls, possibly connected to the players, though they were busy sharing an intense-looking call on the pub phone. No one around looked as though they would recognize a valuable historical manuscript if it bit them on the bum, but Janine was determined to hang on. I drew on all my professional resources and got in some drinks. We then stood and muttered to each other at the heart of the heaving mob—and I mean heaving. Outside of a football terrace or the rush hour tube, I've never been so aware of balance being at the whim of the mass. I drank my sour and cloudy beer fast to avoid spillage. But even in the crush, a local wise-guy had to decide he recognized my companion.

'Seen you on the telly, 'aven' I?'

I chipped in, 'Too right, my friend. She was on *Crime Watch*, and didn't they warn you she was dangerous?'

'Nah. It was that Channel bleedin' Four. She was showin' off wiv a load of interlecturals, in the slot where we was expectin' Sumo Wrestlin'.' And he turned to beckon a few of his fellow aggrieved. The last thing we needed was to become a centre of attention. Without debate, I dragged my academic friend out into the street.

'I could've handled it, Sam!'

'In which accent? Let's face it, your cover was blown, lady.'

She went into a quiet sulk as we slowly walked back the way we came. Then there was a sudden, brief swell of voices behind us. We instinctively ducked into a doorway before peering back to see who had followed us out of the pub. It was our boy! Either he'd overheard the fat wrestlers' fan club, or else he'd spotted our quick exit. After looking sharply left and right, he crossed the street to a public phone. The call was very brief and left him visibly downcast. He didn't re-enter the pub but walked speedily homewards. If he hadn't been so self-absorbed, he might have noticed us in yet another doorway, clinging together. When his footsteps died away, Janine murmured, 'Good job your beloved Dora can't see us now.'

'Or her husband. She says he took a shine to you, chatting over the hedge.'

'That's a fine boost to my ego. Being fancied by a mad vicar. Let's get going.' And we went back on the trail, eventually sneaking into the rear of the van once we could see that the lad was back in his flat.

Our renewed vigil was a short one. A car entered the street and pulled over so that the driver's door was close to the house. Neither of us could make out who was at the wheel. An adjacent streetlight threw the car's interior into deep shadow and the driver wasn't inclined to get out. The horn sounded once, and our biker promptly answered this summons, bowing low to talk to his visitor. It was another short conversation. Within a few seconds the youth reeled backwards, clutching his face.

Janine exclaimed, 'His nose must be broken! If they do that to their own, what have they got in mind for me?'

I was worrying along the same lines, especially after what happened next. As the car moved out and went past the van I caught a quick but clear glimpse of the driver's face, the ghoulish face of the man who with one hand had held me paralyzed while he reclaimed his strip of celluloid pornography.

CHAPTER 12

The Case of the Missing Barmaid

Comes a time in the affairs of an amateur sleuth when it's too late to go to the police. Too late because his or her own activities might appear suspicious. Mere fragments of evidence, if offered to the Force, would at best get a dismissive laugh, at worst lead to the gumshoe's own detention on a twisted-about charge, like—for example—assault by vomit on a 'perfectly innocent' messenger.

Janine was convinced her threatening notes had originated from Rudolph Wescott, the businessman who was trying to export the Heatherstone Library to the States. But if a willing policeman was to convey this accusation to Mr W., what might the latter say? 'Officer, would I really be so foolish, when I already have a highly respectable firm of auctioneers handling the sale for me? And by the by, who is this psychopath I'm supposed to be employing as my intermediary?' Who indeed? The Ghoul was a complete mystery man. No name. No link to any of the locals. Ron and I had never noticed him until he approached us in the pub car park, and Ron was no longer around to back up any of the story. When the Ghoul had advised me at the library to have 'a big attack of amnesia' it seemed a cowardly but sensible path to follow. But now I felt it was vital for Janine's safety to discover who the hell the Ghoul was. Since, to see Ron flaunting the celluloid, he must have been inside the One-in-the-Eye at least once, Josie might have a clue.

'Would you like a drink in a half way decent pub for a change?' I asked. Janine and I were up the front end of my van as I turned off the main road by Woodhouse's Garage.

The forecourt was in darkness at an hour when Ron used to leave on a few neon signs, even thought the place was closed. Slowing to a halt, I stared across at the shadowy remnants.

Janine said, 'I wish I'd met your friend properly, not just over that silly business with the plastic skull.' I nodded. She gave my left hand a squeeze. 'OK, let's go to the terrible village inn.'

'Why terrible?' I asked, driving on.

'All that mock-historical décor. But don't get me on one of my hobby-horses.'

'None of us regulars like what they've done to the posh side, but parts of the structure are very old.'

'Is the posh side where they serve meals? That's the only side I've been. And that was just the once. I'd better shut up!'

The van was left outside my gate. The Eddie was set free. The three of us joined a continuing wake in the public bar. Alfred and Albert had reached a state of mourning which was close to their usual state of crotchety gallows humour. Landlord Koerner had acquired a new anguish on top of the loss of a great regular.

'Josie's gone and left us.'

For a chilled moment I thought this must be another euphemism for death. 'What on earth happened to her?'

'Search me. Marianne took a phone call. The girl was bloody rude, apparently.' I felt immense relief but said nothing. Tony Koerner went on, 'All right. I know the two of them didn't hit it off, and it's been getting worse lately. Even so . . .'

'You should of stepped in,' Alfred called out.

Albert added with emotional extravagance, 'That gal was worth her weight in gold. We might as well stay put in our own houses from now on.'

In a feeble attempt to lift their gloom I said, 'Josie's threatened to quit before now. She'll probably be back tomorrow.'

Koerner grimly nodded towards the other bar. 'You-know-who wouldn't have it. But where am I going to get a replacement who's half way as good?' A moment later Marianne Koerner demanded his assistance. If the vanquishing of Josie pleased her at all she wasn't showing it. The familiar frown deepened when her husband turned to Janine and apologized for having to leave our bar temporarily unattended.

'So you're the young lady what's living in the vicarage orchard as was,' Alfred said as we sat at their table.

'Not all that young, but otherwise, yes.'

'You sound young to us,' Albert said, adding, 'We don't get much female company round this side of the pub.' Suddenly he poked me with his white stick. 'Describe her to us, Sammy, there's a good lad.'

I turned towards Janine and gave her an embarrassed smile. She stared straight back and asked, 'Well? What do I look like?'

'Er . . . she's not very tall.'

In chorus they said, 'We know that!'

'How, if you can't see her?'

Albert, with remarkable clarity for one who'd been drinking for half a day, said, ''Cos of the level her voice came from before she sat down.'

Alfred put in his pennyworth. 'And we know she's a good-looker, so you might as well admit it.'

'Yes, she is.'

Janine gave a bell-like laugh. 'Thank you, one and all. Sam's only being diplomatic.'

'No, I'm not!'

Alfred shook his head. 'No, he ain't. It was obvious the way the landlord had to be dragged off into the other bar. You could tell from his way of speaking. Ain't I right, Albert?'

Albert took a long, serious drink before saying, 'Ron Woodhouse would've liked the extra company. If he'd had a lady-friend maybe he wouldn't have done it. Maybe she'd have kept him on the financial straight and narrow.'

I realized that I had distracted myself—by drink and other means—from giving serious thought to the reason for Ron's suicide. Vague notions had floated into my mind, but I'd pushed them aside on the grounds that, when someone kills themselves, the air becomes thick with glib explanations. Some possible reasons had been aired at the lunch-time drinking session, but money troubles had not been among them.

'Where does this financial stuff come from?' I asked angrily. 'I knew Ron as well as anyone, and he never let on he was short of cash.'

'Don't take it out on us,' Albert said. 'Tony Koerner was the one who brought it up. He heard it from some bloke who came in the other bar after you'd gone off for the afternoon.'

Alfred added, 'It was your new chum who told Tony—Gordon Summing.'

'He's not my chum, and I'm going to sort him out before he starts spreading any more stupid stories.'

Janine said, 'Fair enough, but for the time being, who wants another drink?'

I looked across at the two old boys and sensed that she had just been elected as an honorary regular. Rather than spoil things, I shelved my indignation.

After closing time I walked Janine home. The vicarage was in darkness—just like Ron's garage—but her bungalow had a light on over the front door. 'It's on a time switch,' she said, 'but I don't suppose a burglar would be fooled.'

'I wish you weren't there alone.'

'Me too. But I'm not the easiest person in the world to live with.'

'I didn't mean . . .'

'Of course you didn't.'

There was a brief, embarrassed silence before I came up with a practical solution. 'Look—why don't you borrow Eddie—even if it's just for tonight?' In immediate response, the dog jumped through a gap by the gate and disappeared round the back of the building.

'Did he really understand what you just said?'

I shrugged. 'Maybe he's gone for an out-of-sight pee . . . or worse.'

'I don't care. I'd love to borrow him. There's a limit to my brave front.' A nearly full moon came from behind cloud and showed how vulnerable she looked.

'I'm sorry the pub was such a haven of gloom. You must come there when we're in better sorts.'

'When will that be? Your blind friends seemed inconsolable over the absent barmaid.'

'They'll get over it. What puzzled me was the lack of joy on the landlady's face. She's been trying to drive Josie out for ages. Come to think of it, though, I don't think I've ever seen her smile.'

'I have.' Janine looked towards the vicarage. 'I'm sure it was her I saw coming out of next-door about a week ago, looking very pleased with herself.'

A possible friendship between Marianne Koerner and Dora Philpot was not something I wished to discover. Tony Koerner might have undergone a personality change after Ron's death, but his wife seemed to me an out-and-out hard case.

Gordon Summing didn't live in Miston village. His farmhouse and office lay off a private road some two miles further down towards the coast. In a spacious, clean yard stood a couple of milk lorries. They must have just come back from that morning's dispersal to the electric floats which delivered door-to-door. His drivers, neither of whom I recognized, were off-loading empties into a bottle-washing plant. At least Darren would have given me a greeting. These guys just looked through me, but perhaps it was a lousy job and they couldn't wait to get home. I had left my van in a lay-by down on the main road. This was not so that I could sneak up on Summing, but because I needed fresh air to clear my head. Janine Quibbley had given me an over-generous nightcap of malt whisky before we finally parted company. As I strode up into the Downs, I made myself a promise to ease back on the alcohol—for a few days at least.

'Push the door, please, Mr Bevan.' The female voice through the intercom was slightly familiar, but my concentration was on opening the office door before the buzzing stopped. Once inside, I cautiously progressed along a white-glossed corridor lit by skylights. Machine noises came through the walls on either side, and I decided that the passage had been constructed through the centre of what had once been a very large work-space. A door at the far end opened before I reached it and a face peered round to give me a wink.

'Josie!'

'That's right, Mr Bevan. Please come this way. Mr Summing will be with you presently.'

'You can't work here!' I said, as she ushered me into a very unfarm-like inner office.

'Why not? I trained as a secretary straight after school. I only worked at the pub because I was too lazy to travel into town.' At the end of this explanation she pushed me down on to a three-seat leather sofa. 'Want a coffee?'

'Please. Black, no sugar.' I watched her approach a coffee-maker in a far corner of the office. She was wearing a slim, calf-length, grey skirt. Her white blouse was pinned at the neck with a silver brooch. Her hair gave only the slightest hint of its former spikiness, and her make-up was muted, except for strawberry lipstick.

'It's rude to stare,' she said, handing me a bone china cup and saucer.

'I'm trying to get used to the new you.'

'Don't put me off. I only started yesterday afternoon. I phoned in from here to tell Marianne where to get off.' Her cheerful expression dropped for a moment. 'I was sick when I heard about Ron.'

'We all were. Albert and Alfred are just as cut up about you quitting.'

'Never mind them,' she said tartly. Then she leant close and whispered, 'At least *you*'ll be able to see me regularly.'

'Will I?' I whispered back.

'You are going to take on the job, aren't you?' I shook my head. 'You must. I'm sure something's going on here. Where've you been these last few days, anyway? I've kept ringing your house.'

Footsteps in the passage brought the whispering to a halt. She sprang across the room and pretended to be searching through a box file. Summing entered, halted, looked from me to Josie to me again, and burst out laughing. 'Most impressive. The hard-working secretary totally ignoring her boyfriend.'

'She's not . . .' Josie shot me a desperate look over her boss's shoulder. 'She's not ignored me completely. I got a coffee out of her.'

'So would any business visitor.'

'Well, Josie and I like to keep our relationship a very private thing.'

He pursed his lips and nodded. 'So if you were to accept my offer of employment, I wouldn't expect any canoodling on the firm's time?'

'Absolutely not.'

'Hm. If you didn't, I'd be suspicious.' Josie blew me a kiss over his shoulder. This time he turned and almost caught her at it. 'Josephine, I think it would be a good idea if you took yourself off for the moment.' She went without a word, and moments later typing could be heard from the next room.

'A lot of Miston village boozers are going to be after your blood.'

He shrugged. 'The girl was at the end of her tether in that place. Tony Koerner hasn't a clue how to treat staff.'

'Or he doesn't know how to stop his wife mistreating them.'

'Whatever. But can we get down to the humble matter of my storage buildings. Are you ready to design them and supervise the construction? For a fee of £2500?' I raised an eyebrow. 'All right—£2750.' I was there to complain about his rumour-mongering, and yet I found myself asking, 'What's the time-scale?'

'Two weeks.'

I snorted. 'Why not adapt a couple of ready-made sheds?'

'Because—as I said the other day—a gale force wind would have them in bits up towards Lewes. I want brick structures, totally waterproofed.'

'What's your budget for materials and labour?'

'That's for you to tell me . . . and see if I fall for it. Do you have local people who you can trust with the sub-contracted work?'

'Sure.' If Josie hadn't been on his payroll I would still have turned the job down. 'I'll get you an estimate by Tuesday.'

'By Monday midday.'

'Maybe.'

After a brief hesitation he grinned, and we shook hands. 'I have a feeling we'll get on.'

'Only if you stop spreading rumours about Ron Woodhouse's money troubles.'

His hand dropped away. He slowly moved to sit at his desk. His face reddened slightly beneath the tan, but his voice was calm. 'I am guilty of an indiscretion, and obviously Tony Koerner couldn't wait to spread the word. As it happens, there was a general buzz of discussion about your friend's unfortunate death. All I said—indiscreetly—was that only the day before he'd come to me for a loan.'

'I was with him most of Thursday.'

Summing checked a desk diary, looked up and said, 'Five-fifteen p.m., to be precise. And you were not with him. Apparently you were with a Dr Quibbley at that time.' He paused, then put the question for me. 'How do I know that? Because, as you are well aware, Mr Woodhouse was very free and easy with general gossip, to a degree which makes my slip of the tongue regarding his finances a mere drop in the ocean. Wouldn't you agree?'

'How much did he want to borrow?'

'For that information you'll have to whistle. Unless it comes out at the inquest.'

'Fair enough.' The defence seemed solid enough and it was my turn to blush a little. 'Sorry I overreacted, but the story had spread from the posh bar to the public, and probably well beyond.' I got up and placed my cup and saucer on the edge of his desk. 'If you still want an early estimate I'd better go and do some measuring down at the site.'

He also got up. 'I'd come with you, but I have to make use of Josie. She'll be knocking off at lunch-time.' He walked with me in silence through to the yard. Then he put a conciliatory hand on my shoulder. 'No hard feelings, Sam. I can understand how upset you are on Ron's behalf. I liked him too, you know, even though I found him a trifle uncouth. I only wish I'd been able to help out, but he took my refusal like a man. No attempt to make me change my mind. To be quite frank, since he didn't look all that downcast, I thought he must have a second string to turn to.'

'Perhaps that will come out at the inquest, too.'

'Yes, yes. Must get on.' With another quick gesture of farewell (or dismissal) he left me and headed towards the lorry-drivers who seemed to be moodily waiting for a word. I ambled on my way, irritated at being sharply 'finished with' yet again. Summing's mood swings, his alternations between clumsily elaborate sentences and a sort of telegraphese, still managed to leave me feeling out-manœuvred. As I walked, I found myself childishly wondering how to get the better of him. Then I decided that his very employment of Josie and myself could be his big mistake.

Half way down towards the main road I wished I hadn't left the van so far away. My legs were feeling weak, and my spirits weren't raised as several dairy-workers aggressively passed me, some on motorbikes, some in cars, none of them offering me a lift. Soon I was not so sure who had made the big mistake. I hoped Josie would not be working for long among such a cheerless mob. At least I would be based elsewhere and have finished within weeks. It was only when I reached the van that I realized I'd missed a chance to ask Josie about the Ghoul.

CHAPTER 13

Perfume and Mirrors

Having had enough of Gordon Summing and his schemes for one day, I didn't visit the future building site. Nor did I go to the pub. Instead, I looked in on Dr Quibbley, but found her eager—in the nicest possible way—to see the back of me so she could continue with some academic work. Eddie was welcome to stay on and he made no effort to follow when I left.

Next I called in at Josie's family home. She wasn't back from work yet, but her mother, Mrs Fletcher, insisted I wait. I was provided with a mug of tea and a hot, home-made pasty. 'Just a snack,' as she put it. Soon afterwards, I was joined by Mr Ainsly who had heard my voice through the wall and was keen to talk to me. Josie's mother wore a wearily amused look, suggesting that her elderly relative would use any excuse to come visiting from his adjacent cottage.

'Ron Woodhouse was one of the rudest blokes I've ever known,' Mr Ainsly proclaimed. 'But I'd rather have him and his insults still alive and kicking.'

'Thanks very much,' I responded, feeling not for the first time like Ron's honorary next-of-kin.

'Also, I don't believe that suicide rubbish for a minute. He wasn't the type. I'm old enough to know.'

'What else could it've been?'

'Murder.'

'Honestly, Uncle Jack!' Josie's mother said, handing the old boy his own tea and pasty. 'You and your horrible ideas.' Certainly, Mr Ainsly's mind had a tendency to run on morbid lines, enough to have upset his great-niece when we were up on the hillside reclaiming Darren's bike. But in this case there was a definite dead person, and apart from Summing's suggestion of financial troubles, any motive for suicide was well hidden.

'Have you told the police?' I asked him.

''Course not. First thing I knew, I'd be under suspicion myself.' He clamped his false teeth into his pasty and there was a clattering silence for several minutes. Our hostess removed herself to the kitchen, and after finishing off my own snack, I gazed around the untidy but relaxing room. I hadn't often visited the Fletchers, but there was always a welcoming atmosphere. Josie's parents preferred home comforts to outside pleasures. Their daughter seemed to get on well with them, and was allowed a fairly free life with this nest to return to when she wanted. No wonder she had rejected Darren's offer of an alternative.

'I bet that's my dinner you two've been eating!'

The girl had passed through the room before her great-uncle could splutter a defence. 'I only take what I'm offered. No wonder she works at a public house, the lip she has on her.'

'She doesn't work at the pub any more,' I said. 'She's a secretary at Summing's Dairy.'

'*The* secretary, if you don't mind,' Josie announced as she passed through the room again, coming from the kitchen and disappearing up the stairs.

'I'm always last to get family news!' Mr Ainsly grumbled as he put aside his plate. 'But maybe she'll learn some manners there. Mr Summing's a proper gentleman, and a generous one. He gave a tidy sum to the Church Fund.'

'When was that?'

'At Mrs Philpot's coffee morning last week. He caused a fair old flutter amongst the ladies when he showed up. The vicar and me are usually the only blokes on hand.'

'I bet he made a big show of his generosity.'

'Not at all. He took Steven and myself into a quiet corner.

Mrs Philpot only found out what was up because she came and accused us of looking like a bunch of conspirators.'

This Summing's a clever bastard, I thought, and then changed tack for caution's sake. 'Going back to what happened to Ron—have you any firm suspicions?'

'Only that I bet it was his tongue got him his come-uppance. Folks like me can take a bit of ribbing, but there's those that can't.' I half expected Mr Ainsly to tap his nose and say 'mark my words', the sort of thing that would have provoked Ron into calling him 'a stupid old yokel'.

In spite of the risk, I switched back to matters parochial and asked, 'Is there any news of the vicar?'

'They've only been gone a day. I won't expect to hear anything till mid-week. Reverend Salmon from Woolfield is standing in tomorrow. Will you join us to pray for Steven . . . and for Dora?' This last was said with a challenging expression. Was it possible the earlier references to Summing were meant to put me in my emotional place?

'I don't think my prayers would help much.'

He shook his head, but before a theological debate could get underway, Josie came back downstairs. She had done a lightning change into jeans and a sweatshirt with a picture of Napoleon Bonaparte on the front and 1812—THE RUSSIAN TOUR on the back. She hauled me out of my chair, saying, 'Come on, lazybones.'

'Josie! Don't be cheeky,' her mother called from the kitchen doorway. 'And don't pull Mr Bevan around like a sack of potatoes.'

'He loves it. That's why he's my new boyfriend.'

'Don't believe everything she says,' I protested as she dragged me towards the street, but I was aware of undiluted horror on the face of Mr Ainsly, while Mrs Fletcher offered a great big smile of approval. Both reactions were bad enough, but in a further twist, I imagined Dora ringing the church caretaker with news of her husband and being slipped this piece of false village gossip. Josie pulled the door to before I could put the record absolutely straight. She then hung on to my arm as we walked through the village. From time to time she would wave to onlookers with her free hand. Some responded pleasantly. Others stared in justifiable disbelief. One lad yelled a threat that Darren would sort me out as soon as he knew. Too bloody right, I thought. Josie said nothing until we reached my van where she released me with a flourish and asked sweetly, 'Can we go down to the coast? I fancy eating fish and chips on a beach.'

Glad of a plan which would stop me being a local spectacle, I unlocked the vehicle. As soon as we were turning on to the main road I announced, 'There's no way I can play along with this "new boyfriend" stuff.'

'You've left it a bit late. After this morning, my new boss believes it for sure.'

'OK, but promise you'll tell your family the truth. Tonight. Including your Uncle Jack!'

'I'll do my best. Got any cigarettes?'

'In the glove compartment, but they're old and stale.' She found the packet, and a box of matches. After a couple of drags she threw the unstubbed cigarette out of the window. I heard myself pompously declaring, 'That's the way forest fires are started.'

'Remind me again, when we're in a forest.'

At that particular moment there were fields either side of the car. We were driving through the heart of Gordon Summing territory.

Relations improved a little once we were sitting on a breaker at Rottingdean, eating our fish and chips amid the incoming tide. Josie told me about her initial snooping at Summing's Dairy. 'Looks as though most of the milkmen are doing second jobs for the firm.'

'What sort of jobs?'

'Dunno. The wages details are kept vague. All the bonus payments go under an overtime heading, but the sums don't make any sense for overtime of milk deliveries.' She champed away on her last piece of battered cod in a pretty good impression of her great-uncle. After she had wiped her mouth on a tissue, she said, 'Can't help making a pig of myself sometimes.'

'You're certainly a girl of contrasts.'

'Yeah. But some men like to be kept guessing.'

'Some of you keep us guessing, whether we like it or not.'

'You moping over Dora Philpot again?'

'Never mind her. There's something else.' And at last I told her about the Ghoul, about his threat to Ron and the painful way he had dealt with me at the library. Josie became excited.

'I know exactly who you mean. Just like a walking corpse. Whitish-grey skin tight over his face. He visits the pub once a month. Sits on his own. Drinks vodka and tonic but hardly ever eats. Doesn't seem to be connected to anyone we know.'

'Except the biker who delivered threatening notes to Janine Quibbley!' I described the events which ended with the stake-out at Darren's Brighton flat, slipping in a mention of my first visit to the place.

She heard me out before sharply asking, 'Why didn't you tell me before that you'd been to the flat?'

'Because you'd have wanted us to go back there.'

'So?'

'So it freaked me out discovering I hadn't been alone in the flat. I'm not cut out for detective work!'

'You're a natural. Or else you wouldn't have gone through the door uninvited!'

'I don't know why I did. I only dropped by to see if Darren was at home.' I didn't admit that I had been distractedly chasing information about Dora and Gordon Summing.

Josie looked out to sea for a few moments, then she turned back to say, 'I think Darren's dead.'

'You're being morbid, like your old uncle.'

'I think he's dead. He would have made contact with one of us by now. And I think Gordon Summing's involved. Darren was on that extra payment list.'

'What about the courier people he worked for? Seems to

me Darren was spreading his services far and wide. There might have been a clash of interests.'

Josie pursed her lips before saying, 'He would never tell me what exactly he was getting up to. That's another reason why I wouldn't go and live with him.'

'And it's a good reason for leaving it all alone now. He was clearly deep into some shady business. That flat has had a fortune spent on it. And there were a lot of boxed-up electronic goods.' Josie pulled a face. 'Did you ever go there before you broke up?'

'Never. He tried to force a set of keys on me once, but I threw them back at him.'

'Just as well. Means you can't be tempted to go and check the place out now.' And in case she hadn't got the message, I added, 'I'm quitting before I learn anything it's unhealthy to know.'

'Of course you are.' Josie got up, gathered the wrappers from our meal, and folded them neatly. 'You've got your hands full. There's the wife of a loony vicar to rescue. And a professor—or whatever she is—to protect.' As she walked inland along the concrete breaker she called over her shoulder, 'I'm just a nuisance of a barmaid-turned-secretary!'

I waited in the back of the van while Josie rang the bell to Darren's flat. No response was expected and moments later she rang the ground-floor bell. The delivery boy came to the door, emerging far enough to reveal a colourful bruise across the top of his left cheek. His initial scowl faded as he decided to approve of his caller. Whether or not she stuck to her prepared speech—about having a date with Darren that afternoon—Josie was invited inside. Though this was what we wanted, I felt edgy. Our battered lad might now know that Darren had disappeared—and why. Josie was strong, but, if things turned nasty, the biker was no weakling either. Stage two of the plan—when Darren inevitably didn't show up—was for Josie to ask with sweet innocence if her temporary host could get her into the top flat.

Ten minutes later, Dora walked round the corner and

my vigil was thrown into turmoil. She caught sight of the van and halted. I was desperate to talk to her but I didn't want to get out, in case the biker was looking out of his window. Josie was already taking enough of a risk. Dora slowly started walking again, passing Darren's door with a slight glance, and crossing the road. I crawled through the internal chaos of the van to push open the passenger door as she drew level. She slipped into the seat, almost as if we had an appointment, and, once I was sitting beside her, she gave me a long kiss. 'That's for all the trouble I've been giving you,' she murmured as I got my breath back.

'Any time,' I said.

'Did Mr Ainsly tell you where we were staying?'

'I . . . er . . .'

'Thank goodness you parked a street away. Steve has been sitting by the front window most of the day. He's convinced someone is coming to get him. My sister will be glad to see the back of us. We're going on to a friend's farm in Hampshire tomorrow.'

'Will you give me the address?'

'If you have something to write on—and with.'

I reached back into the chaos and found a stub of pencil. On the dashboard was a scrap of paper. I watched keenly as she wrote out the address. When she finished she turned the paper over, and seemed to freeze for a moment. It was the piece of paper on which Darren had written *his* address. Dora handed it to me, saying, 'That's this street.'

'Yes.'

'Does a friend of yours live here?' Darren's name wasn't with the address.

'Friend of a friend.'

'So you haven't come to see me at all.'

'If I'd known where you were I'd have haunted your doorstep! How long must you stay with Steve?' She gave a deep sigh and rested her head on my shoulder. Rather than press for an answer I said, 'I've been offered work by a friend of yours. Gordon Summing. Did you tell him I used to be an architect?'

'He's not a friend, though he'd like to be. But I heard him telling Steve about plans for some building work. I let him know you weren't just an odd job man.'

'In front of your husband?'

'Yes. I didn't realize Steve's jealousy was pushing him so near to a crack-up. Anyway, you and I weren't lovers then . . . except in my imagination.'

'And mine.'

'There you are!' She kissed me again, but only briefly. 'I have to go. I was permitted half an hour to get some sea air.'

Before I could protest at her virtual imprisonment, she was on her way, not looking back until she had crossed an intersecting street and reached the next corner. By then she was able to see Josie who was opening the passenger door, saying, 'So much for keeping a look-out!'

'I was a bit distracted.'

Josie swung into her seat, and witnessed the distant Dora turning from us to walk off at speed. 'Oh my God! Did she know you were waiting for me?'

'Not until a moment ago.'

'Sorry.'

'Can't be helped. She guessed I must be waiting for someone. They're stopping over with her sister in the next street up.'

'Let's go after her. I can put her straight.'

'Forget it. The husband's waiting in a state of high paranoia. What happened with you?'

'Looked like it was going to be easy. Thingy was very friendly. Recognized me from when Darren used to hang out with a bike crowd in Lewes. He works for the same dispatch firm. Shit!'

'What?'

'I forgot to get the company name. He's called Clarence, by the way.'

'Oh yeah?'

'He can't help it. And he couldn't help me to get into Darren's flat either. There's a mortice lock as well as the Yale.'

'That means whoever was there the other night had a full set of keys. They must have thoroughly locked up behind them.'

'Bit over-careful for a burglar.'

'Too right, but I never believed it was an ordinary burglar. Look, before we go, does one of the bikes over there belong to Darren?'

Josie stretched across me to look. 'It would help if one of them wasn't under a cover.' She sat back, saying, 'You smell very chic all of a sudden.'

I sniffed at my jacket. 'Expensive?'

'About fifty quid for a tiny bottle. You must have had a nice time while I was risking my life.' She opened her door and started to get out.

'Where are you off to?'

'To check the bikes.'

I wound down my window and adjusted the wing mirror so I could secretly watch her. She clearly discounted the bike that had been left to the elements, and while she was lifting the cover on the second bike a car pulled up a few houses away. This time the Ghoul didn't summon his lad with a horn blast. He started to get out, attention locked on to Josie and her investigation until a middle-floor window slid up and an angry male yelled, 'Leave my soddin' bike alone!' Before things could get worse, I started my engine, executed an unbelievably fast three-point turn and halted just long enough to gather up the endangered barmaid-turned-secretary.

'Neither of them's Darren's,' she said as I accelerated away.

'Maybe not, but that was definitely the Ghoul who nearly grabbed you.' At the corner I halted again and leant across to shut her door properly. In the kerb-side mirror I could see the Ghoul calmly gazing after us, perhaps with a smile on his face. The biker had come out to join him, and they seemed to be friends again, united in their consideration of us.

CHAPTER 14

Concealed Entrances

In the second week of June it became official. Ron Woodhouse had taken his own life while the balance of his mind was disturbed. A large, secret debt seemed to be mainly responsible. There wasn't a full inquest, but it emerged that his only chance would have been to sell the filling station and garage. No evidence could be found that he had even looked for a buyer.

Ron had already been buried in a shaded plot on the inmost edge of the churchyard. A simple service, with no threats of eternal damnation, was presided over by Reverend Salmon, the stand-in vicar. No surprise wives, ex or current, or any other relations had turned up. A single stranger had been noticed, though not by me, hovering discreetly at the back of the church. Someone suggested he was a journalist, but no one was approached for an interview. Aside from this 'intruder' perhaps a dozen friends and acquaintances, mostly from the village, had gathered, and the hard core moved on to the Broken Harold Inn. Josie's refusal to cross the Koerner threshold had made this final wake an extra grim, all male affair.

Since the afternoon of the lightning getaway life was much calmer. My 'girlfriend' continued working in Summing's office, but no clues turned up concerning the fate of Darren. Darren's mother had reported her son's absence to the police, so his name was added to an extensive computer file. Steve and Dora Philpot stayed away, presumably at the farm in Hampshire, and I had not had the nerve to attempt a visit. On a happier note, the Ghoul seemed to have vanished from our lives.

I had worked almost non-stop, designing and supervising the construction of the storage buildings.

Throughout the same period Doctor Quibbley was caught up with university examinations, too busy to put much time towards saving the Heatherstone Library. But she did belatedly write to the local paper.

Dear Sir,

I have not been offered any academic post in the United States. If such an offer magically occurs in the near future I shall reject it!

Taking a generous view, I think you have fallen for a childish rumour, put about in order to discredit my campaign to keep the Heatherstone Collection in this country.

In the interests of further accuracy I should like to point out that I am 33 years old, not 41 as stated in your article, and my forename is as below—

Yours correctively,
Dr Janine Quibbley

The next time we met, I said, 'Aha! The truth is out. I'm older than you.'

'No you're not. You're taller, that's all!'

'But I read your letter in the paper.'

'They got it wrong *again*! It should have been thirty-eight, not thirty-three.' She screwed up her face. 'I oughtn't to have mentioned my age. Personal vanity triumphed over the dignity of the campaign.'

'It made you sound human.'

'Rubbish! I sounded like a pompous bluestocking from start to finish. When I saw it in print I wanted to burst into tears. Unfortunately, I was about to give a lecture.'

'On what?'

'On . . . on . . . I don't remember! Give it a rest, Sam! Anybody'd think you're a policeman.'

It was my turn to pull a face. I didn't want to be a policeman, or a private detective, but with the job for Summing virtually complete, I was feeling restless. There were plenty of villagers waiting on my services, but the old pattern of work lacked something.

Late on a Saturday afternoon I complained about my disorientation to Josie and she fingered part of the problem. 'In the old days, whatever job you'd done, you had Ron to go drinking with. A mate your own age. Alfred and Albert are bloody exhausting company just by themselves.'

'You're not my age, but I wish you'd come to the pub with me sometimes.'

'P'raps I will soon. When it's Marianne Koerner's night off.'

At the time, we were taking a walk by the river, partly to give Eddie some exercise and partly because we were both at a loose end. It had rained through the morning, a much needed downpour after a dry fortnight, and the countryside was humming and hissing in the lowering sun. Having watched a few small craft sailing by, we turned inland, not far from Summing's outhouses.

'They're funny-looking buildings,' Josie said.

'Thanks a lot!'

'You know what I mean. No doors or windows. Just those ladders leading nowhere. How d'you get in?'

'Come and have a look.'

The outhouses were really one building with a solid brick partition and a central guttering between the two gabled roof sections. Metal ladders, fixed to the wall, ran up close to the dividing point. We each climbed a ladder to the frustration of Eddie who, having failed to jump his way up the wall, ran back towards the river. Because the heavyweight padlocks were still on order, I was able to demonstrate how the roofs could each slide open a couple of metres.

'They run on tracks but only so far. Otherwise they'd topple off into the field. Summing wanted access from above, and this is more practical than having a hatch system. Also, it shouldn't let the rain in.'

Josie hiked up her already short skirt and swung across, on to the corresponding interior ladder. 'Come on. Let's finish the guided tour.' And she disappeared from view. I clambered over to her vacated ladder and peered down into the shadows. She was standing in the darkest corner and didn't respond when I called her name. I quickly climbed down the inner rungs, ran to the corner, and caught her as she seemed momentarily to faint. As strength came back into her limbs she clung tightly to me and whispered, 'This place is evil!' Since we were in an almost brand-new building, this had to be a wild pre-judgement. But the fearful echo of her voice made me shiver, and I found myself holding her almost as tightly as she was holding me. Then our lips touched momentarily but with a certain seriousness.

Her voice echoed again as she asked, 'Has he ever told you what he wants to store here?'

'Not in detail. Cattle feed. That sort of thing. Stuff he doesn't want to get wet.'

'We're surrounded by a lot of cattle feed, Sam!'

'Eh?'

'It's called grass, and it doesn't mind getting wet at all.'

From above an additional voice said, 'Perhaps I should use the buildings for locking away nosey secretaries.' We looked up to see Summing dangling a pair of enormous brass padlocks over the opening.

'As long as you lock Sam in with me,' Josie said, giving me a final squeeze.

'Then I would have to charge you rent.' He made way for us to climb out. I went first and chatted to him down in the field, but he wasn't listening properly. His attention was fixed on the bare and slender legs of the descending Josie. Once she had reached the ground, he turned and handed me one of the padlocks. 'Shall we affix one each as a ceremony of completion?' I agreed. We climbed back up, slid the roofs into their closed position, slipped the padlocks through the already fixed clasps and turned the keys. We had not gone for the sort that snapped shut, to avoid any farm-workers being locked in by passing kids. During the operation, Summing murmured, 'I think I'm becoming dangerously jealous of you, Sam. It's a situation of some perversity. Here I am with all the material advantages . . . and you have all the women.'

'Bit of an exaggeration.'

'OK. I only have some material advantages.'

'And I only have one girlfriend.'

'Hm!'

Once we were back down beside Josie, he shook me warmly by the hand. 'A job well and truly finished. Congratulations and many thanks, Mister Reluctant Architect.'

Slightly embarrassed, I shrugged. 'They're only a couple of fancy sheds. And anyway, the builders deserve most of the credit.'

'Well, it's you two, not the builders, I'm inviting up to the house this evening.' He checked his watch. 'In fact, you'd better come with me now. I didn't realize it was so late.' He strode off towards the riverside, which confused us until it dawned that he must have arrived by motorboat. By the bank, we found Eddie shamelessly sharing a sandwich with one of the anglers. The dog got himself included in the invitation, and Josie's last-minute fashion worries were brushed aside. 'The whole event is spur-of-the-moment. Everyone will be casual. Most of the food will be done on a barbecue. And you look too attractive already.'

'Ha-bloody-ha!' she responded, though with a broad grin. She turned to me. 'What d'you reckon?'

'You aren't as much of a scruff as me.' This was true. I wasn't in work clothes, but my shirt wasn't fresh that day, and my jeans were verging on the grubby.

Josie sighed. 'Let's go, then. I'd better not show you up any worse.'

As we climbed aboard, Summing explained that he had taken the river route down to Newhaven to collect the padlocks and a few other items. 'If it hasn't completely sunk before I retire, I'm going to live in Venice. I'd much rather go to the shops by speedboat than by car any day.'

'Wouldn't we all, Captain!' Josie murmured, but her boss

didn't respond. He was concentrating on getting us out into midstream.

In a few cases 'casual' meant arriving in the Alfa Romeo instead of the Rolls, or wearing designer jogging gear, but we relaxed when we saw that a fair number of Gordon Summing's guests were not out to earn style points. The river trip had been short and sweet. Our immediate destination turned out to be a boathouse almost hidden amid trees and bushes half a mile downstream from the storage buildings. From there to the main farm we travelled by Range-Rover. Josie sat up front, while Eddie and I bounced around in the rear with the emergency booze. Having helped to unload, I was introduced to several people whose names I immediately forgot. My instant amnesia was partly down to a desperate need for a pee. Josie led me off to the nearest bathroom, but I was surprised when she locked herself in with me. Turning from the door, she whispered, 'You won't get legless, will you?'

'Why not? I'm not driving.'

'Never mind that. We ought to keep our eyes open. See exactly who turns up to this party.'

'I don't care who turns up . . . as long as it isn't the Ghoul. Now, can I get on with my pee?'

'Go ahead. I won't watch.' The bathroom was bigger than my living-room and work-room combined. She wandered off to a distant wash basin, leaving me to relieve myself in comparative solitude. On completion, I turned to find her stripped to the waist, with a towel around her middle. Since the basin was in use, I washed my hands under the bath tap, but then I had to pass close behind Josie to reach the towel rail. She looked over her shoulder and said, 'If you want to be helpful, sponge my back. That designer-shed of yours brought me out in a horrible cold sweat.'

Taking the soapy sponge and setting to work I said, 'This is an odd job I hardly ever get offered.'

'Not even by darling Dora?'

'Nope.'

'Or the Brainbox?'

'Are you kidding!' I reached around her, rinsed the sponge and went on to wipe the suds from her back. 'Just as well your mother isn't around to walk in on us. She'd really get the wrong idea this time. How did she take it, by the way. You never told me.'

Josie turned round. 'Take what?'

'The news that you and I are only friends. You were meant to put her straight about us weeks ago.'

'I never got round to it.' She took the sponge from my hand and lobbed it behind her. It made a gentle splash in the basin. 'P'rhaps I didn't want to confuse her if things changed.'

Eddie the Greedy Guest had been adopted by a group of children who were apparently in exclusive charge of the barbecue. He would probably turn out to be their best customer. A majority of the grown-ups preferred to drink and chat, even ignoring an extensive cold buffet. Josie and I planned to mingle just long enough for 'spying' purposes (though I hadn't much of a clue who we should be looking out for). Then we were going to slip away across the fields to my house, perhaps to continue what had been halted by successive rattlings of the Summing bathroom door.

By the time we had sheepishly emerged into the corridor, there was a queue four or five long—and at the head stood Marianne Koerner. She didn't say a word, but I saw a glint of cynical amusement in her eyes. Later, when Josie and I were temporarily apart, I came across her again. Beyond the crowded patio at the rear of the house were two spacious lawns divided by a low, ornamental stone wall. Marianne sat alone on this wall, nursing a glass of white wine. I ambled over, food and drink in hand, and asked, 'Mind if I join you?'

'Why not! Plenty of room.' Only a few words, but they lacked the normal cold edge. In the early evening light her normally stern features appeared to have softened.

I sat beside her. 'So did you and Tony toss a coin to see who minded the pub?'

'We're both supposed to be here, once he's opened up. I came early to help Gordon's sister-in-law with the buffet.'

'Is that "sister-in-law" as in brother's wife? Or has Mr Summing got a missus we don't know about?'

'Brother's wife, over on a visit from Holland.'

'Ah well, it's a fine, international buffet you've provided.' I raised my plate in salute. 'But wasn't it a bit of a busman's holiday for you?'

She shrugged. 'I'm not much of a one for socializing—in case you haven't noticed—so it's easier if one has a job to do.' I nodded and tucked into my food, not quite sure if she had just admitted to a terrible shyness, or was simply acknowledging what I'd thought of as her anti-social nature. After a pause she said, 'I hope you realize what you've taken on.'

'Pardon?'

'The girl's a born heartbreaker.'

'Is she?'

'I must admit, I was surprised when the regulars started gossiping about you and Josie. It's not long since they all reckoned you were pining away for What's-her-name at the vicarage.'

'That's the trouble with village gossip,' I said enigmatically.

Marianne smiled for the fist time in my presence, though I recalled Janine saying she'd once seen the woman make a cheerful exit from the vicarage. This in turn made me wonder about the reference to Dora as 'What's-her-name'. Meanwhile, the off-duty landlady was saying, 'You're dead right, of course. And village pub gossip's even worse. I don't usually take any notice. Your girlfriend, on the other hand, used to thrive on it.'

I put down my empty plate, took a sip of red wine and said, 'It was probably her way of making the job bearable. And your husband isn't beyond dealing in a spot of tittle-tattle.'

She gave a sigh. 'Don't I know it. Listen, I have no right to warn you off Josie. There was a time, not all that long ago, when we got on well enough. Then it all went to the bad—over lots of petty things.' She lit a cigarette and said, 'Tell her I'd like bygones to be bygones, and I'm glad she's got a proper job.'

'OK.'

At that moment, Tony Koerner found his way through the crowded patio, spotted us and waved. As he headed towards us across the lawn his wife flatly murmured, 'Here comes the life and soul of the party.'

The barbecue kids, having no advice to the contrary, had kept up their duties, disregarding the dishes heaped with uneaten sausages, bacon and burgers. Even Eddie the Canine Dustbin had eaten his fill and lay curled up, with one eye half open. I arrived on the scene at the same time as another adult, a man in his early thirties. He was fair-haired and slim, though his rolled-up sleeves revealed sinewy forearms. Another sporty-type, perhaps, though physically slighter than our ailing vicar. His manner of talking to the junior chefs was pleasant and unpatronizing. He also selected a few burnt offerings to make their efforts worthwhile. Turning to me, he said, 'I'm starving. How about you?'

I pointed towards Eddie. 'My assistant's eaten enough for both of us.'

A little blonde girl chipped in. 'He would only eat burgers, Roo. But he managed nine.'

The man called Roo said, 'Great. But how can we lower the sausage mountain?' As a gesture, I found a new plate and removed four sausages from the crest of a huge pile. The man called Roo patted me on the shoulder. 'Well done. I think it's a shame how the so-called adults just concentrate on getting sloshed. You and I must be the soberest of the bunch.'

'Wine or fizzy beer isn't my tipple.' Also, I had left my glass on the wall beside Marianne Koerner.

'You're a pub man, then?'

'Doesn't it show?'

He laughed. 'I've seen worse. So how do you know Gordon Summing?' We had wandered up to the patio doors. From an inner room I could hear dance music.

'I've just supervised some building work for him. Nothing much. Some farm outhouses.'

'Ah yes. I believe I've heard him singing your praises.' He had nibbled at a few of the items clustered on his plate. Suddenly, he set the residue aside. I did likewise, retaining the sausage I was half way through. While I ate it up, he looked at me with disconcerting interest. 'I'm sure Gordon told me, but what are you called?'

'Sam Bevan.'

'Yes. Your name's cropped up several times. From Miston, am I right?' I nodded. 'Lovely village. I've been negotiating to buy a place there myself.'

'Whereabouts?'

'I'll tell when and if the deal goes through.' He looked at his watch. 'Mm. I'd better collect my daughter and her chum, so we can start taking our leave. Annabel's the one who's been feeding your dog.'

'The one who called you "Roo".'

'Yes. She's a great A. A. Milne fan. But it's also short for my name: Rudolph. Rudolph Wescott.' He held out a hand. 'Good to meet you, Sam. Perhaps we'll do business sometime.'

I shook the hand as briefly as I could. This was not the time to knee him in the groin on behalf of the Heatherstone Library Campaign! Dr Quibbley might not have been proud of me, but I rationalized that I was there undercover, and at last I had come across a definitely sinister associate of our host. As Wescott headed back to the barbecue, I entered the house.

There was no sign of Josie on the dance floor, but as I passed into the main hall I heard a burst of her laughter. This sound was followed by a silence which should have warned me, but my legs were working faster than my brain.

I was up a flight of stairs and almost around a corner before I shuddered to a halt. I pulled back quickly, but in any case, neither Josie nor Gordon Summing had eyes for me.

CHAPTER 15

A Fisherman's Tale

When Rudolph Wescott's modest Volvo Estate slowed down, I was too self-absorbed to refuse a lift. Eddie leapt into the rear behind the daughter and her friend. I joined the Sussex millionaire in the front. 'Do you not have a car?' he asked once we were underway.

'A van. But I got a lift here from the host. By boat and Range-Rover.'

'Very stylish.'

'Not as comfortable as this.'

'Where can I drop you?'

'The Broken Harold in Miston, if you don't mind the detour.' I was dying for a pint, and the One-in-the-Eye was where I could best avoid Josie. Before there was a showdown, I needed to consider my situation. Marianne Koerner's warning about her jostled in my mind with a sudden burst of guilt about avoiding Dora. Why—apart from being overworked and a coward—hadn't I sneaked over to Hampshire? Wescott interrupted these troubled thoughts.

'You're a friend of Dr Quibbley, I think.'

'I certainly am.'

'Hm! I wish it was possible for her to see the library sale from my point of view.'

Was this a joke? To try and find out, I asked, 'Have you ever talked directly to her?'

'No. I'd like to. Could you arrange it?'

'Might have been easier before the threatening messages started.'

He made the turning on to the main road with exaggerated care. Then his politeness fell away. 'What threats? Sounds to me exactly like something that woman would make up.'

'I was with her when they were delivered. By bike. The second time we even caught the courier.'

'And . . . ?' And fortunately I was sober enough to hold back any further details. He didn't tolerate silence for long. 'The point is, if one of my employees has overstepped the mark, I shall find out. Not that I'm admitting any responsibility right now.'

'OK.' I shrugged. 'And for what it's worth, I'll tell Dr Quibbley you want to talk.' He grunted, and for the rest of the short trip to Miston the only conversation was between the children and Eddie.

As the dog and I were being dropped off, Wescott said, 'Let's hope this mess can be sorted out with satisfaction on all sides.' He took a card from his wallet, wrote something extra on it and handed it out through the window. 'There's a private line for your friend to use . . . in case reason prevails. Good night.' I made a gruff response which did not stop him looking highly pleased with himself as he drove away.

Instead of entering the pub, I confused Eddie and marched off to Janine Quibbley's bungalow. She was already in a tetchy mood, and when I unloaded news of my encounter she went berserk. 'Do you know what that bastard's been trying on, do you?'

'To buy your house?' Wescott's now not so casual remark at the party came back to me.

'He's been bloody-well trying to buy this place!' she yelled, not hearing me. 'My landlord rang me earlier. Sit down. I'll get you a whisky.'

'No, thanks, I'm going down the road for a beer in a minute.'

'Don't blame you. I wouldn't stay here with me in this mood.' She went to the kitchen door and opened it for us to leave. Eddie was even more confused. He had crept under the table during the shouting. Now he ran away into the next room. Janine gave a long sigh. 'Well, the dog can stay, I suppose.'

'Come with me. We'll leave Eddie on guard.' She shook her head. 'Come on. It's pointless hiding away here every evening. Alfred and Albert are always asking after you. They think we've fallen out.'

'Tell them . . . I'm useless company.'

'They'd never believe me. You'll have to prove it to them yourself.'

She left the room but returned quite soon wearing fresh lipstick and clutching a purse. 'I look a fright, but I don't care. And don't expect me to enjoy myself.' Once we were in the lane she admitted to overreacting. 'My landlord isn't going to sell, anyway. He's a nice man. He rang all the way from Texas to reassure me.'

'Did you tell him what's been going on?'

'And how! The call must have cost him a fortune, but he wanted to hear the lot. Said he's been missing a good, home-based academic punch-up.'

'Wescott's not an academic.'

'The warring factions who are screwing up the library campaign are. The idiots!'

There was a buzz of excitement when we entered the public bar, a hint of anticipation in the manner of Albert and Alfred which had nothing to do with the beer I was offering to buy them. Janine sat at their table while I waited to be served. It was a long wait so I asked the old fellows, 'What's been going on, then?'

'Nothing!' they chorused, but Albert leaned towards Janine and murmured, 'Don't think I'm being personal, but I hopes you don't want to use the ladies just at the minute.'

'Not at all,' she replied with a grin. 'I went before I came out. What's in there? A bomb?'

'You'll be all right, 's long as you stick by us,' Alfred

whispered loudly. 'And if Sammy stays by the bar till it's sorted out.'

'What are you two twittering on about?' I asked.

'Your double-booking!' Alfred replied with a wheezing chuckle, and at that moment Josie came into view. She stared at me, then at Janine, then back at me (with eyebrows raised), and finally at Alfred.

'You can lose that smirk for a start.'

'Eh?'

'Look at the old trouble-makers! Dying for a fight to break out. Don't know why, since they wouldn't be able to see what went on. Or would they?' Alfred and Albert protested their innocence and sightlessness, mostly in the direction of Janine. Meanwhile Josie turned to me. 'I came to see if you were all right, that's all.'

'I'm fine.'

'Good. I'll be off, then.' And she was gone.

With a hurried promise to be back soon, I handed Janine money for the round and ran out of the pub. Beyond the car park I had to grab Josie's arm to make her stop. 'Listen. It was my mistake. I shouldn't have got carried away earlier. But it was still a shock, seeing you with that . . . jerk.'

'So I noticed.'

'Come off it. Both of you were too busy to notice anything.'

'If you hadn't rushed off you'd have seen me trying to signal—to let you know it was a put-on.' I let go of her arm, only then noticing that she had not struggled to get free. 'Summing was drunk and amorous. He was in the mood to be indiscreet. I thought I would risk a kiss and a grope, for some information.'

'Hope it was worth it,' I murmured. This calculated approach could just as much apply to the intimate way she'd been behaving earlier with me, and I felt deflated for the second time that night. I turned and trudged back towards the pub. This time she followed and grabbed me.

'Be fair, Sam. Do I throw a scene about finding you in there with the Brainbox?'

'She's a friend.'

'All right. What about Dora? The gossips think you've got over her, but only because you've had good use of me as a smoke-screen.'

'You're using me as a pretend boyfriend while you try and find out what happened to Darren, so we're quits!'

'Exactly,' she said, and she repeated the word after a pause during which she seemed to be fighting back tears. 'So what right have you got to storm about the place being jealous?'

'None.'

'Nor me.'

She let go of my arm and looked ready to go. Quickly I asked, 'So why don't you join us? Get to know Janine instead of always thinking of her by a nickname.' Josie looked far from eager until I added, 'There's a connection between Summing and the people threatening her. On top of the coincidence of Darren and the other biker having flats in the same house.' I filled her in on my meeting with Wescott, and then we re-entered the pub to find Janine in a merry huddle with the blind duo. There was no way we could get down to discussing conspiracies with Alfred and Albert present, but at least the two women met and were friendly towards each other. If this was a disappointment to the old men they didn't show it. Instead, they relished a level of female company they weren't used to either in public or at home, since Alfred was a widower and Albert had never married. The evening drifted into a mellow phase until an excited group of anglers came bustling in, defying us to guess what had been caught.

'An old boot,' I said, too tired to be original. Other dismissed suggestions included an iron bedstead, a crate of French brandy, and—most unlikely of all—a bloody great fish! With glee, Ralph, the lad who used to serve petrol for Ron Woodhouse, opened up a large waterproof bag and pulled out a human skeleton—minus its skull. As he held it up, the lower portion disconnected itself and clattered to the floor.

Josie had already gone pale. Now she angrily shouted, 'Get the sodding thing out of here!'

An embarrassed Ralph tried to stuff his catch back into the bag, but the bones seemed to have other ideas, twisting this way and that. Janine had told Alfred and Albert what was happening and Alfred asked, 'Shouldn't you have called in the coppers?'

'Ah well, that's the other surprise,' said Ralph getting the lower leg and foot out of sight, ''Course, I had one helluva shock when I reeled it in. But guess what I discovered when I looked close?'

Janine and I chanted, 'It's plastic!'

This caused Josie to murmur, 'I forgot that little detail. But it still gets on my nerves.' Nevertheless, she relaxed a little, whereas poor Ralph looked completely crestfallen.

I joined him at the bar and said, 'Sorry. We should have let you tell it. Can I get you a drink?'

'No need,' he replied sulkily.

'It's for a favour. Didn't Ron ever tell you? He and I and Josie were with her great-uncle up in the Downs when he discovered a plastic skull. It was hidden inside Darren's bike helmet, like a curse.'

Ralph looked ruefully across at Josie. 'No wonder she didn't like my catch, then.'

'Never mind. D'you reckon you could show me where you pulled "dem bones" out?'

'Just as easy to tell you. You were near enough when you got aboard that motorboat this afternoon. I was about fifty metres up from there.'

'I didn't spot you.'

He grinned. 'No. You only had eyes for her. Don't blame you either. Your dog had a couple of biscuits off me, though.'

The pub session lasted till closing time and beyond. With the Koerners still off at Gordon Summing's party, their staff took a laid-back view of the licensing laws. I found myself drinking very slowly, causing a few sly comments from Albert and Alfred about the state of my emotions. The threat of Josie's waspish tongue kept them under control for most of the time, and she herself stuck to soft drinks. Janine, on the other hand, was in a mood for mixing it. She didn't get completely legless, but occasionally Josie and I had to prop her up on the way back to the bungalow. Unlike me in an equivalent state, she recovered quickly, without any wild vomitings. After that, the three of us were able to sit and discuss the dark deeds of Messrs Wescott and Summing. Summing's dubious activities were still a matter of speculation, but he had let slip a miniature hint when Josie got into her huddle with him.

'Remember when he found us this afternoon? How we were talking about what he was going to store in your new buildings? Well, he admitted to me it wasn't likely to be only cattle feed.'

'And . . . ?'

'And that's it. He didn't get a chance to tell me any more, because I saw you getting the wrong idea and running off. I was daft enough to try and catch you before you left.'

Janine took in this exchange with great interest. Later, when I was supposed to be brewing up a pot of tea in her kitchen, she caught me standing just outside the back door, gazing up at the dark windows of the vicarage. She said, 'Suppose her ladyship never comes back.'

'Eh?'

'You heard.'

'OK. If Dora doesn't come back . . . I'll be disappointed. But she said it wouldn't be long before she was able to leave her husband.'

'Maybe she's a liar. You certainly are.'

'Me?'

'All this stuff about you and Josie pretending to be together. If it's pure pretence, I'm chair of the Rudolph Wescott fan club!'

'I like her, that's all.'

'No. I am the one you like, Dora's the one you've got a belated schoolboy crush on, and Josie's the one you're going to miss your chance with because you're a fool. Now get indoors and make the tea!'

By the time I carried in the tea-tray, Josie was fast asleep in one of the super-chairs. Janine had been jotting things on a spiral notepad, and she amazed me by saying, 'Would you come with me if I went to see Wescott? I know it's a lot to ask.'

'No, it isn't. Especially since I like you.'

'Smart-alec!' she murmured with a grin. As I poured two cups, she explained, 'It just might be that a deal is possible. And he's probably easier to negotiate with than my idiot colleagues.'

'Before he told me his name at the party, I quite liked him. But he must have already known who I was, so he's definitely devious.'

'I'll be prepared for that.' She looked across at the sleeping Josie, and added, 'Now—there's one who isn't quite the female Machiavelli she thinks she is. You're going to have to be ready to rescue her when she gets in over her head. What with that, and backing me up, you're going to be a busy man!'

It wasn't long before Josie surfaced from her snooze and wondered where she was. Then she struggled out of her chair, saying she must get to a proper bed. I offered to walk her home, and Janine countered with a request that Eddie should stay on at the bungalow. I didn't object, especially since I'd noticed a stack of canned dog food in the kitchen. Eddie was always better fed away from home, so I could hardly spoil his fun.

A bank of heavy cloud had passed in front of the moon leaving most of the lane in pitch darkness. It was after one in the morning and most of the houses gave off as little sign of life as the empty vicarage. Also, there was next to no street lighting, and, especially in the winter months, it was a habit of careful villagers to carry a pocket torch at night. In summer and in a state of percolating emotions Josie and

I did not have a torch between us. But we did halt for a while, to let our eyes adjust, and as we waited, it seemed sensible to hold on to each other. Still intertwined, we eventually moved off, but at the junction which led leftwards to her family home we somehow found ourselves going right, towards my house.

If Gordon Summing or anyone else was waiting to spy on us, we didn't give a damn.

CHAPTER 16

The Guilt Trip

I was back, huffing and puffing my way up the steep stairs to Darren's flat. But this time I was well prepared with a set of keys and a torch. Safely into the hall, I turned the power on at the mains. Only after wandering into the big room did I start to feel uneasy. The boxes of electronic equipment had been removed and the bed was stripped back to its mattress. A fat, domestic spider dangled casually from the skylight. I didn't remember a skylight from before. Perhaps it had been blacked out in some way.

I retreated to the kitchen where I found a completely different atmosphere. A little table was set for two. Glasses of white wine had been poured. A saucepan of potatoes was bubbling away on the gas stove and something was in the oven. If no one was hiding on the premises waiting to enjoy their meal I would have to be a good neighbour and turn the gas taps off. First I decided to check out the bathroom.

I should have minded my own business and gone away. Darren was kneeling with both hands in the tub. I called out his name, but without seriously expecting a response. His face and bare arms were drained of colour. Truth to tell, there must have been something wrong with my eyes. Everything was shaded from white through grey to black. The bath water, near to an overspill, was very black.

As I stood taking in this macabre tableau, I began to puzzle over Darren's pose. Could it be that his arms, backed up by the weight of his slumped body, were keeping another human form submerged? I forced myself to peer down into the densely clouded water. I could see nothing. And then, as I was about to turn away, two female hands bobbed to the surface.

I rushed back to the kitchen and turned the knobs on the gas stove to zero. As the potatoes slowly ceased to boil, I opened the oven. Inside was a roasting dish, containing a motorcyclists's helmet. The visor had melted, and the paint on the remainder was sizzling.

Before I could make any more weird discoveries, a telephone started to bleep in the near distance.

In the hall of my house the real phone was ringing. Josie remained fast asleep as I slipped out of bed. According to the alarm clock it was eight-thirty, a bit early for a Sunday call. Drowsily I shuffled downstairs and it was only as I floated a hand towards the receiver that I came sharply awake. My hand dropped and I moved back a pace or two. I felt sure it was Darren getting in touch at last. People often went missing for weeks, months, years even—and then they came back and ruined the new lives set up by those they'd left behind! The ringing seemed to relish my imaginings, seemed to get louder, with no inclination to stop. Taking a deep breath, I stepped across to shut the bloody thing up. The caller hardly gave me time to say the number.

'Sam?'

'Yes?'

'I came to the party last night to see you and you'd already gone.'

'My God! I wouldn't have, if I'd known.' If I had known Dora was coming to the party a few things would probably not have happened. But I didn't, and they had. I felt very shaky.

'After that I went to your house, but you weren't there either.'

'I was in the pub.'

'At half past midnight?'

'No. Not then. I was having tea with some friends. Like a sort of pub overspill.' As I spoke the last word, I recalled Darren, elbow deep in the blood-filled bath. But who was the woman under the water? 'Look, I must see you. I should have come ages ago. Is Steve any better now? Would it be safe for me to drive over?'

'What's the point?' She hung up.

As I replaced the receiver there was a scuffling from the top of the stairs. I caught a glimpse of Josie's bare legs before she disappeared into the bedroom. By the time I joined her she was almost dressed. 'Loved the bit about "tea with friends" and the "pub overspill". Very tactful!'

'Tact is all it was, Josie. I'm going to tell her the whole truth, but I have to do it in person.'

'Why?' Josie pulled her hand away as I tried to take hold of it.

'I hate it when brush-offs are done by phone or letter.' Or by courtesy of a drunkenly considerate friend, which was how I learnt my marriage was over.

'OK, act the fucking gentleman!' She pushed past me. 'But I bet she won't want to hear it.'

'That's her problem,' I said, grabbing a dressing-gown and following her down to the front door.

Josie turned angrily. 'No. The problem is this. You're playing the innocent Mr Nice Guy. But what you hope is she'll do something to try and get you back under her thumb. What am I talking about! She's already whistling for you and you can't wait to go running. Good doggie!'

She stormed out but failed to shut the door in my face. Keeping pace with her, I said, 'Just before the phone went I was having a horrible dream about Darren.'

'Tough!'

'Thanks, but the point is, because of my dream I was convinced the caller must be Darren. Which was a possibility I could hardly face. And when it turned out to be Dora . . .'

She stopped walking. 'Yeah?'

'It was just as difficult to cope with. Those two were the people I least wanted to talk to straight after last night. Which was wonderful. For me.'

Josie gave a curious smile. 'How wonderful?'

'Exceptionally wonderful. The best for years.' This was not a lie. I would never have admitted it at the time, but my evening of passion with Dora hadn't been perfect. She was more than slightly drunk, and her mood occasionally suggested that she might be about to match her husband's nervous breakdown. Also, my own nerves were not exactly robust after the events in the bell tower.

'I had a wonderful time, too,' Josie said. 'And I think you look really cuddly in that dressing-gown.' To prove it she threw her arms around me.

'Er . . . look . . . this is very nice but why don't you come indoors and let me make you some breakfast?'

'Only if you promise to take me along when you go to do the right thing.'

'Eh?'

'Even if I stay in the van I want to be nearby, as back-up in case the vicar runs wild. After all, he doesn't know you've given up his missus!'

Mr Ainsly caught me as I was sauntering out of the Miston Stores with a Sunday newspaper. I had left Josie doing the washing-up. 'Shame on you!' he said, waving his walking stick. This angry action almost caused him to topple over and I thought I heard an ethereal laugh, as if Ron's spirit was at my shoulder still enjoying the Ainsly antics. What fascinated me was the precise timing of the old man's outrage. He had barely spoken to me since Josie made the shock announcement that I was her boyfriend. Now he was spluttering, 'After early Communion I dropped by to have a word with Josie, and what did I find?'

'She wasn't there?'

'She hadn't been home all night, as you very well know!'

'Maybe. Um . . . were her mum and dad upset?'

He obviously wished he could thunder out threats of vengeance on the parents' behalf but Mr Ainsly was painfully honest. 'No, they weren't. They let the girl get away with all sorts. But that don't make it right!'

'If it upsets you so much,' I said with a deep sigh, 'we'll have to get married.'

'That's not what I'm getting at at all. Truth is, you two aren't suited, and you know it. She's much too young for you. And anyway you're already married.'

'Divorced.'

'Still married in the eyes of God.'

'Even though we didn't get wed in church?' This nudged him into a grumpy silence. 'What was it you wanted to see Josie about? Can I pass on a message?'

'Whatever it was, I'll tell her myself.'

I shrugged, guessing it had been nothing but an excuse. Being a nosey old so-in-so he was probably in the habit of checking on his relatives next door. But in the past Josie must have spent the night away with Darren, so why was he making such a big thing of it this time? Feeling a touch unsettled, I changed the subject. 'You should have been in the pub last night, Mr Ainsly.'

'Why?'

'Ralph Scott fished a plastic skeleton out of the Ouse yesterday. He brought it in to show us all.'

'Are you pulling my leg?'

'No. The only bit missing was the skull. I expect he'll be round to see you today.'

There was a rustic bench outside the stores. Mr Ainsly checked its surface for bird droppings and the like before risking his Sunday suit. 'This needs some thinking about. It makes no sense at all—to dump the bits that far apart.'

'Perhaps it was only the skull that was really needed—to put the frighteners on Darren.'

He gave me a sharp look but didn't launch into an accusation that I had stolen Darren's intended. Most likely he thought we were equally unsuitable for his great-niece. After a pause he said, 'I wonder where you would buy such an item.'

'At a joke shop?'

'Don't be daft. It's much too pricey for that. I'll ask at the medical centre tomorrow. I've got a doctor's appointment.'

'Aren't you well?'

'With all my worries?' he snorted but didn't go on with the intimate details because fisherman Ralph came into view. He was in an excited state again but looking very serious. He nodded a greeting to Mr Ainsly but spoke to me.

'You know you made that joke last night about me catching an old boot?'

'Did I? Sorry.' I thought he had been more upset because I knew the skeleton was plastic.

'That's all right. But the thing is, one of the lads did catch a boot this morning. A newish leather boot, like a biker would wear. 'Cept it was waterlogged, of course.'

I froze from head to foot.

Mr Ainsly said, 'Never mind boots, Ralph. What about this skeleton?'

Ralph leant in close to him, even though the old man wasn't deaf. 'The police might want to talk to you about that. I already told them how you found the head and I pulled in the rest.'

'But there's no connection with boots, leather or otherwise,' Mr Ainsly complained.

Ralph stood back, immensely pleased with the potential of the case. 'What if the boot belonged to Darren, though? That's what the coppers are working on. They've got divers down that section of river right now. I watched a long while after they questioned me. Had to come away in the end. I'm starving hungry!'

By midday a wind had got up. My van was tight against a hedgerow. Beyond the hedge was a field of barley, and beyond the field sat the Hampshire farmhouse where Steve and Dora Philpot were supposedly staying. Notions of water and death were enough in my mind, so I didn't much appreciate the rippling crop's impersonation of the sea. I turned to Josie and said, 'We can't get the van any closer without it being recognized.'

'Pity you haven't got binoculars. We could check the scene out from here.'

Josie's manner was not exactly neutral. She couldn't totally erase signs of anxiety, but for the most part she was impressively under control. When I had told her of the river search she said we should get out of Miston straight away. 'It's our last chance to even scratch ourselves without someone taking note.' My paranoia told me that we were probably under the microscope already, but as we drove off there was hardly a soul around to take notice. Perhaps a lot of villagers were down by the river watching the police divers at work.

We found a gate not far from our parking spot and crossed into the field. The previous day's rain must have been heavier in that part of the country because mud stuck to our footwear in great clumps. Soon we would be too weighted down to run away, but we recklessly crept onwards. Then, half way down the side of the field, a loud bang scared the life out of us. We ducked our heads and stayed still, trying not to breathe too heavily. But no angry shouts followed. No burly, red-faced farmer burst upon us ready to fire the second barrel of his shotgun. Josie slowly stood up, made me do likewise, and pointed to the middle of the next field where smoke drifted from an automatic scarecrow. The relief only partly mended my shattered nerves. 'This is crazy,' I said.

'Yes. I told you. The best way would have been to drop in, friendly-like, at the front door.'

But we trudged on, ending up crouched behind a woven fence through the cracks of which we could see an overgrown garden and the farmhouse itself. Almost immediately, I spotted Dora. She was standing at a sink, just inside the kitchen window. Her gaze was mostly directed out at the garden, but her hands were working away out of view, possibly preparing vegetables for lunch. Her face had a better colour than when I last saw her, but it was markedly thinner. The curve of her cheeks had virtually reversed, and yet far from making her look haggard, the effect had shifted her appearance from cheerful prettiness to a melancholy beauty. My reaction to this was perverse, even allowing for other events. This Dora simply wasn't the one with whom I used to be in love. I wanted to convince Josie of my liberation straightaway. She appeared far from happy as she stared through her own spyhole. But before I could speak, we were distracted by a regular, swishing sound which started up beyond the fence. Whoever was responsible was too close to be identifiable, though I caught a glimpse of a scythe as it sliced without mercy through the long grass and even through an innocent cluster of poppies. I glanced back to Dora who managed a thin smile and a limp wave in the direction of the demon mower. From that moment it was pretty obvious whose hands controlled the blade.

Josie and I exchanged 'Let's get going!' looks, but in that instant a voice rang out. 'What the hell are you up to?' A man stood at the corner of the fence. He was short, skinny and sallow, but he did carry the essential shotgun. Fortunately, the twin barrels were inclined towards the ground —for the moment.

'Er . . . can you help us?' Josie asked.

'Why should I? Why are you spying on my house?'

'We're looking for some friends. Is this Waterman's Farm?' I asked, and gestured back up the hill. 'We left our vehicle at the top. We've taken so many wrong turnings the petrol's very low.'

'What friends?' he asked, ignoring my waffle and not looking any friendlier himself.

'Steve and Dora Philpot.' I spoke loudly enough to be heard the other side of the fence but the scything continued. I would have expected Steve to show his face, or was he now so unhinged that he couldn't recognize my voice or even his own name?

'Wait here!' the farmer said. He about-turned and disappeared round the side of the house. The scything came even closer to the fence, as if the blade would soon cut its way through to us.

'Want to run for it?' I asked Josie.

'After last night I don't have the energy.'

'I hope we manage all that again.'

'Do you?'

'Often—if our friendly farmer doesn't come back with a shoot-to-kill policy.'

'Or if the other one doesn't get us first.' She nodded towards the garden. Occasionally the fence shuddered, suggesting that Steve the mad mower must be catching the posts. I was about to take Josie in my arms for a possibly final embrace when the farmer returned. This time he had left his gun behind.

'Dora says will you come in the house?'

'Our shoes are very muddy,' Josie said, not eager all of a sudden.

'You can take them off at the door.' He didn't wait for any more excuses. We had little choice but to follow him. The path around the house turned to gravel and we scuffled off some soil on the way.

Dora was not at the door, so by the time she clapped eyes on us we were uneasily shoeless. I was kissed on the cheek and introduced to the farmer, who was unfittingly called Tom Cherry. To Josie she said, 'I'm sure I should know you, but . . .'

'Josie Fletcher,' I said. 'Mr Ainsly's great-niece.'

'Of course! I'm so sorry. Josie, of course. It's very nice to see you.' She continued this unconvincing gush, telling the farmer, 'Mr Ainsly is our church caretaker back in Miston. A wonderful old man.'

Josie offered a piece of counter-patronage. 'We thought it was about time someone from the village dropped by to see how you and the vicar are doing.'

Dora gestured towards to the window. 'Steve's as full of energy as ever.'

And there he was, scything away, though there was little left to cut down. But at least one mystery was solved. He hadn't heard any goings-on from beyond the fence because he was wearing headphones. A bright yellow personal stereo hung at his belt. Dora rapped on the glass. She must have found a gap in the music for Steve instantly turned, seemed to recognize us and gave a jaunty wave. Then he continued scything. Farmer Cherry announced that he was going off to fetch his wife from somewhere or other. As he made a moody exit, I wondered if the man was suffering from hospitality fatigue. When the door was shut, I asked Dora, 'Any chance of your coming back soon?'

'God knows!' She reached into a handbag and pulled out a packet of cigarettes. Noticing a glint in Josie's eye she offered her one. 'I'd given up for five years before all this,' she said, and when she had obliged with a lighter, 'Look, Josie—would you mind going out and having a word with Steve? He gets obsessive about tasks. It would be wonderful if someone else could make him stop for once.'

Josie took a drag on her cigarette and said with a half smile, 'We're here to help.'

Dora showed her the way through to the back door. When she returned she asked, 'Drink?'

'No, thanks. I'm driving.'

She poured herself a large, straight Scotch, but barely sipped it before setting the glass aside. I was gestured towards an armchair and she stood before me once I'd sat down. 'So how is it with you and young Josie? The real thing, or a clever pretence to get in here and see me without Steve suspecting?'

'It was never supposed to be the real thing. We were friends, and . . .' I made a feeble gesture.

'What about her other boyfriend? The one with the motorbike?'

'That's over. He hasn't been around for a while.' I

paused. She said nothing, so I went on, 'You know a bit about her, then.'

'Of course I do. But did you expect me to receive her with total sweetness and light?'

'No.'

She laughed. 'No. You no longer think I'm a good and kindly person, do you?'

'I know I haven't helped very much.'

'Hm! I'd say you've helped yourself quite well. Gordon Summing dropped some heavy hints about you and his new secretary when I turned up at his party. I think he was hoping for something on the rebound.'

'The guy's a shit.'

'Yes, well, perhaps you'd know. Anyway, I gave him no satisfaction. And then a woman, who I think has something to do with the pub, seemed to think I'd be interested to know you'd left the party on your own. She was right, as it happened. That's why I came on to the village and risked calling at your house.' She stubbed out her cigarette with some venom. 'Last night was my longest break from Steve in weeks. I was amazed when he agreed to my going. What a waste of time!'

'Sorry.'

She sighed and shook her head. 'I have no rights over you. In a way I'm even glad for you. My life is such a shambles. You never deserved to get tangled up in it.'

'Why did you ring me this morning?'

'I hardly slept a wink. I was up early, alone and feeling sorry for myself.' She reclaimed her glass of scotch, adding, 'I also wanted to make you feel bad.' She laughed again. 'I never thought your conscience would drag you out this far.'

'It would all have been different if you hadn't made everything so mysterious. For instance, why did you stand me up at the Brighton Pavilion?'

Perhaps she would have told me at last, but inevitably we were interrupted. Steve almost bounced into the room ahead of Josie. He grabbed my hand and pumped it up and down. 'I was beginning to think we'd never be visited by folks from home.' The headphones had slipped down around his neck but the tape was still turning.

'You're wasting your batteries,' I said.

'Eh? Oh, thanks.' He switched the cassette-player off. 'Do you like *Motorhead*? Wonderful stuff to wield a scythe to.'

I glanced at Josie. She gave a shrug, not showing much surprise that the vicar should be listening to bikers' music. I said, 'I've never been that keen on Heavy Metal. The Blues are more to my taste.'

Dora, who had been yawning during this artificial conversation, said, 'It's a pity we didn't know you were coming. I'm not sure that lunch will stretch.'

'Don't worry, it's just a flying visit,' Josie said, and I mumbled in agreement. I had expected some curiosity from Steve about events in his main parish, but he seemed determined only to talk about neutral topics. After five more minutes of pointless exchanges we did get as far as reclaiming our shoes at the doorstep. There we were rescued from a hymn to the perfect design of a scythe by a phone going somewhere back in the house. Steve strode away to answer it.

'Grab your chance, while he's occupied,' Dora said flatly. 'I'll say goodbye to him for you.' Even though it was all over, I wanted to make a gentle farewell, but she practically shooed us on our way.

As we set off down the lane, hoping it would circle round to where the van was parked, I could hear Steve's voice booming from within the house. 'My word, you'll never believe this, Mr Ainsly! We've just been having a visit from your great-niece! Yes, she turned up with that chap who does odd jobs in the village. I was quite touched that they should make the effort.'

CHAPTER 17

Telephoto

'Don't strain your eyes. Borrow these.'

I turned to find Gordon Summing urging a pair of binoculars in my direction. I hadn't heard him approach, so intent was I on the doings of the police diving team. The public were being kept well back from the river bank, and several groups of onlookers had retreated to the top of the field, aiming for a grandstand view. A surprising number were armed with field glasses, like a bunch of misplaced race-goers. Summing was also sporting a camera with an enormous add-on lens. I said, 'Now I know what you get up to in your spare time.'

'What?'

'Taking candid snapshots of the Royal family for foreign magazines.'

'Wish I did. Damn sight more lucrative than running a dairy farm.' He fiddled with the camera for a moment. 'This is a recent acquisition. Earlier, I was getting some fine pictures of a family of coots near my boathouse. Then one of my chaps spoiled things by telling me what was going on up here.' Summing seemed to me an unlikely ornithologist, but after all, I still hardly knew the man. I was less surprised when he gestured at all the people around. 'By rights I ought to charge these people for hanging about on my land.' We were in one of the fields just south of the storage buildings. Apparently, the search party had first worked a long stretch upstream, towards Lewes, on the logic that the boot would have drifted seawards. Now a reverse theory—that the boot had got lodged, while the body (if there was one) drifted—was sending them just down beyond their starting point.

Josie and I had arrived back in Miston by the middle of

the afternoon. We had looked in on her parents and learned that no further discoveries had been made down at the river. Darren's mother, whom I hardly knew, was also at the Fletcher cottage, waiting to hear the worst. Josie had stayed on to boost the protective circle. I'd gone off to my house, tried to read the paper, failed to concentrate, and finally gave in and joined the watchers. So now I was standing with Gordon Summing at my shoulder, and yet my previous night's fit of jealousy lay almost forgotten until he said, 'Pity you left the party early.'

'I wasn't too keen on walking home,' I muttered, edging the binoculars into focus. 'Your pal, Rudolph Wescott, offered me a lift.'

'But you left Josie behind.'

'There was someone else I had to see. Josie and I met up again later. I took her home an hour ago.'

Lowering the glasses, I glanced across to see how he received the last detail. It was difficult to tell. Summing's squinting face was partly masked by the camera, but he said, 'Another lady-friend of yours turned up later. That attractive wife of the vicar. She seemed very disappointed that you'd gone.'

'I expect I'll see her sometime,' I said, looking through the binoculars again. At that moment a wet-suited arm surfaced from the river and made a sign to the officers inland.

'Take care, Sam. It doesn't do to be over-casual.'

'Because there's always a rival waiting to grab his chance?'

He didn't answer, perhaps because it was all action down by the river. In trying to get a sharper view, my clumsy fingers sent the glasses right out of focus. I was soon to wish they'd stayed that way. When the blur was gone, I saw, bobbing on the water, a familiar leather jacket surmounted by something which hardly looked like a human head at all. Darren's stay among the creatures of the river had rendered him beyond normal recognition. A whirr and click came from Summing's camera, and then he suddenly let it fall with a clatter against his belt. 'What the hell am I doing?' he said angrily.

With a visibly shaking hand, I returned his binoculars, saying, 'It'll hardly be one for the family album.' Summing glared at me for a moment. Then he loosened his camera from its leather case, opened the back and exposed at least part of the film. While he was fitting the camera back in its case he muttered to himself in a foreign tongue. Not quite German, I thought. Maybe the man was speaking in Dutch, but he stalked off before I had a chance to ask. As I made myself turn back towards the river I heard the Range-Rover's engine starting up, roaring unnecessarily before the vehicle pulled away.

I wanted to be with Josie as soon as possible after the body was found, but there was the problem of Darren's mother. I was aware my presence might add to her grief. Mrs Glover had earlier let slip a remark suggesting she still considered Josie her son's girlfriend-in-suspension. As it turned out, a uniformed policeman was on the Fletcher doorstep excluding callers whatever their claim to intimacy. I didn't try. Instead I loitered on the other side of the street, hoping Josie might spot me through the window. After a short while, a man I didn't know emerged from the cottage and beckoned. I approached him, but instead of taking me inside he placed a hand lightly on my shoulder and guided me in the direction of the church lane. His hand soon dropped away, but I felt as though I was being invisibly guided as far as the churchyard. Nothing was said until he had lowered himself on to a flat, yellow-mossed gravestone, and even then it was left to me to break the silence. I said, 'I've heard psychoanalysis is a bit like this.'

'Like what?'

'The shrink provokes the patient into pouring out his heart by hardly saying a word.'

He pushed out a lower lip, then pulled it in again. 'You'll have to excuse me. This should have been my day off. I'm still adjusting.'

During another long silence, I wondered, was he adjusting to the horror of finding a corroded corpse, or to the shock of losing his spare time? I had never knowingly observed a plainclothes detective before. He was, I guessed from the lines on his neck, somewhere in his mid-forties, though his casual dress—dark blue chinos, green denim shirt, slightly shabby grey and white trainers—and lack of flab suggested a younger age. He wore his hair over the collar at the back, though someone (the man himself?) had recently given the front and sides a brutal trim. His lower face sported a pepper and salt stubble over which he occasionally rubbed a hand. Perhaps he was trying to decide whether or not to grow a beard. Whatever the case, he suddenly shook himself and said, 'My name's Wyatt.'

'As in Earp?'

'As in Francis Wyatt.' And he flashed an identity card at me which showed that while he was some sort of law officer, he wasn't local. Mind you, the card was so quickly in and out of my sight that he might as well have come to read the electricity meter.

'I'm Sam Bevan.'

'So Mrs Fletcher told me.'

'I was hoping to talk to Josie.'

'The daughter?' He slowly shook his head. 'You'll have to wait your turn. Last I saw, she was in a huddle with the deceased's mother. But Mrs Fletcher asked me to say she doesn't want you feeling out of it.'

I shrugged and smiled. So keeping Josie out all night really hadn't turned her folks against me. With a slight recklessness I said, 'It's a bit of a problem when your girlfriend's ex-boyfriend turns up dead.' He made no response until I added, 'Even though Josie and I got together after Darren went missing from the village.'

'It's all right, Mr Bevan. Try and relax. It may even turn out that Darren Glover simply fell in the river of his own accord. But—just in case—I'm hoping you can slip me a few useful facts.'

'Not half!' I said, with a huge, probably unwise sense of

relief. And I narrated in detail the saga of the bike on the hill, Darren's offer to 'hire' me, the empty flat and all. I finished with an apology. 'I know we should have come to the police earlier.'

'Nah. The local lads wouldn't have thanked you for it.'

'They got to work quick enough when that boot was fished up.'

'That was just showing off.' Then, grudgingly, 'Still, they did come up with a body.' From one of his shirt pockets he fished out a slim notebook and a pen. I had wondered at his not taking notes, but he wasn't about to start. Instead, he wrote down a Lewes phone number, tore out the sheet and handed it to me. What with the other cards and slips of paper I'd been given over recent weeks I was turning into a walking filofax. 'I'm not based at the local cop shop,' he said.

'So will I have to go through everything again with another policeman?'

'Maybe. Maybe not. They're short-handed and I'm being allowed to help out. I'll bung them a copy of what you told me.' From his other shirt pocket he produced a tiny tape-recorder. 'That's if the batteries haven't run out.' He ran the tape back a little and held the machine tight against his ear. 'No, it's OK.' With a groan or two he got to his feet.

'Will you be talking to Josie?'

'Yep. And to you again when you remember what you didn't tell me just now. That's why I've given you that bit of paper.'

'I thought I'd told you everything.'

He laughed. 'We never tell anyone everything, even if we want to. I must get back.'

We left the churchyard and walked past the bungalow garden. Janine waved from behind her study window and Eddie came hurtling round the side of the building. He squirmed through a hole in the front hedge and swamped me with affectionate attention. 'Sorry about this,' I muttered.

'Don't mind me,' Wyatt said. 'You're obviously a popular lad. Local dogs. Mrs Fletcher. Miss Fletcher. Not to mention that good-looking woman.'

'This is my dog, actually. I've been lending him to Dr Quibbley. She's had some threatening letters specially delivered to her bungalow.'

He gazed in Janine's direction with an interest which might have been more than professional. 'Is that Quibbley, like in the Whatsit Library Campaign?'

'Heatherstone Library. And what about this for a coincidence? The biker who delivered the letters lives in the house where Darren had his Brighton flat.'

'I said you hadn't told me everything.'

'Yeah, there's also the business of this guy we call the Ghoul.'

'Another biker?'

'No, just a thug.'

'That'll have to wait. I can only take in so much at a time.' As he started walking on, I turned and gestured to Janine that I'd be back. Eddie and I caught up with Wyatt as he was passing the vicarage. Glancing up the drive, I was amazed to see the Philpots' car parked half way into the garage. The detective nodded up and back towards the first floor. 'That's another good-looking woman. Beautiful, even. But she doesn't look so friendly. I don't know her, so it must be you who's in her bad books.'

CHAPTER 18

Headless Wonder

When Inspector (or whatever) Wyatt found me in the pub at lunch-time the next day, he brought an intriguing piece of news. Having collected Ralph's fished-up plastic skeleton as possible evidence, he had gone on to Mr Ainsly to see if the skull was a true match. He had been welcomed in with much blather from the ancient church caretaker, but when the moment to produce the skull arrived it was no longer in its hideaway beneath the cottage stairs. This disaster delighted our eavesdroppers.

'Jack Ainsly wouldn't find his own backside if he didn't talk through it half the time,' muttered Albert.

'Remember when he lost the bell tower key for a month? Lovely and peaceful it was,' murmured Alfred.

Wyatt turned on his bar stool and asked, 'So you think this skull is just mislaid?'

The white-sticked duo pretended for a daft moment that their own conversation was entirely disconnected from ours, but Wyatt asked to be introduced all the same. Then he repeated his question.

Alfred sucked on his few remaining teeth before asking, 'Was Jack sure about where he put it in the first place?'

'Yes. He'd stored it in a particular cardboard box, which was taped shut in case it gave his cleaning lady a fright.'

Albert almost choked on this one. 'Take more'n a plastic skull to put the wind up Eileen Smight.'

Wyatt shrugged, and then guessed they wouldn't see the gesture. 'You obviously have a poor opinion of Mr Ainsly —but would he tape up an empty box?'

'Was it properly taped?' I asked.

'Re-taped. You could see where the earlier tape had broken the surface of the cardboard. Mr Ainsly admitted to using the box on previous occasions, but he couldn't remember sealing it, except the once. I must have a pee.' He sprang up and was out of the bar in a moment.

Alfred shook his head and asked me, 'You sure he's a copper? They don't usually let on so much about their doings.'

Albert snorted. 'How would you know?'

'Because my cousin George was in the force, and you couldn't get a word out of him.'

'True enough. I met him once, or three times. You couldn't get a pint out of him, neither.'

When Wyatt returned, he cast further doubt on his

authenticity by buying a round, but Albert and Alfred quickly dropped the subject of Cousin George.

'So who would be likely to visit the Ainsly cottage in search of a plastic skull?'

The old boys gave him a generous list which included me and even the late Ron Woodhouse, allowing that the evidence might have been stolen a while ago. I issued a personal denial and was about to protest on Ron's behalf when it struck me how often he and Mr Ainsly used to spark each other off. Wyatt wasn't taking notes, but I assumed he had set his recorder going while he was in the gents. Later, outside in the car park I had a private word with him. 'The skull just might be somewhere down at Woodhouse's Garage. It's been locked up and left since Ron died.'

Wyatt jangled a set of keys before my face and said, 'It was already on my agenda for the day. Want to come with me?'

I was supposed to be erecting a trellis for Mrs Leigh-Harcourt, so I popped in to ask if she minded me starting late. 'As long as you're here by tea-time,' the old lady said, adding with a twinkle, 'Then I can tell you the latest about my neighbours across the back.' She could only mean Dora and Steve and I was tempted to hang about long enough to get the gossip, but Mrs L.-H. didn't give me the option. 'Away with you. My lips are sealed till you come back.' I left Eddie with her to show my good intentions.

Some weeks back a gust of wind must have knocked over the metal CLOSED sign at the garage. I had to tug it free from groundsel and other weeds. It made me shudder to think that Erasing Nature could move into action so quickly. Wyatt unlocked the workshop, and we slid back the big doors. Even though it was a bright day, the inner shadows were barely moved. A coating of oil on the floor seemed to set a grim tone for the entire space. Only a computerized diagnostic machine stood out brightly from the mass, its dials and screens still promising to root out any faults your motor might have hidden away—except that there was no electricity to power it. Wyatt brought out a small but bright torch and we worked our way through a few cupboards. No plastic skulls were waiting to grin at us, but what we did learn was how neat and organized the workshop was beneath its gloom.

Up at Ron's house, the front door mat was buried under a pile of mail. There were a lot of trade catalogues and general junk but Wyatt said, 'We'll have a look through, just in case. The executor obviously isn't taking much of an interest.'

'Who is the executor?'

'An accountant in Lewes, called Alan Langley.'

'Never heard of him. I wonder if he was the mystery man at the funeral.'

'That was more likely to have been me.'

'You?'

Without further explanation, Wyatt speedily checked and cast aside most of the mail. Towards the end he handed me a telephone bill and asked, 'What do you make of that?' The bill had an attached sheet itemizing calls which had clocked up over a certain amount of units. The day before he died, Ron had made several lengthy calls to one particular number. There was also a call to the same number on what must have been the actual morning of his death. Moving my gaze back up the page, I registered the number's regular appearance. 'Recognize it?' Wyatt asked.

'Yes. It's Gordon Summing's number. He's the dairy farmer Darren used to deliver for. I designed and organized some building work for him.'

'Doesn't Miss Fletcher work for this man?' I nodded. Wyatt smiled. 'So presumably you call her on that number now and then.'

'Now and then.'

'How is she bearing up, by the way?'

'All right, considering there are a few smart-arses around who behave as though either Josie or I must have pushed Darren into the river. Or else he drowned himself out of a broken heart over her.'

Wyatt gave one of his shrugs. 'Maybe he did. Our scientific geniuses haven't come up with much beyond that he did drown.'

'So why didn't the body pop back up to the surface by and by? Aren't they supposed to?'

'The boot that didn't get fished up was wedged under a root and him stuck in it. He could've kicked himself into the trap while thrashing around under the water.' I shuddered visibly and even found myself feeling a little short of breath. Wyatt nodded. 'Gives me the creeps, too.'

'Josie says she'll be glad when the funeral's over and done with.'

'That should be soon. They've released the body—but there's not to be a cremation. Just in case a later look is needed.'

I could hardly see the point of that. According to my view through the binoculars, a lot of evidence had been cancelled out by the time the body had spent in the river—but my stomach asked me not to pursue the matter. Instead, I asked, 'Will you be winding up your investigation—if there's nothing to go on?'

Wyatt gave a crooked smile. 'Maybe and maybe not. I like it round here. And besides, I haven't talked to Dr Quibbley yet.' He pocketed the phone bill. 'Shall we look around for this death's head?' I'd almost forgotten that was what we were there for and I felt a belated, sharp guilt at poking around in Ron's private world. It was not long since I'd finally convinced myself of his genuine suicide. Now the ghosts of doubt were trying to make a comeback as we went from room to room. In spite of the odd phone bill, I felt a measure of relief when we were crossing the forecourt twenty minutes later. Nothing further had turned up, but Wyatt seemed satisfied with a cursory search. 'I didn't really expect we'd find the damn thing.'

'I never saw the upstairs before.'

'And?'

'It was so tidy. Like the workshop.'

'Like the man himself?'

'No. Ron was . . . no, he wasn't untidy, but there was a certain looseness about him.' I gave a dry laugh. 'Makes me feel a bit ashamed. I live alone, and usually my place is a complete tip. Especially my workroom.'

'I've a wife and two kids, and the house is in permanent chaos—unless there are secret periods of tidiness when I'm away. Which is a lot.'

We went back to the centre of the village in Wyatt's car. I got out near the pub and he drove on in the direction of Janine Quibbley's bungalow. Walking around the corner to Mrs Leigh-Harcourt's house, I found myself wondering how seriously married-with-two-children this curious policeman was.

To demonstrate that I could still be a true professional, I erected the trellis before accepting tea and gossip. The day had clouded over all of a sudden, getting so dark at one point that several houses resorted to electric light half way through a June afternoon. Not so the vicarage, which I couldn't help glancing at now and then. Signs of life were so absent I could hardly believe Dora and her husband were back. This negative impression contrasted greatly with Mrs Leigh-Harcourt's experience of her neighbours.

'One has to admit, they're a lively couple.'

'Another shouting match in the garden?'

'No—not actually so noisy this time, and not so late. About half past eleven last night. I was closing my bedroom curtains before putting the light on and a glint of metal caught my eye.'

My stomach tightened, thinking back to Steve and his manic wielding of the scythe back in Hampshire. 'What was it? A knife, or something bigger?'

'It turned out to be a garden spade. And she was only there at the start. They did seem to be having one of their arguments, but this time it was all *sotto voce*. Then she stomped off and left him to his digging.'

The notion of Dora 'stomping' didn't ring true to me, in spite of all her recent transformations, but I concentrated my interest on the vicar. 'What do you think he was burying?'

'I couldn't tell. He was in the small space between their shed and the corner of my wall.' Mrs L.-H. blushed slightly. 'Also, he looked up in this direction twice. Probably he didn't see me, but I couldn't help feeling like a nosey old so-in-so.' With a burst of laughter, she added, 'Which, of course, I am.'

'Me too.' And we both tucked into tea and cake with a hearty appetite. A little later I asked, 'Would you mind if I went back down the garden for a minute?'

'I thought the job was finished. The trellis looks very nice from here.'

'I want to give the posts one last check over. Don't want my handiwork collapsing the moment a wind gets up.'

'You're so thorough, Sam,' Mrs Leigh-Harcourt said, with a sweet smile. 'And you will tell me if you find anything interesting, won't you?'

Somewhat sheepishly, I let myself out by the back door. Eddie came with me and tested one of the trellis posts in the time-honoured canine fashion. I tapped him on the nose and told him to behave. In a sulk he ran back to the house, while as casually as possible I edged my way to the furthermost corner of the garden. Unhelpfully, the dark clouds had moved on, but there was still no sign of life in the vicarage; no angry staring face; no twitching curtains. Hurriedly I peered over the wall at the space behind the shed. Mostly there were nettles and piles of cut grass. No tell-tale patches of tamped-down earth. But then I spotted a mound of loose soil and a fresh hole perhaps a metre deep. It seemed very likely that Steve Philpot hadn't been burying anything at the dead of night. He had been digging something up.

CHAPTER 19

Commercial Break

Rudolph Wescott's office building, overlooking the Hove seafront, consisted of three formal floors and a penthouse flat. Janine Quibbley and I were aware of these details even before we crossed the corporate threshold. They were there for anyone to read on a huge estate agent's LEASE FOR SALE hoarding alongside the front entrance. Janine muttered, 'Now I bloody well know what's coming!' and stormed ahead of me through the revolving door.

Since the two antagonists knew badly of each other but had never come face to face, I was girded up to make a fairly futile introduction. But the moment a smart young male assistant showed us into the chairman's lair, Wescott grasped Janine by the hand, almost whispered, 'So much grief could have been saved if we had met before this,' and led her, talking all the while, across the full length of the office to a picture window. For several minutes I stared at the two of them and beyond to the glistening sea. Wescott continued to speak very softly and I gave up trying to listen in. Instead, I started to feel fairly pissed off with la Quibbley for bringing me along. It was bad enough being ignored as much by her as by Wescott, but why was she keeping her earlier aggression so thoroughly on hold? Were Wescott's (presumably honeyed) words going to wipe out the Heatherstone Campaign just like that? Was Janine corruptible after all? In the end her voice, sharp and clear, shook me out of my brewing resentment.

'You must think I've just fallen off the Christmas Tree!'

Wescott turned and acknowledged my presence for the first time with an appeal for support. 'Why doesn't your friend believe me, Sam?'

'Believe what?' I said, perversely irritated that he should remember my name.

'I've just offered Dr Quibbley two months in which to get a British consortium together to buy the Heatherstone Library for half what I've been offered elsewhere.'

Recalling the valuation quoted in a newspaper, I did some simple maths and asked Janine, 'Is £600,000 out of reach?'

'Possibly not—if my colleagues would suspend their in-fighting for five minutes.'

Wescott pulled a semi-amused face at this. 'That part really isn't my concern.' He leant across a desk to respond to a beeping intercom. A female voice told him that his next appointment had arrived downstairs.

'Why the change of heart?' I asked.

Janine answered for him. 'Apparently, our campaign finally got to his conscience.'

I had grudgingly moved to meet them in the middle of the room, and while she spoke, I looked closely into Wescott's face. Her barely disguised cynicism appeared to provoke melancholy more than anger. To me, he said, 'I am a businessman. But I value my homeland. And I've only now become aware that there is such a thing as cultural conservation—as well as the kind that deals with animals and natural resources.'

Very pretty sentiments, I thought. Aloud, I said, 'So I hope the counter-campaign is already cancelled. Like trying to buy Dr Quibbley's house from her landlord.'

'Buying your house?' He turned to Janine, looking shocked and hurt.

'That's what the man said.'

Wescott shook his head. 'I did tell Sam I was trying to buy a house in Miston. But the deal fell through.'

'Don't I know it!' said Janine triumphantly.

'I don't see why you should, unless you are a close friend of the Hannatt family in Rudge Lane.'

Rudge Lane was tucked away in the north-west corner of the village. The few houses in it were big, and sat amid generous amounts of garden. I said, 'I did some work for the Hannatts once. I didn't know they were moving.'

'They aren't any more. Keith Hannatt's health failed just as his firm was about to transfer him to Canada. A bungalow would hardly suit my growing family, Dr Quibbley. Someone else must be after it.' Janine looked unconvinced by his disclaimer, but Wescott went on to surprise us by saying, 'I must, however, apologize about the unpleasant messages you received.'

'Oh yes?'

'They're only connected with one of my companies by the sheerest accident. But I accept responsibility all the same.'

'Oh yes?'

Janine's repeated, frosty response threw him for a moment, but he pressed on with an explanation which in turn gave me a chill. 'At the end of last year I acquired a local distribution company.'

'To distribute what?'

'Anything you like. The fleet of vehicles range from container lorries down to modest vans, those being for self-hire or with driver. And in a distant corner of the operation we have a small motorbike dispatch unit.' Which suggested to me that Darren had worked for both Gordon Summing and Rudolph Wescott!

Janine was angrily saying, 'So one of your keen employees took a dazzling initiative and decided to bike out the threats! Terrific!'

Wescott stayed calm. 'It wasn't like that at all. A customer—acting through normal channels—paid for the deliveries to be made. My people, of course, had not the slightest idea what was in the envelopes.'

'What customer?'

Wescott shuffled slightly. 'A . . . Mr M. Smith.'

'Brother of the more famous J. Smith?' I inquired drily.

'While there are many real life M. Smiths, it probably was a false name. Especially since there was an address for the client which turned out to be a derelict house. I'm very sorry.' His intercom beeped again and while he was answering it, Janine turned and walked out of the room. Before following her, I lingered to ask, 'As a matter of interest, why is the lease of this building for sale?'

Wescott gave a slow smile. 'We're not going bust, Sam. We need more space, that's all. To which end the library sale will be helpful, so please tell Dr Quibbley to get in touch again soon. My offer has a very strict time limit.'

I made my exit and nodded goodbye to the male assistant who was waiting outside with a man I didn't recognize. And yet, as I reached the lift I realized that the name twice mentioned over the intercom was one I'd heard recently—Alan Langley. Alan Langley, the indolent executor of Ron Woodhouse's estate. I turned to have a second look, but both assistant and visitor had disappeared into the boss's office.

A lot of unnerving things had happened to me in recent months, but being driven by an angry Quibbley outdid the lot! I kept praying for friendly, rescuing sirens, but perhaps the Metro was hurtling at a speed beyond police visibility.

'We must have lost them by now,' I ventured, as we tore out of Brighton by the coast road.

'What?'

'Nothing.'

'You want to walk?'

'Er . . .'

'What?'

'Nothing.'

We both fell silent, but at least she slowed down by about five miles an hour. Eventually, sticking to the longer route home, we steamed into Newhaven. Literally. The car's temperature needle was flirting with the danger zone.

'Mind if we stop?' Janine asked.

'Not at all,' I replied bluffly.

Leaving the vehicle with its cooling system a-burbling, we wandered down to the dock area. The swing bridge was opening up to let through a medium-sized cargo vessel. I watched the ship with the childlike fascination a land-lubber has for things nautical. Janine's mind was understandably elsewhere and she dragged me away to a café where we ordered coffee and sandwiches.

'If Wescott's a crook, he's quite a clever one,' I offered dully.

'*If* he's a crook!'

'But this deal about the library . . . is it a bargain? Or is there a catch?'

'I need an offer on paper, whatever. And even then I don't know who will believe it. Some of my male colleagues will be convinced I must have slept with the man.' She looked furtively at the shelves behind the café counter. 'I'm dying for a cigarette.'

'Me too, but I'll stick to the coffee.' She pulled a face but didn't give in to temptation. I went on, 'Why did the bike-boy refuse to say the messages were from a Mr M. Smith? Even under threat of your hockey stick? What was there to be afraid of?'

'We only have Wescott's word about the false name. And maybe secrecy is part of the usual procedure. Remember what your chum, the Ghoul, did to the laddie! Even if it wasn't because he'd reported our tracking him down, it was a severe piece of discipline.'

Without great enthusiasm, I said, 'Perhaps I ought to check out the Wescott delivery headquarters. See if I can spot the Ghoul working there. Watching from a healthy distance, if possible.'

Janine gave me a pat on the hand. 'Forget it. I'm not expecting you to take any more risks. We'll leave it to a professional.' She nibbled along one edge of a ham and cheese sandwich, in the manner of an attractive but distracted rodent.

Trying not to smile I asked, 'So—how was it yesterday with Francis Wyatt? Good interview?'

'More like a gentle gossip. He hardly comes across like a policeman.'

'That's what they all say.'

'Do they?' She started eating properly and when her own sandwich was gone she eyed the remaining half of mine. 'D'you want that? I never had any breakfast.'

'Help yourself.' She grabbed it before I could change my mind. While she ate, I pondered on the Hove meeting. 'You didn't look like you believed Wescott's version of house-hunting.'

'Maybe not. The trouble is, thinking back to the phone call, I don't think my landlord told me it was Wescott. I think I filled in the name as soon as he said an approach had been made.'

'Didn't he recognize it anyway?'

'No. The offer came through a property dealer—and as we know, our Mr Wescott controls a lot of different companies . . . so I made an assumption.'

'Which I backed up because of what the legendary millionaire said while giving me a lift. So maybe he was telling the truth about that at least.'

'There still could be a Wescott connection. I'm going to call Texas, get the name of the property company and have it checked out this end. I'm sure Francis Wyatt will do that for me.'

'Yes,' I murmured as my attention was caught by some familiar faces in the precinct outside. 'I'm sure he will.'

'I do know he's married, Sam. But don't begrudge me a bit of easy-going flirtation.'

'Not at all.' I looked back to see that she'd reddened slightly. Embarrassed myself, I pointed towards a doorway opposite, where Marianne Koerner and Gordon Summing were making earnest conversation. 'In their case, she's the one who's married. He isn't. As far as anyone knows.'

'Are there any couples you actually approve of?' Janine asked tartly.

'I didn't mean to sound disapproving.' She sniffed. 'Even about those two. It's just a bit of a surprise to see them here together. Though she did help out with the catering at his party.'

Deciding to give me the benefit of the doubt, Janine

peered out into the precinct and pronounced, 'Not lovers. Plotters, maybe. But I think it's more a hand-holding session, with her the one who needs comforting. Who are they, anyway? Is that the woman from the Miston pub? The one I saw coming smiling away from the vicarage?'

'That's her. And he's the guy I did the farm buildings for. Josie's boss.'

The café windows were covered by net curtains, but I felt uneasy when Marianne and Summing turned and looked our way. They slowly crossed the precinct and appeared to be consulting the large blackboard menu which was propped between curtain and window. Janine and I turned to face each other. We sipped our coffee, waiting for the bell on the door to tinkle. A minute passed and no one came in. I took a quick glance back at the window. The others had moved on, either because they were untempted or because they had somehow seen us through the gauze.

The remainder of the trip back to Miston was taken at a sane speed, dictated by the vehicle itself. There was no further discussion of flirtations and the like. Even Wescott and his doings were sidelined as Janine coaxed and swore at her car by turns. Whatever her tone of voice we never got above 50 m.p.h. We were approaching Woodhouse's Garage and the Miston Village turn-off when she cried in desperation, 'It's no bloody good to me like this. I'll have to see if this place can sort it out.' And even as I tried to warn her, she swung off into the garage forecourt.

'You're wasting your time. This place has been shut down since Ron died.'

'Bugger it. I forgot. Sorry. But where can I take it?'

'Into Lewes is the nearest now.' And as I spoke, the engine died.

Janine turned the key and got a pathetic cough in response. 'Tremendous.' She slumped back in her seat, turned my way, said, 'One day I'll take you on a decent outing.'

'Thanks.'

Then she squinted past me. 'Hang on, though.'

I tracked her gaze across to the workshop. The doors were closed, but leaning against the corner of the building was an unattended motorcycle. Janine sounded her horn in three long blasts and one of the sliding doors opened, shifted from within. A figure in an overall and a baseball cap came out. 'We aren't open,' he called. I say called, but his voice was not much above a hiss. He gestured towards the sign which had stayed upright since I rescued it from the weeds.

I sank low in my seat, and tried to mutter another warning, but Janine leaned across me and called through the open window, 'I didn't see the notice. But I think my battery's packed up. Can't you help at all?'

'We're not reopening till next week. We've only taken over the business today. Get your friend to push you somewhere else.' And the Ghoul turned and walked back towards the workshop where the young man he'd once punched so viciously stood waiting, and grinning.

CHAPTER 20

Rites and Wrongs

Recently, Josie had been going to work in a Renault 5 which someone in her extended family had saved from the scrap heap. I phoned her at the farm office and warned her not to let this vehicle break down within the vicinity of Woodhouse's Garage. I then phoned the special number given me by Francis Wyatt. I was told, 'He's out, but he'll get back to you.' Which he didn't.

Luckily, I hadn't had to suffer the indignity of pushing Janine Quibbley's car away from the Ghoul and his sidekick. The starter had suddenly come back to life, suggesting a loose connection rather than a flat battery. Whatever the fault, I was greatly relieved, though my level of panic had been well above that of my companion. Janine hadn't recognized either of the men till I jogged her memory. And then, since the Ghoul hadn't actually attacked us, she wondered if I'd been turning him into too much of a bogeyman. As I still remembered his paralysing grip in the Lewes library, I wasn't about to soften my view. When she had dropped me home and driven off in search of a more friendly car mechanic, I made my urgent phone calls.

Next day was the day of Darren's funeral and through the morning I made more fruitless calls to Wyatt's office. Gordon Summing had insisted that Josie take the whole day off and I'd postponed my odd job bookings. The service was set for 2.30 p.m., and with a couple of hours to go, Josie popped around to her parents' cottage to fetch a change of clothes. Moments after she left, the phone rang. Wyatt returning my calls at last, I thought, but it was Darren's mother. I said, 'Hang on. I'll call Josie for you. She's only just gone out the door.'

'Don't bother with her!' The woman's voice was remarkably controlled as she went on, 'It's you I want to speak to. Josie'll be coming back to the house straight after the service, and I'm not expecting you to join us unless you specially want to. But is there any chance you and me could have a chat later? Like when the family and all have had their tea?' I could hardly refuse, and with a rough time agreed she rang off leaving no clue as to what we would be discussing.

When we entered St Olaf's, I was surprised to see Dora sitting near the door. She didn't look our way as we passed, but it was only when we reached our places that I relaxed a bit. Darren's mother and collected relatives took up the first two rows, which meant Josie and I could be fairly inconspicuous tucked in behind them. Even so, I longed for the whole business to be over. Ron's funeral had been a tightly-knit affair—if it had occurred in winter one could have described the few mourners as huddling together for warmth. This day the church was nearly full. As a private eye, I'd have preferred to size up the assembly from further back. Even as a semi-official mourner, I turned briefly and picked out Wyatt and a couple of the local detectives doing their best to look respectful of the general grief. Late in at the back came a few strangers, whispering together with the air of tourists checking out a quaint aspect of English village life.

When Steve Philpot got going it was difficult to believe this was the first service he had conducted since his nervous collapse. If Dora was there to monitor the state of her old man, she needn't have worried. The power and confidence of his voice was so impressive and fascinating that I was distracted from the sorrowful folk around me. It took a nudge from Josie, requiring a tissue not for herself but for her mother, to remind me I had a practical role in what was going on.

One grim advantage of being up the front end of a funeral congregation is that you leave the church or chapel first. As I made my slow way down the aisle, with Josie tightly holding my arm, I allowed myself a modest scan of the waiting faces. Gordon Summing was there, as I would have expected. Next to him were the Koerners, though Tony the landlord stood between the previous day's 'conspirators'. Marianne Koerner's face was shaded by a wide-brimmed hat. Elsewhere, Mr Ainsly was grouped with Albert and Alfred, an unholy alliance but that their three voices had rung out clearly and tunefully above the apologetic mumble which most of us substituted for hymn-singing. Dora, who seemed totally disconnected from those around her, looked directly at me. It wasn't an angry stare, as when Wyatt and I had walked past the vicarage. It was more like a heavily restrained plea for help, which was puzzling, given how well her husband had run the service. Not knowing how to respond, I switched my gaze and kept walking. The various policemen had slipped away into the side aisles, moved close to the main door and were in their turn watching the central exodus. When I came near him, Wyatt raised an eyebrow and tilted his head, which I read to mean, 'See you round the corner', but the interment would have to come first.

Only a small number progressed from church to graveside. Inevitably, emotional tensions stretched among the family, but although I was still on comforter duty, Josie did not break down. The Revd Philpot said his stuff with more conviction than his stand-in had managed over Ron Woodhouse, but even my companion's attention started to wander. Just as the coffin was being lowered, she gave a start. I squeezed her hand in sympathy but she responded by tugging my arm down. I followed her eyeline and saw what she was on about. Well back in the churchyard, though not obviously hiding, stood our Brighton dispatch rider, the surprisingly named Clarence. My eyes scoured the surrounding area, all but the patch directly behind me since I could hardly turn my back on the grave itself, but unless he was in the blind spot there was no sign of the Ghoul. Turning my concentration back to young Clarence, I was amazed to see him dab at his eye. Perhaps he and Darren had been better friends than we knew, but we were not about to find out. As the burial amen-ed itself to a close he rushed off to the lane, and a departing bike could be heard above the coughs, sniffs and sobs of the mourners.

I was given a second dispensation not to attend the after-funeral tea. Josie sent me on my way to find Wyatt and discover what the police knew of Clarence and his wizened foreman. My first stop was the pub, which Tony Koerner had arranged to open early. Wyatt wasn't there, but I stayed for a quick one anyway.

'You two and Mr Ainsly were in fine voice,' I said to Albert and Alfred.

'Jack led the choir when we first joined as nippers,' Alfred recalled.

'Bossy as hell,' Albert added. 'But you forgot that when he did a solo. As pure a tenor as I ever heard. Could bring a tear to the eye.'

Alfred called out to the landlord, 'Your missus seemed

to take on a bit, Tony. Sure I heard a few sniffs from her direction.'

Koerner dismissed the notion. 'You're lucky you didn't hear a few sneezes with all those flowers about the place.' Though it was the height of the pollen season, I'd never noticed Marianne as a sufferer. But her husband went on to make it sound serious enough. 'She's locked away upstairs at the moment with her pills and an ionizer.' And a fairly boring discussion about ionizers, fringe medicine and the like got underway. The subject which barely seemed to be on the agenda was Darren. Possibly they were waiting till I had gone, so I finished my pint and rose to give them a chance.

'You got your nerve up to join the family gathering after all?' said Albert.

'Maybe, later. Before that I need to find Francis Wyatt.'

'The scruffy policeman?' Tony Koerner asked. I nodded even though I hated the man's obsession with neatness of dress. At least it meant he kept his eyes peeled. 'I saw him going off up Church Lane.' With a wink he added, 'To a certain bungalow, I'll bet.'

The old boys and a few others chortled at this, suggesting the spread of a latest Miston myth—THE POLICEMAN AND THE PROFESSOR. Janine would be far from pleased, but the gossip gave me somewhere to look next.

After the dignity with which Steve Philpot had conducted the funeral, I hardly expected to hear raised voices coming from the vicarage. The shouts—from both husband and wife—were particularly audible while I stood waiting at the back door of Janine's bungalow, though the verbal content had reached the 'I will'/'You won't!'/'I will, and just you try and stop me!' stage. My eavesdropping could make no sense of the debate beyond its heated nature.

The bungalow door opened and Wyatt greeted me with a fleeting smile. He leaned out, listened, tutted and said, 'D'you think they're suited?'

'Haven't a clue!'

He stood back to let me enter the kitchen. When the door was shut, he murmured, 'That was a curiously noncommittal answer for one who so recently carried a torch for the lady.'

'Thanks for keeping a confidence, Janine!' I called towards the next room, but there was no response. 'Where is she?'

'In London, trying to get £600,000 together. A written offer of sale came from Wescott in today's post.' A touch sheepishly, he added, 'She's lent me a key—so I can have somewhere to relax now and then.'

'Does your office know where you relax? I've tried to phone you yesterday and today.'

'They know, but yesterday I was out of the country till late. In Rotterdam. This morning I was in Haywards Heath and Eastbourne. What's up?'

'I expect Janine will have told you already.' I outlined the developments at the garage.

'She mentioned it. Wescott's bought the place.'

This was stated very casually, and I recalled the presence of Ron's executor, Alan Langley, at the Wescott office building. But the nuts and bolts of the deal didn't lessen my outrage. 'That boy delivered two lots of threatening mail. Can't he be had up for it?'

'He'd claim not to know what the contents were.'

'So why did he prefer to take a beating rather than reveal who sent him?'

'Possibly because he didn't know what the contents were.'

'Eh?'

'Let's suppose he was generally used to delivering packages, etcetera, which were not exactly legal. In that case, he would automatically react against being quizzed about where they're from.'

I followed him. Just. 'Does this mean the police know Wescott's distribution company is crooked?'

During this conversation Wyatt had been gnawing at a ragged thumbnail. With this crude piece of manicure done he conceded, 'Let's say we've got an eye on the organization in question.'

'Great! So you won't be wanting amateurs like me muddying the water?'

'Not for the moment.'

This wasn't the total 'keep-out-of-our-way' I expected (or wanted) but I didn't query what my future role might be. I said, 'Do I take it, from the general police presence at the funeral, that Darren's death is suspicious? Maybe even connected with Wescott and associates?'

'Dunno. Is that how you take it? Personally, I'm going to take tea. Join me?' He moved to fill a kettle at the sink.

'No, thanks. I've just had a pint.' Wyatt plugged the kettle in anyway, and I tried another tack. 'At the church I thought you had something to tell me.'

He faced me with a boyish smile. 'My trip to Haywards Heath involved a visit to a property company. Jan called Texas last night and got the name of the firm that was after this bungalow.'

'Another Wescott subsidiary?'

'Nothing so convenient—but this time the client hadn't left a false name. Careless. I called to check with Jan before she left for London. She recognized it.'

'What was the name?'

'Nathan Pearce.'

It meant absolutely nothing to me, and Wyatt seemed more interested in the freshness of the milk he'd brought out of the fridge. 'So who the hell is Nathan Pearce? One of these male academics who seem to hate our Dr Quibbley so much?'

'An Eastbourne dentist.' The milk was deemed useable. 'I called in at his posh surgery and hinted that in exchange for on-the-spot discretion from me, he might like to own up to a little note-writing. Which, after some huffing and puffing, he did.'

'Have you arrested him at least?'

'No. And before you do your own huffing and puffing, listen. The recipient has yet to make an official complaint.

My guess is that she won't.' At first I thought Wyatt was pulling my leg, but his smile faded as he went on, 'The vestiges of love and all that.'

'The guy's her ex-boyfriend?'

'Yep.'

'And he's a dentist?'

'Private and doing well.' He added in a murmur as he merged tea and hot water, 'She was only the dentist's girlfriend, but she certainly knew the drill.'

'Do us a favour!'

'Sorry. Sure you won't have a cuppa?'

'Positive. I ought to go and see how Josie's getting on. But don't you think it's odd that Mr Pearce aka Smith used this particular courier service?'

'Originally he was going to bung the messages in the post. Then he realized it would be best to do this from another town. Then he decided motorbike delivery would be more menacing, and he picked a Brighton firm at random from the Yellow Pages. He was stunned when I pointed out the connection with Wescott. Genuinely, I happen to think.'

So that corner of mystery had been cleared up, though I still felt edgy about the local presence of Clarence and the Ghoul. I was about to leave Wyatt to his tea when a jacket hanging on the inner door started to bleep. He fished out a mobile phone, spoke his surname and listened hard before saying, 'Got it,' into the phone and, 'Shit!' at the phone as he put it back. A burst of traffic noise came from the lane.

We ran out to find that two police cars had blocked the lane immediately outside the vicarage. A group of slightly embarrassed uniformed officers waited as another, unmarked car pulled up. Chief Inspector Niles and his sergeant, the local detectives at the funeral, got out. Niles marched straight towards the vicarage front door while the other stepped our way for a moment. Smugly, he said to Wyatt, 'Turns out not to be your business after all. Sorry about that, sir.' And he chased off up the drive. As they gave the bell a long ring and banged fiercely on the door, my stomach turned over. Were they going to make a terrible mistake and arrest Dora? Neurotic she might be, but I flatly refused to believe she could have killed Darren. Had Steve's distorted jealousy re-emerged to such a degree that he would believe anything of her, even to the point of falsely turning her in?

'What did they tell you on the phone?' I was being presumptuous but Wyatt answered all the same.

'My people had just been tipped off about this farce. Your vicar rang the local HQ and confessed to drowning Darren Glover back in May.'

'But why would he do it?' I asked, hiding a grim notion that Steve might just as easily have ended up confessing to murdering me.

'To protect mankind. Whatever that's supposed to mean. He wouldn't explain further.'

We had drifted back from a gathering of onlookers, but this didn't stop Steve Philpot from spotting me as the detectives led him down the drive. He burst through the crowd and grabbed my hand. 'Sam, you must help Dora through this. You're her one true friend. Promise me.'

'I'll do my best,' I muttered feebly as the officers caught up and directed him to their car.

'God bless you,' he shouted over his shoulder, and again as he was being ushered into the back seat of the vehicle, 'God bless you, Sam!'

Once all the cars had sped away, the crowd, as if choreographed, turned to stare at me. Wyatt murmured in my ear, 'What are you waiting for?'

'Pardon?'

'You've been appointed the lady's champion. You'd better go and see her.'

'Not while this mob is hanging about.' I went back towards the bungalow and stopped by the gate. Wyatt joined me, hands sunk in pockets. I said, 'You don't think he did it, then?'

He shrugged. 'It's out of my hands either way. Basically,

I was using their investigation as a cover for looking into something else.'

'So do you pack up and go home till they find they've got the wrong man?' He didn't reply. 'Dr Quibbley will be disappointed if you do.'

He gave a convincingly heartfelt sigh. 'In a way it would be best if I did push off. Before my life starts to get as complicated as yours.' I pulled a face. Whatever complications faced me, they weren't what I would have expected a month or so back.

The lane was fairly deserted now. Time to do my duty and find out how I could help Dora. Wyatt went back inside the bungalow, muttering that his tea was probably stewed. I walked slowly up the vicarage drive. I was about to ring the bell when a breathless Mr Ainsly appeared as from thin air. 'Wait!' he gasped. 'Leave . . . leave it to me.' He leaned on me for a second or two. Then he straightened up and said firmly, 'Someone told me what the vicar said to you, but I'll take charge till the mistake is sorted out. You go to Josie. I'm sure she needs you.'

Since he disapproved of me and his great-niece being together, this directive was a surprise, but I felt I couldn't simply walk away. 'Let's both see how Dora is. Then I'll leave you to it and find Josie.' He grumbled but gave in, and we rang the bell.

At the third ring a hoarse voice called out, 'Go away! I don't want to see anyone!' And a ripping noise came from just inside the front door. Immediately after that, an inner door slammed so hard that the front windows shuddered. Mr Ainsly called through the letter-box to identify himself, but that got us no further. 'This just won't do,' he muttered, and he defiantly pressed the bell again. No sound came from within.

'She's torn out the wires,' I said. Putting an arm across his frail shoulders, I gently wheeled him about. 'Let's try again later.'

'But I've got responsibilities,' he said with a sob in his voice. 'I never thought things would get this bad.' We walked slowly to the lane. 'Steven called me straight after he called the police. Told me it was him that took the skull from under my stairs. He was there the day after we found it. Saw me taping it up in its box. But how was I to think he'd do such a thing when my back was turned?'

'He wasn't well at the time.'

'He still isn't! But I won't believe him saying he's a murderer. Especially after he claims he's the one who put the motorcycle up the hill. How could he have, with his vertigo?'

How indeed, except by the sheer force of will which got him up the bell tower, though it had made him vomit with fear. I said nothing of this to Mr Ainsly, but I remembered that there had been a pool of vomit by the stile, not far from the bush where the bike was found. There had also been that acrid smell in the bathroom of Darren's Brighton flat, a flat reached by an extremely steep set of stairs.

CHAPTER 21

Extended Contract

Laurel Glover lived in Elm Tree Close, a cul-de-sac of council houses on the eastern fringe of the village. She was an original resident, having moved in eighteen years back with her farm worker husband and their young son even before the road was made up. Eight years later, the husband died of a lung infection which ran riot. And now the son, an only child, was also dead. All but a few of the trees which gave the Close its name had been felled.

The private wake was on its boozy last legs when I arrived, and the cousin or whatever who opened the door greeted me with a belch of disapproval. 'You've got a sodding nerve turning up here. Even if it wasn't you that killed him.'

'He was specially invited by me,' came an angrier voice

from the depths of the hall, and Darren's mother pushed her way through the torpid, all-male gang. She seemed to be the only sober person in view. Though we hardly knew each other, I was kissed on both cheeks and led into the sitting-room where a mixed group of mourners whispered over the few remaining sandwiches. Having positioned me by an ornamental fireplace, Laurel Glover called in the hallway drunks. Three or four grumpily obliged. 'For those of you who don't know, this is Josie's young man, and I want to tell you all what I feel about that.' She paused and the complete silence suggested that she had everyone's attention. 'Even if my Darren was alive, I think Josie would be better off with Sam.' This provoked a few low murmurs, though they were impossible to interpret. Laurel went on, 'So if any of you disapprove, you can bugger off out of my house!'

I expected a mass exodus, but the gathering held together, at least for the moment. An elderly man—Uncle Something-or-Other—asked what I wanted to drink. 'After an introduction like that, is there any chance of a stiff scotch?'

He padded away while Laurel Glover explained, 'I know I gave you the wrong impression the afternoon they were diving for my lad, but I was in a fucking awful state, as you can imagine.'

'Today can't have been any easier.'

'It's had its moments. But there's been loads of things to keep me busy.'

She was a small, wiry woman in her late forties. Before Darren's disappearance her hair used to be dyed a lifeless black. Since then she had let it emerge silvery grey, which actually made her look younger. As soon as her relative returned with my whisky, I was taken out to the kitchen where Josie and her mother had started the washing-up. Mrs Fletcher gave me a hug and made herself scarce so that the rest of us could have a serious talk. Josie kissed me on the lips and said, 'After Laurel's little speech you'll have to stick with me—or else!'

—

'What about those out there who still think the opposite?'

'They're all wind and piss,' said my sponsor as she jammed a chair under the door handle to prevent interruptions. 'Now then. Darren hired you after that business with his bike to try to find out who had it in for him. Right?'

'Yes, but he disappeared without giving me anything to go on. I must give you the £150 he left with me. I'll bring it round tomorrow.'

'Josie says you've been earning it.'

'He's done lots of investigating,' Josie said, 'Though he's always pretending to give up.'

'So keep the cash,' Laurel said firmly. 'And I'll pay you some more.'

'Absolutely not,' I spluttered. 'Funerals and so forth are incredibly expensive.'

'Too right! But Darren left me with more than I want anyone out there to know. And since the police have decided to cock it up, I'm asking you to keep your eyes and ears open for the real killer.'

'You don't think it's Reverend Philpot?'

'No, I sodding don't! It's got to be someone connected with whatever Darren was caught up in. Trouble is, I never got out of him anything more than a wink or a grin . . . and too much cash for me to sleep easy. That's why I said that about you being much better for Josie.' The women sadly hugged each other. I, in the meantime, thought: she could be paying me to end up in the river myself! But Laurel went on, 'I don't want you taking any risks, mind. Once you have a suspicion, just bring it to me.'

I wasn't about to encourage her plans for unofficial revenge, even if it was a temporary fantasy thrown up by grief. Coolly I responded, 'If I took evidence to anyone it would be to Francis Wyatt.'

Josie reminded her, 'He was one of the policemen at our place on the Sunday. The very laid-back one.'

Laurel grimly asked, 'Why should he be any bloody use?'

'He doesn't believe Steve Philpot did it. But there's some

sort of internal rivalry which means he can't interfere—unless he has solid proof.'

Josie said, 'So Sam will get the proof for him.'

'Sure,' I agreed, trying to sound as though we were doing more than humouring a bereaved mother. It hardly mattered. By then Laurel was not looking well enough for us to talk much longer. I quickly told her, 'I'll see what I can find out, and I'll keep the £150, but forget about any further payment.' She nodded in agreement, at least it seemed like a nod at first, but her head and rest of her upper body kept going forwards until we caught her.

With huge relief, I threw off my suit jacket and was loosening my black tie when Josie demanded help. 'I'm surprised I wasn't the one to faint. I've outgrown this dress since my gran died.'

We had left Laurel Glover in the care of her two sisters. Her fainting fit had been brief, but it provided an overdue excuse for the house to be cleared of hangers-on. Josie and I were planning to go for a walk, but first we needed to change and to collect Eddie from Mrs Leigh-Harcourt.

'You're not exactly overweight,' I murmured, edging down her zip.

'I must have filled out somewhere,' Josie said huskily, and then gave a giggle. As she didn't move away, I went on to loosen the soft brassière which had caused her to present an occasionally distracting profile during the funeral. Since the discovery of Darren's body we had, by a mutual though scarcely stated agreement, limited ourselves to comforting embraces. Now, as my hands touched the breasts I had tried not to think about when Darren's soul was being commended to a higher place; now, as Josie let her clothes drop and turned to press her open mouth against mine, it was clear by mutual consent that we were ready to move on.

Very gently, very slowly we made love.

Later, while we lay in a wonderfully cosy post-climactic haze, I thought the phone might be ringing downstairs.

Josie didn't seem to hear it, and I didn't bring it to her attention. She was draped on top of me, and my hands rested in satisfaction on the smooth backs of her thighs. We could manage a shallow, rhythmic breathing, but for a little longer neither of us shifted a limb. I doubt we could have reacted if the house was on fire.

Josie preferred to wait in the van while I collected Eddie. 'I know what I look like,' she claimed. I thought she looked great, blooming in fact, which turned out to be the point. 'Even an old lady like Ma Harcourt would sense what I've been up to. And I feel shy about it today.'

'Don't I look the same?'

'I dunno. Could be you've just had it, or else you've just downed a highly satisfying pint.' She kissed the tip of my nose. 'Whichever way, it's your dog that needs fetching . . . so get on with it, lover.'

Mrs Leigh-Harcourt was more interested in a quiz show than my appearance. I was let in with barely a glance as she hastened back to her television. Even the news about her neighbour across the gardens went for nothing. When I thanked her for looking after my dog yet again, she simply waved us goodbye, keeping her eyes on the screen. Eddie, who wasn't always so keen to leave, went bounding out to the van. He seemed to give a smirk as he scrambled past Josie and into the back. Getting behind the wheel, I said, 'Mrs L.-H. was too busy watching the box, but I think Eddie's guessed.'

'Just as well. He'll need to get used to it. Won't you, doggie?' Josie usually took little notice of Eddie and he was amazed to be addressed directly. In response he stretched a paw over the back of her seat. She gave the paw a brief shake, turned my way and said, 'Walkies, then?'

Normally we would have gone all the way on foot, but this time we drove to the top end of the dirt lane beyond the Garden Centre. It was mid-morning and we wanted to reach proper fields before the light started to fade. The riverbank had been chosen for our walk because Josie still felt a need to say a personal farewell to Darren. This area seemed more fitting than the churchyard. But it was a different ghost that caught me unawares. Having strolled past the rusty, abandoned Volkswagen, we were going through the metal gate when I found myself shivering from head to toe. Josie anxiously asked, 'Do you want to go back?'

I shook my head. 'It's OK. Just that the first time I came down this track was the morning Ron killed himself. There were sirens in the distance and I didn't know they were to do with him.' At that moment Eddie the Totally Rational spotted a few rabbits and tore off towards the river. Arm-in-arm we followed.

'One good thing happened near here,' Josie said. 'You kissed me when I was spooked inside one of your horrible buildings.'

'My pleasure. Though they're Gordon Summing's horrible buildings.' The outhouses, possibly still unused, were not far away, but we didn't let ourselves be drawn towards them. Instead, we scaled the rise of ground which masked that stretch of river. There were no anglers in view, but a couple of canoeists paddled past, heading for Lewes. From further south, towards the sea, came the drone of a motorboat. 'Hope it's not your boss. I'm not in the mood for another of his parties.'

'Nor me. Though at least he would behave himself this time.'

'How d'you know?'

'He apologized when I went in on Monday. Said whatever happened was a bit of a blur but he thought he might have overstepped the mark. I told him I'd already forgotten all about it.'

'Even his indiscretion about what might be kept in the storage buildings?'

'Yeah, I told him I'd particularly forgotten that bit! What d'you think I am?'

'I think you're the true detective round these parts. I'm just a romantic bumbler, and even Francis Wyatt's too busy falling in love.'

'With the Brainbox?' Josie smiled broadly. 'That's great. Isn't it?'

'Not for Mrs Wyatt and all the little Wyatts, perhaps. But at least I know where to start looking for him if we ever come up with the famous "proof".' The motor craft we had heard now came in sight. It was not unlike Gordon Summing's boat, but the two-man crew weren't familiar, and they sailed past us with barely a look. 'Phew—that was a relief,' I said, but Josie had lost her smile.

'How the hell are we going to find out who killed you, Darren?' The question was addressed towards the disturbed waters of the river, but I tried to offer up an answer.

'By accident. That's the most likely way. Or else the police will release Steve Philpot and get on with the job themselves. He's only "helping them with their inquiries". That doesn't always lead to the "helper" being charged.'

Josie started to cry and this was not a moment to offer comfort. Moving inland a little, I was joined by Eddie the Frustrated. The rabbits had outrun him, which was probably just as well. I wasn't convinced he would know what to do if he caught one. More to the point, I was sure I wouldn't know what to do if he caught one. In a feeble attempt to boost the dog's self-esteem, I sought out a stick and threw it a modest distance for him to fetch. He trotted off a few yards but then he circled around, came back to me, and looked up expectantly. I was about to give him an ironic pat on the head when my attention was diverted to a running figure up the top end of the field. I squinted and came to the conclusion that it was a woman. She had come from the main road but through a gate which was to the south of our dirt lane. Josie came up quietly behind me, slipped a hand into mine, looked where I was looking, and said, 'I thought you told me she was ill!'

I squinted again and realized that the runner, suitably kitted out in jogging suit and trainers, and even wearing a colourful headband, was indeed Marianne Koerner. 'Her pills and ionizer must have worked wonders.'

Marianne did not run in our direction. She made for the

gateway to the next field along, reversing the route which Summing's driver had taken all those weeks ago. I shivered again. Josie clung to my arm and murmured, 'Let's go home, love.'

There was an oddity concerning Marianne Koerner which had bothered me in the few moments when my other worries and considerations gave it a chance. This lay in the contrast between her smiling exit from the vicarage as witnessed by Janine Quibbley, and Dora's off-hand reference to a woman at Summing's party who 'had something to do with the pub'. Since Marianne was definitely not going to be on duty, I persuaded Josie that our journey home should include a stop-off at the One-in-the-Eye. By the end of five minutes I was in a mood to rename the place the Tear-in-the-Eye. Even though she had been there when Ralph brought in his fished-up plastic skeleton, all the solid regulars behaved as if Josie was making her first appearance since quitting as barmaid. That it was the day of the funeral must have had a lot to do with it, heightening everyone's emotions. I took solitary refuge in my beer while she was greeted with hugs, kisses, and not a few sobs by one semi-drunk after another. Caught short of a handkerchief, Tony Koerner could be seen dabbing at his eyes with a bar cloth. Since he was clearly off-guard I asked him, 'How's Marianne feeling now? Any better?'

'Almost right as rain. Those pills are a wonder.'

'And the ionizer helped, I expect.'

'So she says. Though to top it off she's gone for a run. Apparently the evening air will finish the job. Thanks for asking.'

'Not at all.' I ordered a second pint, even though I was only half way down the first. Josie, who scarcely touched alcohol, had already been offered enough drinks to last her a month. 'Of course,' I murmured, 'there's been a few interesting developments since I was here a few hours back.'

Tony Koerner laughed loud and genuinely. 'I've taken a tidy sum from the Gentlemen of the Press, as well as from the usual layabouts.' I looked around and saw no strangers, only the regulars and Josie. Tony said, 'They haven't hung about, Sam. Only came in for off-sales, to sustain their vigil up at the vicarage.'

This was an obvious development which I hadn't thought about. 'Is Mrs Philpot still refusing to see anyone?'

'Anyone as has tried,' Albert called across.

'Which is not many, given the disgrace,' added Alfred. I turned back to the landlord.

'Perhaps your wife ought to try when she's back from her run. Dora Philpot must need help, and they are friends, aren't they?' Tony Koerner looked blank. I tried again. 'I thought Marianne popped into the vicarage now and then.'

'Sure you should have this second pint?' Tony asked, with a leer. 'It's not my missus that used to pop into the vicarage. It's you! Before our Josie got you on the straight and narrow. Dear, dear! I hope you aren't going to have a relapse just because the vicar has been unavoidably detained.' This provoked a burst of laughter from those nearest the bar.

Josie, freed by her welcome committee at last, joined me just as Alfred said to Albert (and to anyone else in earshot), 'Didn't someone say the handyman was knocking on the vicarage door before the prison van was out of the lane?'

Before Josie could wade in on this, I quickly said, 'For once you've heard something that has a grain of truth in it, Alfred. Although it was a police car, not a van. And although I waited a good few minutes before doing what Steve Philpot *asked* me to do, I definitely went to see if his wife needed any help. And just in case I was tempted to misbehave, I had your dear old friend, Jack Ainsly, with me. But she didn't let us in, anyway.'

Instead of feeling suitably sorted out, Alfred merely muttered, 'That's not how I heard it.' And Albert backed him up.

'That's a relief,' Josie announced loudly. 'If you'd heard it the way Sam told it I'd suspect he really had been up to no good!' Her fans, including Eddie who gave several loud barks, received this wisdom raucously enough to drive Albert and Alfred into a grumbling huddle. Meanwhile, Josie whispered to me, 'You ought to have known better.'

'Eh?'

'Never try and talk sense to them two, especially this late.'

This was one of those disconcerting times when I felt as if I was the nineteen-year-old and Josie was a stunningly-preserved thirty-something. She patiently sipped at a half of lager shandy while I downed my second pint, and then we left the pub.

As we approached my house, I looked up and thought I saw a flicker of light from inside the bedroom. Unless it was a reflection in the window, of a shooting star or the lights on an aeroplane. Or else my imagination was on the loose again. Josie settled for the latter after we had waited for a reoccurrence. 'Remember how jumpy you were down by the river?'

'Absolutely,' I said, with only a faint slur. 'Time to pull myself together.' Mentally consigning all spooks to the regions from whence they might have come, I unlocked the door, but as we entered the hall, Eddie began to growl softly. My attempts to calm him failed, even when I took him through and pointed out that the back door was securely bolted. And so the three of us systematically checked out the sitting-room, the kitchen, and finally the workshop. The catch on the back room window was still in a state of semi-repair. I had never finished the job I started while Darren was trying to hire my services as 'a sort of detective'. The lower window was slightly open.

'Did you leave it like that?' Josie asked.

'Haven't a clue. I could have. I quite often do. Sometimes, anyway.'

'Very helpful!'

'Still—' I squatted and looked beneath the workbench. 'No one's under here.'

'That leaves upstairs, then.'

Indeed it did, and I suddenly started to pick up on Eddie's unease. Supposing I hadn't imagined the flicker of light. Supposing the spooks had refused to be consigned. As there was no obvious sign of breaking and entering, could we be suffering a genuine, supernatural invasion? I kept these fears to myself, and, although it would be no use against a phantom, I grabbed a large hammer.

We crept up the stairs, which seemed pointless given the amount of noise we'd already made down below, and the landing floorboards did us no favours as I led the way to the main bedroom. It was in complete darkness except for a small red dot in the furthest corner. Coming in last and being both brazen and practical, Josie switched on the light.

Crouched against the wall was Dora, pale and dishevelled, and only the cigarette she was clinging to prevented her from looking like a ghost.

CHAPTER 22

Hiding to Nothing

'Those bloody journalists were giving me no rest, even though I wouldn't let them in the house.'

'How come they didn't follow you here?' Josie asked, helping our visitor to her feet.

'I tricked them,' Dora said with a hint of pride. 'I opened the bedroom window and shouted I was going to come down and talk to them in five minutes. Then I sneaked straight out by the back door, climbed over the wall and knocked on Mrs Leigh-Harcourt's window. She let me through to the next street without any fuss. I think she was more interested in what was on television.'

'And you got in through my workshop window?'

'Yes. I'm sorry.'

'Don't worry,' Josie said brightly. 'We'll hide you till they get fed up and push off. Isn't that right, Sam?'

'The spare room bed's not aired, but . . .'

Josie cut in, 'An even better place would be my mum and dad's. They could put you up in my old room.'

Dora hardly seemed to hear this. She said, 'Those people won't go away. Even when the police let Steve go. He didn't do it, you know.'

'We don't think he did!' Josie said, and I kept any doubts to myself. Instead, I added, 'Nor does Darren's mother. She wants me to find the real killer. I need to talk to you, to see if you know anything that can help.' It was a little disconcerting, the three of us standing about in the bedroom, so I suggested a transfer to the kitchen where we could relax with a hot drink. As for later on, I couldn't help hoping that a room in the Fletcher cottage would be available.

Not long after we had all moved downstairs, Josie announced that she was going off to sound out her parents. Following her to the front door, I whispered, 'Why not phone them?'

'Dora needs to talk to you alone.' She pressed the back of her hand against my groin. 'And I'm prepared to trust you, just this once.'

'You know it's all over, whatever little there was in the first place.'

'Hm! There's one thing I didn't realize till just now. She's been in that bedroom before.'

'What on earth makes you think that?'

'Female instinct, my little innocent!' She gave me a fleeting kiss and went off down the dark road.

Back in the kitchen, the kettle had boiled and Dora was fetching down a box of camomile teabags. In the process she noticed her Canterbury Cathedral cake tin on the next shelf. Suddenly embarrassed, I said, 'I haven't had a chance to wash that out yet.'

She handed me the teabags and turned to inspect the tin. Weighing it in her hands she said, 'You never got round to eating the cake, either.'

'Sorry. Iced sponge isn't my favourite.'

'I know that, Sam.' She prised the lid off and exclaimed, 'Lord, that's exactly what I brought you!' She quickly closed the tin and put it back, muttering, 'I was in a terrible state then—just like now.' She forced a smile. 'I'd like to visit you one day when I'm feeling fine.' The smile faded. 'Some bloody chance!'

I put my arms around her and she clung to me, sighing but not crying. Eventually she said, 'For weeks and weeks, I've needed someone to hold me. In fact, I think you were the last.'

'This is different.'

She looked up at me with a snuffling laugh. 'Yes, I've well and truly lost my chance.' We separated and she sat at the far side of the table while I set her teabag to soak. 'I should have left Steve there and then. But someone had to look after him. And I wasn't sure how serious you were. All the same, there was a genuine spark between us, wasn't there?'

I nodded, passing over her tea and turning to pick up the instant coffee I'd made for myself. After sitting opposite her, I said, 'The truth is . . . I don't think you'll ever leave your husband.'

'Won't I?'

'However bad things are between you. So, if you want me to help prove his innocence, will you answer some difficult questions?' She gave a listless shrug. Not a great encouragement, but I dived in at the deep end. 'Was Darren ever your lover?'

'No.'

'Steve must have thought so. He's admitted to that business with the motorbike and the skull. Why bother unless he thought you were having an affair?'

'That is what he thought. But we weren't.'

'It was a very elaborate way of scaring Darren. Why not just have it out with him?'

'The simple way is not Steve's way. Whatever he thinks is always counterbalanced by enormous doubts. He wanted to secretly put the wind up Darren and see if it provoked a guilty reaction.'

'Darren's reaction was to offer me money to find out who had it in for him.' She said nothing but was clearly taken aback. 'That evening and night I had visitors by the yard. First Darren. Then Janine Quibbley, who'd accidentally adopted my dog. Then you. Then Josie, checking up how the detecting was going, since she'd sent Darren to me. And finally your sedated but still deranged husband!' From a state of surprise, her face had drifted back into neutral. 'To cap it all, next lunch-time I met Gordon Summing for the first time, and it turns out even he was outside this house the night before, around the time Josie left for home.'

Dora regained a small measure of animation and said, 'Steve had you and Gordon Summing lined up as alternative suspects.'

'So when he came here and asked me to act as a go-between to try and save your marriage . . .'

'He was testing you out.'

This convoluted approach fitted in with Steve's claim that he had climbed the church tower to prove how desperate he was for my help. But then, maybe a sudden jealous urge had made him push me over the edge. Perhaps the supposed accident was attempted murder after all. In which case—my suspicions couldn't help but run on—did he also kill Darren, after all? To try and complete the sequence, I asked, 'What daft system did he use to try and get an admission out of Summing?'

'He never got round to Gordon. Letting me go to the party was his way of proving that the jealousy crisis was over.' She stubbed her cigarette out on the saucer and immediately lit another. 'Instead, he's moved on to surrogate guilt.'

'Pardon?'

'Remember the phone call when you were leaving us in Hampshire? It was Mr Ainsly with news that divers were searching the river.' She made a curious sound deep in her throat, like a suppressed shriek. 'Once Steve knew Darren was probably dead, he couldn't wait to get back and bury him. And from then on he force fed his fantasy of guilt until he was ready to take the blame. Because Jesus died for the sins of the world, a few unhinged Christians try to hijack other people's crimes.'

Since this could be her fantasy about his fantasy, I asked a practical question. 'Where did he get the plastic skeleton?'

'From me. My sister brought it back as a present from Japan. Years ago. That's why it's all on a slightly small scale, I suppose.'

'A weird present.'

'I once had a ridiculous ambition to become a medical student. The skeleton was Clara's little joke.'

'This is the sister who lives in Brighton? Just up the road from Darren's flat?'

Without being drawn on Darren, she said, 'After our brief stay the other week we're not speaking. Otherwise I'd have found a way to reach her tonight. My liberal academic parents gave up on me because I married a priest. Steve's folks are missionaries in West Africa.' She paused for some serious, silent smoking. I quietly waited for her to continue. 'After we were married the skeleton was stuck away in a trunk. The first I knew he'd got it out was the evening after you and I ended up in bed.' She gave me a wide-eyed look as she stubbed out the half-finished cigarette and sipped her tea. 'He'd sneaked the skull back from Jack Ainsly and I found him burying it in the garden.'

'Where it stayed till he dug it up the other night.'

'I knew someone must have been watching.'

'Mrs Leigh-Harcourt had noticed something going on but didn't know what. I looked over the wall while I was working in her garden and saw the hole.'

'Detective Sam Bevan.' She almost smiled. 'Perhaps you are the one to sort all this out.'

'Only with a lot of help. For instance, are you ready to tell me why you couldn't meet me in Brighton?'

She gave me another wide-eyed look while she slowly slipped a hand inside her blouse to straighten a strap. When the operation was finished, she said, 'For two hours I was locked in the bedroom at the vicarage. After I'd caught Steve with the skull I told him I was taking the car, to go and see my sister. While I was changing my shoes he locked the door.'

'And drove into Brighton himself?'

'I doubt it very much. He locked himself in with me.'

If she was telling the truth this shot down my notion that, guilty or not, Steve Philpot had been the hidden presence in Darren's flat. The acrid smell in the bathroom must have come from something other than his vertigo-induced vomit.

Before I could make any sensible adjustments to my view of the case, Dora released further details. 'Streaming with tears, he told me the lengths I'd driven him to—leading to the bike and skull trap. He refused to unlock the door until I had told him I still loved him. He said he was prepared not to question me about where I'd been the night before. This, by the way, after an entire day of refusing to talk about where the hell *he'd* been the night before.'

'He already knew part of where you'd been. I told him you'd come here to apologize for tearing me off a strip in the bell tower. That's all. Then he got shirty because I couldn't confirm anything about your lover. The other one.'

Dora stood up and yelled across the table, 'I had no other lover, damn you! Not Darren, not Gordon, not anyone!' She fell back on to her chair, which rocked slightly. 'I refused to give in. At that moment there was no way I could tell him I still loved him. We were there for two hours, at opposite sides of the room. I suppose the miracle was that he didn't beat me up or try to take me by force. In the end, he crept off to his study. I wanted to run away, but I was afraid of what he would do to himself. Much later, he announced that he was going off to sleep in the shed. It was too stupid for words. I laughed at him, but away he went. I should have left him to it, instead of making a scene for all the neighbourhood insomniacs to enjoy.'

So that was why Mrs Leigh-Harcourt and Janine Quibbley saw what they saw. Or not. But at the risk of another fit of rage, I coolly asked, 'Why was Steve jealous of you and Darren?'

No rage. With exaggerated concentration, Dora lit another cigarette. 'He saw us talking, once, after an evensong to which Darren had brought his mother. It was the anniversary of his father's death. Once at the sports field. They had both played in a soccer match. Steve and Darren, I mean. Not the mother.'

'Hardly incriminating.'

'Except to an insanely jealous man. But what pushed him over the edge, which I didn't know about until a row we had this afternoon, was he'd had a visit from that pub woman, the one who tipped me off that you had left Gordon Summing's party alone.'

'Marianne Koerner.'

'If you say so. She told Steve she'd spotted me and Darren a couple of times in that lane with the rusty car. Instead of asking me outright what I'd been up to, Steve took Darren's bike after dark from outside the pub. It was a ridiculous risk. He could have been arrested as a thief.'

'Better than as a murderer. But . . .' My line of questioning almost faltered. '. . . Why did you meet Darren in the lane?'

She blinked at me. 'Can't you guess why I would meet a man in out-of-the-way places if he wasn't my lover?' My mind rushed to an unwelcome conclusion which she confirmed before I could speak. 'As the tabloids will gleefully describe it sooner or later, Darren was my pusher.'

It is a long standing tradition—in the public bar of the One-in-the-Eye at least—that the village of Miston had been named by a passing weather-forecaster. As in, 'There will be mist on that village tonight,' which his not-deeply-concentrating companion heard as, 'There be Miston Village to the right.' This tale only holds water if the travellers were heading south, on the road from Lewes to the coast. Otherwise, the village would have been to the left. The part about the companion not hearing properly I believe entirely. Whenever a weather-forecast is on the radio or television my attention drifts after the first few sentences.

Dr Quibbley once tried to persuade the pub's amateur historians that in pre-Norman times Miston had been larger than a village and had taken its name from the Saxon bishop, Almis; as in Almis-town. Most of her audience found this far too likely to be believable.

Since Bishop Almis might well have frowned upon the (possible) doings of our present-day vicar, I felt it must be the spirit of the wandering weatherman who stepped in to help us late that night. The thickest mist for months was sitting on the village as Josie, Dora and I left the house.

'It wasn't anything like this when I came back just now,' Josie said.

'Wonder how the members of the Press are taking it,' I responded, fiddling with an old, half-broken torch. The beam sprung to life but faded after we had taken a few paces. 'Bugger it!'

Dora said, 'Better to leave it off and let our eyes adjust.' After all the questions and confessions of the past hour, she sounded remarkably level-headed. I put the torch into my jacket pocket and suggested that Josie lead the way. We set off again in close single file with me bringing up the rear. Gradually it was possible to see two or three yards ahead, but we kept to a snail-like pace. To compensate for the reduction in vision, the mist made me super-aware of night calls from local sheep, cows and poultry. A number of wild birds also joined in the general racket, and as we skirted the tiny village green occasional bursts of human sound identified the unseen pub. Once or twice car headlamps broke through the dark grey swirl, but no vehicle stopped near us and we reached the Fletcher cottage without meeting any pedestrians.

Soon after we set off on the return journey, Josie asked, 'Did she tell you anything useful?'

'Could be.' Could be useful, and could prove to be dangerous, I thought, if I was daft enough to go on pretending to be a detective.

The mist had thinned a little and we were back in the area of the village green. The lights of the pub were like a faint blush in the near distance. Josie stopped walking and faced me. 'Whatever she said has upset you, hasn't it?'

'It might upset you too. Darren used to supply Dora with amphetamines.'

'Did he?' She sniffed. 'I knew he did a little local dealing, even though he would never admit it.' She sniffed again. 'I sort of told you that's why I broke up with him. He always refused to discuss it. He expected me to hang around at his beck and call, but I must never know what he was getting up to. For my own safety, he said. Treated his mum the same way, but she had no way out of it. I didn't need the cash.' She finally blew her nose on a tissue.

'Well, thanks a lot for telling me my fee came out of drug money.'

'I thought it would put you off the whole investigation.'

'Too bloody right!'

'But it could have come from something else, anyway. The dope scene round here is very small stuff. Amphetamines is a surprise. Kind of old-fashioned.'

'Up-to-date enough to ruin Dora's life! And all because of some quack doctor. She had a serious weight problem a couple of years before they moved here. Went to a clinic. Came out slim and hooked.'

'Did her husband know?'

'He went into a total panic when he discovered she wasn't getting her supplies from the GP. So she went into clinic number two, where she was cured of the effects of clinic number one. Trouble is, once they moved here she started plumping out again—at least that's how she saw it.'

She squeezed my hand. 'So you used to fancy her when she was hating how she looked.'

'Seems so. Anyway, one day when she was visiting her sister over in Brighton she bumped into Dr Darren and they came to an arrangement. There's money on that side of the family, and the dealing was originally done through the sister, but then she had to be away for a while. Dora and Darren had a couple of meetings down in that lane by the Garden Centre, and the vicar was tipped off—by Marianne Koerner for some peculiar reason.'

'To spite me, probably. Hoped to cause a fuss. She hated the likes of Darren using the pub.'

'Well, the vicar didn't know these meetings were strictly business. He got an attack of old-fashioned jealousy. That led to the bike business. And Dora didn't dare tell him it was because she was on the pills again—even after she'd weaned herself off them while they were away in Hampshire.'

'She got thinner there.'

'By will-power alone. And smoking.' It was a grim irony that her latest cure might prove fatal in its own right. While I was thinking this, Josie moved half way towards lighting up a cigarette of her own. Then she put it back in the packet.

'If I can get through today of all days without one, I reckon I'm seriously off it.' She clung to my arm and we started slowly walking again. As we passed the entrance to Church Lane she said, 'Did she say anything about why her husband gave himself up?'

'Their doctor prescribed a powerful sedative for him the evening Darren disappeared. But Steve surfaced out of it. He remembers taking the body part of the plastic skeleton down to throw in the Ouse. He remembers Darren showing up on the riverbank. Then there's a blank, until he arrived at my place.'

Josie stopped again. I felt her shiver. 'So he could have done it.'

'No. Now's the first time I feel convinced he didn't. It would have meant a big struggle, and there was no sign of it when he came to me. There's a hell of a difference between tossing a load of plastic into the water and drowning someone as fit as Darren.'

'He could have knocked him out first—with a rock or something.'

'It would still have taken a huge effort getting the body

into the water. Steve's clothes weren't muddy or damp. And I'm sure he was too doped up to have gone home and changed.'

Josie hugged me tightly. 'I want you to forget about looking for the real killer. I think we should leave it all to the professionals.'

I nuzzled her cheek. 'What's brought this on?'

'I've just had this clear picture of how it must have been for Darren, fighting for his life by the river. I don't want that happening to you.'

'Or you.'

'Or me.'

We kissed and clung to each other a little longer, feeling strangely safe in the mist. I murmured, 'Shall we go home and celebrate this wonderful outbreak of common sense?'

'You bet!'

And off we strolled, getting up a reckless speed through the low visibility. Animal and bird noises seemed to have died away. Only our footsteps, slightly echoing, disturbed the calm of the night—until I heard a distant barking, coming from beyond my house. I had left Eddie in the back garden. At first I thought it was simply that he wanted to be let in. Then I realized we were hearing a warning too late. There was a chuckling sound from a nearby patch of mist, followed by a huge, engine roar as two motorcycles were started up. Almost instantly, Josie and I were trapped in a pair of crossed headlamp beams. The operation might have been rehearsed, so slickly did a circle of perhaps twelve non-riders materialize. My hand felt for the broken torch. It was the nearest thing I had to a weapon. At the same time, Josie started calling out their names, identifying the guilty in advance. I recognized a couple of the sturdier drunks from Darren's wake, but some of the foot-soldiers were not familiar to me, while neither of the motorcyclists turned out to be Clarence. I gave up any notion of trying to talk my way out of things after Josie paused in her roll-call and yelled that whatever they'd come for, they'd better make a complete job of it. Otherwise she'd make sure they were hunted down 'to the last sodding one!'

CHAPTER 23

Conditional Rescue

I thought our hopeless situation had driven Josie crazy, yet when she challenged them to do their worst, the gang stopped in their tracks. Some house lights went on, noticeable because a breeze was now lifting the mist. But our luck didn't last long. When none of my neighbours came from the safety of their homes (and I don't blame them) the lads unfroze. They didn't give a damn that people might be simply watching. Josie was bundled to one side, though it took three of them to restrain her. The rest closed in on me, finally coming in a rush. I flailed about with my torch which smashed to pieces on the first head I contacted. After that, it was a chaos of fists and feet as the attackers merged like a rugby scrum-down, with me as the ball.

This was the first time since my schooldays that I'd been beaten up. I wasn't enjoying it at all, and the only defence I could think of was to bring at least one of the bastards tightly down on top of me. Not an intimacy to relish, but at least their target area would be severely limited.

Through the maze of bodies I could hear Josie still yelling. At one point an ill-advised character must have tried to gag her with his hand. First her voice went muffled, then came a cry of male pain, and then Josie was shouting clearly again. The lass had healthy teeth and lungs.

Soon after this a car arrived on the scene. My spirits weren't lifted much. I imagined only that reinforcements of Darren's Avengers must have been waiting for the tip-off. In consolation, I had miraculously achieved a shield of two squirming idiots who were painfully receiving blows on my behalf. In the dark—and perhaps thanks to an excess of booze—most of the gang weren't being particular about their target.

The next, very curious development was a pattern of yelps and groans which weren't coming from me or my two involuntary bodyguards. This quickly led to mob panic, and as soon as I was sure a retreat was on, I stopped embracing my 'shields'. Both of them scrambled to their feet and vanished, but as I tried to sit up Josie almost knocked me flat again. She was on her knees, crying, 'It's all my fault! I should have known the stupid fuckers would try something today!'

'Are you in one piece, Sam? Or should we send for an ambulance?' With only a little pain I turned my head to confirm that one of my rescuers was Gordon Summing.

'I'm going to be bruised all over, but it doesn't feel like anything's broken.'

There was another, blurred figure who kept his distance while Summing rubbed the edge of his hand, murmuring, 'It's a long time since I had to put my karate training to practical use.'

'My darts training didn't help me at all,' I said. 'It's lucky there were so many of them. They got in each other's way.' As Josie and her boss helped me to me feet I asked, 'Who's your friend?'

Summing gestured for his companion to come closer. 'This is Lewis Spencer. He and I were just leaving one of Tony Koerner's private, after-hours sessions. We heard Josie shouting her head off.' Almost before Mr Lewis Spencer emerged into the lights of Summing's car, I knew who he must be.

'Thanks for dropping by,' I said to the Ghoul.

He nodded and then wheezed a remark which I didn't catch. Summing spoke back to him in a low voice and then turned our way. 'If you're sure you can manage without us, we'll be off.' And without lingering for another medical assessment or for further thanks, they got into the car and drove away. At that moment Eddie came bounding down the street and I was nearly knocked flat yet again. It had taken him maybe ten minutes to work out that he must go round the back way to save his master. But it was the thought that counted, and I preferred having him unhurt.

When Francis Wyatt and Janine Quibbley dropped by I was lying in a warm bath. Two officers from the local police, alerted by the neighbours, had turned up as I was limping through my front door. Since the fight was over and the attackers had disappeared (along with the mist) they merely took a few notes and moved on. It wasn't my intention to press charges. I hoped my feud with Darren's pals would die of natural causes.

Our next visitors were just back from a late supper in Brighton. Janine had needed cheering up after a terrible day in London and she was limited in her sympathy for my bruises. 'They'll clear up in time. I'm suffering from terminal humiliation.' She sat on the covered toilet while Wyatt perched alongside Josie on the edge of the tub. My modesty was protected by a mass of Badedas bubbles but I felt I'd been crowded in enough for one night. My claustrophobia only eased when Janine started on her big revelation. 'Wescott's cut-price offer to us was pure bullshit. The chances of an American bid for the Heatherstone Library vanished days ago. Unlike our in-fighting committee, they found out almost straight off that water from an overflowing cistern has damaged a lot of books and papers.'

'A cistern in the castle library?' I queried.

'Two floors above. But water has a way of flowing downwards, don't you know! And the damage is real and irreparable. Our Professor Craglen, who hates my guts, has just been hired by the insurance company. He came to the meeting I'd called direct from his first inspection visit. Told us the news with a sickening mixture of regret and glee. I can hardly be blamed for the flooding, but Craglen will try to make sure I'm viewed as a "headstrong young gel". If I've a career left, it's just leapt back ten years.'

Wyatt blandly suggested, 'Why not write a nice, racy book about it all? Make a fortune.'

'I'm a serious historian, if you don't mind!' And to back up the claim she flicked some of my bubbles at him.

'At least you found out,' Josie said, getting up and handing Wyatt a towel. 'And Sam says you've discovered who was behind your anonymous messages.'

Janine gave up blowing at the bubbles still stuck to her hand. 'Pity it had to be Nathan. I was really hoping to nail Wescott with that one.' Then she suddenly dropped her self-pity, laughed and said, 'Were you embarrassed, having the Ghoul come to your rescue?'

'He was hardly around long enough for me to even thank him. But it shows the connection between Summing and Wescott must be more than social.'

Josie said, 'Would you believe the Ghoul's real name is Lewis Spencer?'

'Sounds more like a department store to me,' Janine replied, standing. 'We'd better get going before the rest of those bubbles pop.'

Wyatt started to follow her out to the landing, but he turned back to ask, 'These attackers of yours—were they all friends of the late Mr Glover?'

Josie pulled a face, possibly in objection to the official-style reference to Darren, but she replied, 'Three or four of them are workers up at the Dairy. Not really mates or relatives of Darren's like the rest.'

Wyatt stroked his stubbly chin. 'Could have been a partial set-up. Summing's men encouraging the others to take action.'

Josie was furious. 'It *had* to be a bloody set-up. The dairymen kept on the edge of the fight. They just slipped away when the boss showed his face. I thought at the time they must be worried about their jobs. But it makes much more sense that they were actually *on* the job! Tomorrow morning I'm going to resign—after I've wrecked the office!'

Francis Wyatt's laid-back manner disappeared for a moment. 'If you want to be more helpful, you'll tell Mr Summing how grateful Sam still is for being rescued. Then maybe we'll find out what favour he wants in return.' Before

I could protest that Josie and I were ex-detectives, he threw me by adding, 'By the way, the word is, my local chums will have finished with your vicar in the morning. He should be home for lunch.'

'On bail?' I asked.

'No. Walking free. So if you know a way of getting word to his wife, it might be as well to warn her. Apparently she isn't answering the phone.'

It was a little after ten o'clock when I arrived at the Fletcher cottage. Josie had driven off to do her Saturday morning stint at the farm office. She was also keen to act on Francis Wyatt's advice. In our joint anger at being manipulated, we had voted to come out of retirement and help uncover Gordon Summing's darker dealings.

I found Dora half-heartedly nibbling at a piece of dry toast. As soon as I told her the news about Steve she rushed away to try and make herself tidy. While I waited, Josie's mum quickly made me a bacon sandwich and slipped Eddie a plate of scraps. We were both grateful to be fed. Thanks to recent distractions, all that was left in my kitchen was a stale, iced cake.

Dora, Eddie and I approached the vicarage to find several reporters sprawled on the lawn, eyes closed against the warm sunlight. Even their standing colleagues hardly seemed to register our arrival at the foot of the drive. As there was no reason why they should recognize Dora, I thought we might slip into the house with a minimum of fuss. Unhelpfully, my companion shouted at the sunbathers, 'Kindly remove yourselves from my lawn. Otherwise I shall call the police.'

They certainly did remove themselves, to form a yelling, agitated cordon between us and the front door. At the same time, Dora realized she had left her keys behind during her backdoor escape the previous evening. She had scaled Mrs Leigh-Harcourt's wall clutching only her cigarettes and lighter. These details were whispered to me as she totally ignored a barrage of reporters' questions and big money offers. Finally, as if it was my fault, she said, 'So how are you going to get me out of this mess?'

Perhaps I should have checked earlier about the keys, but since she was wearing jeans they could have been in her pocket. So I felt rather grumpy as I shuffled a few options in my weary mind. Even if we managed to break through the blockade, there was no immediate access to the rear of the house. From my decorating days at the vicarage I remembered there was a way through the garage, but the garage itself was locked. It was too far and too late to chase around to Mrs L.-H.'s, but we might be able to get across from Janine Quibbley's back garden. Otherwise we would have to seek sanctuary in the bungalow. I took Dora by the arm and led her down the drive. Inevitably, we were followed. The more athletic hacks overtook us, some of them jumping over the garden railings. Few were put off by Eddie's growls, and the general jostling was not doing any favours to my bruises. As one grinning fool pointedly placed himself between us and Janine's gate, my patience snapped. He was of medium build, but to his surprise (and mine!) I managed to lift him clear of the ground, spin round and hurl him into the midst of his colleagues. 'Follow us any further and you'll get a lot worse than that,' I snarled at them, and turned to usher Dora through the gate. Eddie raced ahead.

Only when we were approaching the back door of the bungalow did pursuing footsteps announce that my bluff was about to be called. The leader of the pack had a familiar face and I was surprised I hadn't spotted him before. As if reading my mind, he smugly returned the compliment. 'I never realized it was you, Sammy! What with all that extra muscle. Very impressive. Now—how's about arranging a quick exclusive for old time's sake? You and the lady seem to be interestingly close.'

Eddie had been scratching at the kitchen door until both Wyatt and Janine stepped out. I passed Dora into their care and returned to talk terms. 'Exclusive means exactly that. Your chums'll have to bugger off.'

'Sorry, lads,' Clive Buxton, the one who knew me, said with a twisted smile. 'Who dares and all that.' Perhaps his rivals would not have given up so easily, except that distant, excited voices suggested action back in the lane.

'Do you have some form of contract?' I asked. 'Mrs Philpot won't talk on a verbal assurance alone.' Buxton pulled out a form and offered it for examination. I took the sheet of paper with my left hand and at the same moment slammed my fisted right hand into his stomach. He gasped and doubled over in traditional fashion. I was about to deliver a Ghoul-style second punch hard into his face when Wyatt caught my arm.

'Point made, Sam.'

Janine gave me a pat on the back, but Dora looked at me in surprise, perhaps even in fear, as Wyatt propelled me into the kitchen. Incredibly, Buxton tried to follow us. He had enough breath back to say, 'You people are witnesses. That was assault. If I don't get an interview I might think about calling the police.'

'Forget it,' Wyatt said, holding up his identification. 'And just be glad I stopped you running against Mr Bevan's fist for a second time.'

Buxton stepped back, sniffing. 'OK. OK. I've already got something juicy. Your Mr Bevan's motivation is a story itself.' He shouted in, 'How many years are you hoping the vicar'll get, Sammy?'

Francis Wyatt stepped up to Buxton and put a hand on his shoulder. 'Here's a friendly tip-off. That racket out the front will almost certainly be my colleagues bringing the Reverend Philpot home.'

Buxton's disbelief was short-lived. 'Bugger it!' he muttered, and he pushed off with an overacted clutching of his stomach.

Dora stared at me with a cold expression on her face. 'What's come over you? There's enough trouble without you hitting reporters on my behalf.'

'It wasn't all on your behalf. He's the shit my wife went off with. I've been wanting to thump him for years.' I turned to Wyatt. 'You stopped me making a proper job of it. Thanks.' I whistled to Eddie and the two of us walked out. I'd had enough of chaperoning Miston's queen-of-the-mood-change. As we passed the vicarage drive, a nearly-recovered Clive Buxton was barging his way through to the little group of police officers who were aiding Steve Philpot in entering his front door. I'd had enough of mad vicars as well. My main aim in life was to get to the van and drive off to the peace and quiet of a supermarket.

Two hours later, with the shopping unpacked and Eddie dished up with some proper dog food, I was about to go upstairs for a well-earned nap. Psychic intuition made me turn for a moment and stare at the phone, daring it to ring. It rang.

'Sam. Gordon Summing. Josie tells me you've made a pretty good recovery after your spot of trouble last night.'

'I'm better than I would have been if you and your friend hadn't turned up.'

'Glad to have been of service.' He cleared his throat. 'Actually, my friend has come out of it worse than you by the look of things. He has a badly sprained shoulder.'

The Ghoul being injured was a hard one to swallow, but I said, 'I'm very sorry to hear that. Is there anything I can do?'

'What Lewis needs is a few days' rest, but I desperately need someone to stand in for him on a job late tonight. Any chance of your being free? It would mean popping round to the farm at ten o'clock, preferably not after a heavy session at the pub.'

'No problem,' I said quickly, hoping to keep any edge of apprehension out of my voice.

'Terrific. Josie's already agreed to lend a hand, so I'll see the two of you later.'

CHAPTER 24

Cooked Books

'All he said was, it involved moving a few heavy items. I'm to be there as back-up in case Sam isn't strong enough.'

Janine said, 'You should have seen him this morning, thumping one of the reporters.'

'Yeah, he told me.' Josie hadn't been impressed by my tale of late-in-the-day revenge.

We were lounging around in the bungalow's sitting-room. Francis Wyatt took it to extremes and lay stretched out on a futon which had been unrolled beneath the front window. Staring at the ceiling, he asked, 'Did Mr Summing explain why he couldn't call on anyone else for help?'

'He said he was lucky not to have a strike at the dairy. Being so keen to rescue us last night, he didn't realize he was injuring some of his own workers.' Josie snorted. 'Pretending to believe him wasn't easy. I'd already seen a couple of them around the yard. Looked a bit shifty when they saw me, but they weren't limping much!'

'So—what do we do?' I asked in Wyatt's direction. 'For instance, if whatever we're supposed to transport is highly illegal, are we going to find ourselves arrested?'

'I'll make sure my people and the locals know you're acting on my behalf.' Wyatt got slowly to his feet and added, too casually for my liking, 'All we have to do is find out where you're doing it.'

Where we weren't doing it was at the main farm. Eddie had been left with Janine Quibbley, and my van was left in the dairy yard while Josie and I travelled with Summing to his boathouse in an otherwise unladen Range-Rover. There we switched to the motorboat, which also contained no heavy items. It was only then that Summing eased up on the general secrecy and revealed that we were dealing with export, not import. We would find the cargo stored in one of the new outbuildings, ready to be taken on board and shipped down the river and out to the sea. He was apologetic about involving us at all, blaming a complicated series of exchanges which were impossible to cancel. As we made our way upstream, he promised that we wouldn't be handling anything deadly. No hard drugs, no arms or explosives. Our part in the scheme was perfectly legal. The tricky stage would come later, as he sailed single-handedly through the harbour at Newhaven and out into the Channel. Wondering if Wyatt might have over-estimated the man's deviousness, I asked, 'Aren't you taking a risk telling us all this?'

He gave an exaggerated shrug while keeping his attention on the river ahead. 'Through force of circumstance I need your help to load my boat in the middle of the night. A fool could guess that the next stage must be at least slightly illegal, so I might as well own up.'

'Is it only slightly illegal?' Josie asked.

'I think so, given that most of the population do a little bit of smuggling once in a while.'

'That's usually by sneaking stuff into the country, not out,' I said.

'I'm a businessman. I look for profit in as many directions as possible. I also reward my employees well, as you might both acknowledge.' We managed an embarrassed mumble of agreement. 'Which, along with the gratitude you claim to feel after last night's little fracas, I hope disposes you not to go telling tales.'

'Oh, we're both eminently corruptible,' I said in such a clear and determined voice that Summing swung round to stare at me for a moment. Josie remained uneasily silent.

'All I'm asking is a modest discretion,' Summing said, turning back to his wheel. 'In return for two hundred and fifty pounds apiece.'

'A summer bonus!' Josie murmured, trying to lighten the atmosphere.

'If you like. Though it won't go through the books. You'll get it in cash as soon as we've loaded up.' After this he fell silent and concentrated on turning the boat shorewards without snagging the motor on a mudbank. His physical skills as a sailor were clinically efficient, in contrast to the often rambling nature of his speech. Feeling practically spare, I kept out of his way and pondered on the coincidence of his offering us £250 each. Darren had offered me £250 all told. Perhaps it was the standard basic rate among Sussex villains, like plumbers charging £20 just to walk through anyone's front door. I preferred doing the odd plumbing job, even for a fiver.

A few minutes later we were stepping ashore within close view of the outbuildings. I glanced up towards the top hedge and across to the dirt lane, hoping Wyatt had gone for this as the obvious spot for late-night skulduggery. As Summing, Josie and I walked inland, some vehicles went by along the main road but they did not stop. From nowhere did the Law burst forth, whistles ablowing. If there was a police presence they were biding their time, perhaps puzzled that we were as yet empty-handed.

Summing scaled an outer ladder, undid one of the padlocks and slid a roof section open enough for all three of us to get through and climb down inside. Josie was put in charge of a powerful flashlight while he separated out the mystery cargo which had been hidden under the sacks of cattle feed. There were four wooden boxes, each about half the size of a tea-chest. It was too late in the day, but I wished I had incorporated a pulley system in my design. As it was, I had to mount the inner ladder with a box perched on my shoulder and pass it over to Summing who was waiting to descend in a similar, uncomfortable fashion. Josie insisted on taking the final climb, and passed up the flashlight which I operated from a perch on the adjacent roof. It was no surprise that she was more adept at the job than me. For all his nasty skills, the person I could least imagine doing this particular task was the Ghoul. His shoulders were far too narrow.

'I reckon it's dirty books in these crates,' Josie pronounced as she passed the last box over. An odd gurgle came from Summing's throat which I first took for a laugh, but it was a cry of panic. His grip was slipping and within seconds the box hit the earth with a muffled crunch. I watched this from my perch and immediately played the flashlight's beam down on to the few spilled contents of the broken box. Summing went into an unexpected fury and yelled at me to kill the light. I obliged, leaving him to scramble down in the comparative dark. Unlike the night before, there was at least a faint glow from the thinly clouded moon. While he gathered up what I'd already seen to be large, leather-bound books, I gestured to Josie and we scrambled over to the far side of the closed roof. As we sat on the very edge, with our legs dangling over, the drop didn't look too bad. Our landing had to be softer than coming down on the floor of the bell tower and I'd managed that. On a whispered count of three we jumped. Apart from squelching one foot into a fresh cow-pat, I was fine. Josie was rubbing her right ankle but claimed, 'It'll be all right. You won't have to carry me. Now what?'

It was a simple question which I could have answered straight off if I knew which way round the buildings Summing might come to look for us. I tossed a mental coin and chose the side furthest from the river. I hoped Summing's attention would stray more towards the direction of his boat. The choice turned out to be partly right. He was concentrating on carrying the damaged container towards the river as we sneaked off in the direction of the dirt lane. Our flight was only spotted when we were half way to the metal gate.

'Come back here, you fools! I haven't paid you yet,' he yelled.

I turned and shouted back, 'Forget it. We were just returning a favour.'

Josie added, '*Bon voyage.*' But Summing started out after us and there was a sudden burst of red light and a fierce, snapping sound. We started running again; running, stumbling, tripping once or twice, until the ground at last levelled out near the lane. Summing let loose two more pistol shots before we almost hurdled over the metal gate. This was Josie's undoing. She landed hard on the already dodgy ankle and by the time we were approaching the rusted Volkswagen she was crying out with pain at every step. We would have to lie low at least for a few moments, so I led the way into the narrow gap between the wrecked car and the hedge. Even though I managed to stamp down a mass of nettles without getting badly stung, I suddenly discovered a limit to the space for hiding. A solid object, which was not part of the disintegrating VW, blocked the way. I still had Summing's flashlight in my hand and I switched it on for a brief moment. Josie was hard on my shoulder, leaning on me, in fact, and she gasped, not in pain but in surprise, 'It can't be!' She squeezed past me, saying, 'Put the torch on again for a sec.' I flicked the switch but kept the beam angled as low as possible. Josie then proceeded to search the pannier of Darren's motorbike. 'OK! Got it!' she said pulling out the key. Thank goodness Darren must have been too preoccupied, even after the hillside incident, to change his careless habits. I killed the light again and we rolled the bike onwards and out beyond its skeletal companion. Since she knew how to operate it, Josie got astride the beast ahead of me.

As I sat behind her, I said, 'The cops will love us for moving a prime piece of evidence!'

'Screw them!' she cried, and then, with a wince of pain she remembered her damaged ankle. 'You'll have to kick the starter for me.' She guided my foot into place and I pressed down hard. The engine puttered and fell silent. Not very far behind us the metal gate rattled. Without looking back to check if it was Summing, I kicked down again and the engine fired. If more shots were about to be aimed at us there was no way we would hear them. The bike roared out defiance as we found ourselves accelerating towards the main road, cheered on, I felt sure, by the ghosts of both Darren and Ron.

CHAPTER 25

A Suspension of Humanity

Wyatt wasn't at the bungalow, but Janine emerged bleary-eyed, woken by a combined racket from Eddie and the motorbike. She helped Josie to hobble indoors while I wheeled the 'piece of evidence' into its latest hiding place, between some fir trees and the carport. After that, I borrowed the phone to call Wyatt's special number in Lewes. Getting through to an answering machine, I simply said we were back at the bungalow. Back in the kitchen, I found Janine applying an ice-pack to Josie's ankle. 'What a fuss!' the patient muttered, but she was clearly glad of the attention.

'No one's there,' I said, 'But I've left a message. If Francis checks his machine, maybe he'll call here. The trouble is, I really ought to go and get my van. I don't fancy leaving it in the dairy yard.'

Janine, who had been receiving a high-speed, potted version of events from Josie, said, 'We can fill him in. But shouldn't you wait for a police escort?' I gave a cold laugh. 'Yes, it might be hours,' she admitted. 'Suppose I drive you there. If anyone's on guard we could sort of dash in and surprise them.'

'Thanks, but I'd rather sneak in by myself. Perhaps I'll take a short cut over the fields.' The exhaust on her Metro was noisy enough to alert a security-minded dairyman at half a mile's distance. Also, I didn't want Josie left alone.

As an alternative, Janine offered the use of an old push-bike. 'It's a leftover from my student days, but I even oiled it and pumped up the tyres this week. Must have been in a sentimental mood.'

The Quibbley bicycle turned out to be a classic, with a front basket, no crossbar, and only three working gears. It suited my slow and wobbly style perfectly. I pedalled through the dozing village hardly able to credit that I had been shot at not so far away. I was longing to collect my van and try once more to return to a quiet life, but on the outskirts of Miston I ran into a distraction. The forecourt of Woodhouse's Garage, just ahead of me on the other side of the street, was an area of gloom, as it had always been since Ron's death. In contrast there were lights on all over the attached house. In her sentimental overhaul, Janine had forgotten to replace some very worn brake blocks, so I skidded to a halt by putting my feet down. Being cautiously nosey, I shifted myself and the bike into the deep shadow of a hedge which lined the pavement opposite the garage. For the moment nothing happened, but before I could cancel my curiosity and get cycling again, someone slipped through the hedge and put a gloved hand over my mouth. A voice whispered, 'Keep it quiet and come this way, if you please, sir.' The man's official politeness almost made me laugh aloud but I got myself under control and followed him through the gap which he then plugged with a movable section of brambles and branches. In addition to my guide, there were five or six darkly clad figures ranged along the inside of the tall hedge. They looked more like a squad of marines than a bunch of British bobbies. A couple even had camouflaged faces. I was taken over to their boss who said softly, 'I've just been talking to Jan and Josie. So Mr Summing lost his cool, eh?'

'Yeah, thanks to you being here, not down the road.' Wyatt put a warning finger to his lips. I lowered my voice. 'So what's going on over the way?' Before he could speak one of his men made an urgent signal. I followed Wyatt closer to the hedge.

'Look through the existing gap. Don't go rattling the branches about,' he advised me crisply.

I shrugged and obeyed, stepping up to a spy-hole which allowed me a wide-angled view across the way. The front door of Ron's old house stood open and a perfectly fit Ghoul was sauntering towards the garage forecourt. He disappeared briefly behind the workshop building but re-emerged to view beyond the petrol pumps where he gazed south along the main road.

I kept my voice down but muttered angrily all the same, 'That bastard was supposed to be injured!'

Wyatt ignored my comment. He checked his watch and murmured, 'It's still too early. Let's go in the house for a chat.'

The centre of Wyatt's operation was an apple orchard attached to a late-eighteenth-century house on which I had once repaired some loose guttering. The owners, a couple called Bill and Miranda Pallish, seemed thrilled to have a police operation working out of their property. Most of the windows had been blacked out, to disguise a hive of well-lit activity inside. The Pallishes, who were not much older than me, pretended it reminded them of a war they were born several years after. In spite of his commando-style clothing, Wyatt was more like his usual self as we sat nursing mugs of hot cocoa. He said in a drawl, 'You'll find it a late comfort, but Summing wasn't chasing you seriously.'

'When you think you're being shot at with real bullets you don't bloody stop to ask if it's serious! And are you telling me you had someone there?' He nodded. 'Who didn't lift a finger to save us?'

'Since your pursuer turned back quite quickly, our cover didn't have to be broken. Much to the relief of everyone involved further down the line. Just as well Summing needed to get on his way to the Channel to make his rendezvous on time.'

Still annoyed, I asked, 'Didn't your man see him following us into the lane? Josie had twisted her ankle badly. We might easily have been caught.'

'That was my man in the lane, not Summing. And very surprised he was when you took off on a motorbike. So was I when you cornered past us here. Bit of clever pre-planning on your part.'

Feeling perversely disappointed that we had been in less danger than we thought, I said, 'We discovered it by accident—it's Darren's bike that went missing the same time as him. I've hidden it at Janine's.'

If this was of any interest to Wyatt he didn't have time to show it. One of his men, who had been talking on a radio phone in the far corner of the room, called across, 'Courier A is just re-approaching port, skip. C.G. will board Exchange 1 in ten minutes.'

Wyatt took a sip of cocoa and explained. 'The Coast Guard's waiting until Summing thinks he's safe on the home run before impounding your crates.'

'Full of old books!' I said, dismissively.

'Mm. They just might happen to be some items from the Heatherstone Library which were supposed to have been destroyed by water.' He checked his watch. 'Anyway, Courier A should be back with his return cargo in less than half an hour. Unless he stops off for late-night fish and chips.'

The scale of this operation was dawning on me at a rate of knots, as was the extent of inside information which hadn't been shared with us. I also had a new view of Wyatt's official status. The age of the house we were in seemed apt, given that smuggling had been a thriving activity along this coast before and after the year in which Landlord Piggens was legendarily eaten by all the dogs of Miston. Putting on a Long John Silver voice, I challenged Wyatt. 'You be a Cap'n of the Revenue, I'll be bound!'

'Only by secondment, Sam, for a joint effort linking Customs and Excise and a few other interests, including the noble, if sometimes confused, lads of the local CID.'

Since he was starting to come clean, I asked, 'Given the way Summing acted tonight—even if he had to give up chasing us—do you think he killed Darren?'

Wyatt shook his head. 'That one's still a puzzle. Though there still might be some useful prints on the bike. But we think he did kill your friend Ron Woodhouse.'

Twenty minutes later we were back by the hedge. After giving me the not totally surprising information about

Ron's murder, Wyatt had been called away for a series of phone calls and huddled conferences. Our return to the orchard had occurred without my having a chance to put any further questions. But at least, as we stood at adjacent spyholes, Wyatt didn't make me feel I was only there on sufferance.

Almost on cue, Gordon Summing's Range-Rover turned off the main road and cruised down the side of the forecourt, behind the workshop, finally stopping very near the front door of the house. The Ghoul and Clarence came out to help unload—except that the return-trip cargo was able to unload itself.

On the way back from the house Wyatt had slipped me a pair of compact binoculars. I now focused on the four, shiveringly bewildered figures jumping down from the Range-Rover. Three girls and one boy, aged between eight and twelve, as far as one could guess. Their South-East Asian features brought back to my mind in full horror the 'stills' or whatever on the strip of celluloid which the Ghoul had reclaimed from me at the library in Lewes. Clarence ushered the kids into the house while Summing and the Ghoul talked earnestly. Perhaps they were even discussing what might eventually have to be done about Josie and myself, but I didn't care. I wanted to break through the hedge, to rush across and smash the bastards to pieces! Smuggling out old books and papers was nothing compared to this.

No one on our side made a move. Summing got back in his vehicle and drove in an arc, passing even closer before our eyes. 'What the hell are you waiting for?' I hissed.

'He'll be stopped on his merry way home,' Wyatt murmured. 'So calm down.'

'Are you calm?'

'As much as I can be. Now's the time for action. Outrage has to wait.'

And yet all around me was inaction. They—we—waited and waited. And perhaps they—but not I—could keep their minds clear and efficient. This artificially suspended humanity was almost impossible for me to bear. I couldn't help seeing it as a distant reflection of the sheer inhumanity of Summing and his associates. Also, I felt guilty because I had seen that transparent catalogue, displaying the abuse forced on maybe these very children, and I had done nothing about it. Now I was left to wonder, how would the purchasers deal with their 'goods'? Pass them off as newly-adopted members of the family? Or were these modern slave owners rich enough simply to keep their little pleasures hidden away, blackmailed into staying put because they were illegal immigrants? That civilized human beings would even desire such a debased and debasing sexual side-dish was not even a surprise any more. Evidence came to public notice by the week, if not by the day. An active lobby for legalization was probably lurking around the corner. 'Vote for the right to screw any child who takes your fancy!'

'Here!' said Wyatt, and the tissue he was offering me almost shone in the dark. As I dabbed away the tears that had been quietly running down my face, the sound of approaching vehicles evoked almost tangible relief along our side of the hedge.

In an uncanny fashion, four cars turned on to the forecourt in quick sequence, all having driven south from Lewes. As if drilled, they continued on and stopped in a neat, curved line near the house. Assuming their purpose, I burned with hatred towards each driver, but one in particular had me again wishing to smash through the hedge and deliver some form of devastating retribution. Rudolph Wescott appeared almost to be in a fit of schoolboy giggles as he got out of his Volvo and shook hands with the awaiting Ghoul. Wescott, whom I'd seen with his own daughter, whom I had thought well of for his unpatronizing manner with youngsters!

Wyatt and company still didn't make a move, but there was a certain amount of low-voiced chat into mobile phones or radio sets. I only hoped they were setting up absolutely cast-iron road blocks. However, when the newcomers had gone into the house and come back out with a child apiece,

Wyatt patted me on the arm, as if to say it was almost time. It was almost time for me to have kittens! Wescott's Volvo was the car nearest us, and when he had led his dazed female 'import', albeit with his superficial grace and consideration, to be strapped in to one of the back seats, he looked across to our hedge. Beckoning the Ghoul, he said in a voice audible to us, 'What's that bike doing over there, would you say?'

'Leaning against the hedge,' the Ghoul replied perceptively, and less wheezily than usual.

'I hope it doesn't belong to the village bobby,' Wescott said with a chuckle. 'I should hate to think of him waiting to jump out on us.'

And with ruthless timing Francis Wyatt gave his team the 'go' sign, thereby activating a nightmare version of Wescott's simple fear. Not only did the lads and lasses burst forth from the orchard. Moments later, police cars, lights flashing, sirens blaring, also converged from nearby hiding-places, to block off any motorized exit from Woodhouse's Garage. Clarence the biker was as reluctant as ever to be trapped. Seeing there was no way of riding to safety, he scrambled over the bonnet of a police car before the occupants could get out. Wyatt had given me a luminous armband to show my non-criminal status, but having no official orders to follow, I was standing on the pavement side of the hedge feeling frustrated. As soon as Clarence started running towards the heart of Miston village I hopped on to my borrowed bike and gave chase. I must have been going at twice my usual speed by the time my front wheel clipped his heels. Down he crashed, and he gave a terrible squeal as momentum took the bike on up over his back. At least I managed to steer past his head. As a following policeman dragged him to his feet, Clarence clutched his nether regions, glared my way, and croaked, 'Run down by a sodding antique!' I resented this on behalf of myself and the bike, which seemed undamaged as I rode it back to its former resting place.

Over at the garage, all the purchasers had been caught

and arrested. I made a bee-line for the handcuffed Wescott, but Wyatt grabbed me and said, 'Don't go hitting him, Sam. The sort of lawyers he can afford will fuck us for it.'

I promised to behave. Nevertheless, I walked on up to Wescott and said, 'All I hope is no one does to your daughter what you were planning for that kid in the back of your car.'

Wescott said nothing, presumably would continue to say nothing until his solicitor was present. He looked my way, but with no sign of having taken in my remark. Perhaps, behind the blank, unemotional face, he was busy calculating his options, or perhaps the shock of it all had completely emptied his normally scheming head. I didn't have long to think about this because, to my utter disbelief, I spotted the Ghoul standing by the house, unhandcuffed and talking to Wyatt. As I stormed towards them the wheezing voice said, 'I think it's about time you told him, Francis.'

The implications were obvious, but in case I was still about to risk an attack, Wyatt quickly said, 'Sam, this is Detective-Sergeant Ted Griffin.'

'So what happened to Lewis Spencer?'

'He self-destructed the second my colleagues came charging through the hedge. Though your bike gave me a nasty last moment undercover. I thought Wescott was ready to bolt.'

Remembering the number of nasty moments the Ghoul had given me, I didn't apologize. Instead I said, 'Will you answer some questions for me?'

'Maybe.'

'Do you know why Gordon Summing was so keen for me to help him tonight?'

'He was genuinely short-handed.' Griffin, aka the Ghoul, screwed up his eyes. 'But there was more to it than that. He's had this fixation about you for weeks. Reckoned you had lots of skills and qualities going to waste. But he wasn't sure how best to recruit you into the criminal side of his set-up. There's a few times he asked me, "Is Sam Bevan corruptible?"'

'Nice to be wanted, eh?' Wyatt said with a wink.

'Gives me the bloody creeps!' I said, vividly remembering Summing's look in the boat when I pretended that Josie and I were definitely on for corruption.

Griffin added, 'He got his answer when you and Miss Fletcher legged it tonight. Once these poor kids had been collected, I was supposed to meet him back at the farm. To plan how to sort out the two of you.'

'The same way he sorted Ron Woodhouse out?'

'More likely some type of traffic accident. I can't imagine anyone holding down your girlfriend long enough for carbon monoxide fumes to get her. He told me Woodhouse had almost passed out drunk before he was put in his car.'

'In the morning? Ron didn't drink till midday!'

Wyatt said, 'By all accounts he was in a very agitated state, hence those long phone calls. Summing had already been using your friend's house for goods in transit. Including porn videos and drugs.'

'But the pictures on that transparency made him ill. Summing must have killed him for wanting to back out.'

Griffin shook his head. 'He was wanting double the money. To put the pressure on, he stole that strip from Summing's office and threatened to flash it around in public. I was called in to get it back with as little fuss as possible.'

'Ron told me he found it down by the river.'

'No way! And I haven't got all night to talk about the little toe-rag!' Griffin walked briskly away from us and joined the rest of the orchard team who were gathered in a high-spirited circle near the workshop. Uniformed officers were leading the villains across the forecourt to a secure van. The children were talking with great animation to a young woman who appeared to know their language fluently.

'You even had an interpreter ready!' I said to Wyatt, feeling a spark amid my general depression.

'It seemed sensible, since we had a good idea where they

were coming from. You don't speak any oriental dialects, do you?'

'I can hardly even speak French. Look, is it all right for me to push off? I'd like to go on and collect my van from Summing's farm?'

'Sure! And we'll talk tomorrow. Have a drink and relax.' He walked with me across to the bike. 'I can understand you feeling a bit down. I've been hit that way when close colleagues turned out to be on the take. But maybe your mate Ron was in two minds. He let you see those pictures. Perhaps he hoped you would screw up the deal in some way.'

A clear but negative memory came to me. 'After your undercover sergeant got the transparency back, Ron persuaded me it was pointless going to the police. That doesn't show much of a guilty conscience, does it?'

Wyatt patted me on the shoulder. 'Never mind. You've done your bit, since. Now you deserve a good sleep. Like the rest of us.'

As I got on his lady-friend's bike, I asked, 'Just one thing—is your Lewes office in somewhere called Ladd's Court?'

'Yep.'

'I spotted Lewis Spencer as he was called then coming out of Ladd's Court weeks and weeks ago.'

'Just as well I only told you the phone number, then. Last thing I would have wanted was a country gumshoe rumbling one of the best undercover jobs I've ever known.'

The van was where I'd left it. But it wasn't alone. As I gave up cycling and started to push the bike up the last half of Summing's private road, I noticed the sidelights of an unfamiliar car in the dairy yard. My first impulse was to retreat. Sheer exhaustion would prevent me doing one last battle with some leftover of the criminal empire. Then I remembered that I hadn't given Wyatt back his mini-binoculars. I focused on the yard and saw a uniformed arm stretching from the car window to throw away a cigarette. This gave me cause for relief, and for more alarm. If this was the official police reception, Gordon Summing hadn't come back to base. In fact, he might well have spotted unexpected visitors even further down the link road than I did. The dairy yard was on a rise which allowed it to be seen from the main road turn-off point, and Summing was the possesion of some very powerful field glasses.

I glumly pressed on and spoilt the quiet vigil being enjoyed by the two waiting officers. Given that Summing left the garage an hour back, I asked why they hadn't wondered at his non-appearance. 'Nobody told us how long he'd be,' one of them said.

The other added, 'And that arm-band doesn't mean you can tell us our job! Sir!'

'OK,' I said, slightly embarrassed that I hadn't taken the arm-band off. 'Is it all right if I take my van and go?' I received a grunt for an answer. They were too busy discussing how best to let their boss know that Gordon Summing could well be in the next county by now, if not somewhere out to sea.

I stored Janine's bike in the back of the van and slumped into the driving seat. At least my engine started without a fuss. As I backed and turned, the police car's radio was transmitting a few angry words from Francis Wyatt. I didn't bother to wave goodbye but drove off at a careful speed. At the junction with the main road I paused to wind my window right down. Then I set off again, hoping the flow of night air would keep me alert all the way home. Half a mile later my drowsiness was banished completely. I realized that the vehicle behind me was a Range-Rover, and its driver had no intention of travelling at a safe distance.

CHAPTER 26

Rear-View Terror

'Can't you just think it over?' I yelled. But, even if he could have heard me, it was clearly too late for anyone to tell Gordon Summing to calm down and get rational. The man had decided that my being a protégé who didn't live up to expectations was a capital offence. During at least thirty minutes in which he could have been speeding away from capture, he must have been determinedly waiting for me to come and fetch my van. This suggested that I above all others was being blamed for the unravelling of his Grand Criminal Design. The shots fired in the field, even if his pursuit of Josie and me was short-lived, had already hinted that he was dangerously unhinged. Now he had moved on to the stage described by Sergeant Griffin, aka Lewis Spencer, aka the Ghoul, as fixing 'some type of traffic accident'.

'Why me?'

That's what I shouted when the Range-Rover drove its grid of nudge bars against the rear doors of my van. He clearly didn't care that we were charging back into an area where the Law would be waiting in great numbers. Or perhaps he thought I would be trapped in a burning wreck before we got that far.

'Why me?'

Another mile of this, supposing I did stay on the road, and my poor old van would be concertina-ed a few feet shorter than when I started out. Yes, I knew this was structurally impossible, but I was reaching a stage of panic when only a surreal salvation was worth clinging to.

'Why me, you sodding idiot!?'

This time the nudge nearly made the van swerve out of control. It rattled against the overhanging hedge on my left for a minute or so, collecting a few leafy branches which blanked out half my windscreen. Fortunately, the air flow drove them off quite quickly. At least Mother Nature was on my side.

'Where the hell *is* everyone?'

There were no other cars on the road. There hadn't been any when I cycled to the dairy. This had to be because the cops had sealed it off and set up a diversion. But where the hell were they when I needed them again?

'Oh—for fuck's sake!'

Both my back windows shattered under the same impact. Thank heavens Eddie wasn't riding with me. Or Josie. Or my mother and father. Or anyone else who was dear to me, but I wasn't going to get into that one. Summing was pissing me off too much for me to start saying mental goodbyes! Instead, I started swerving from side to side of the entire road-space on purpose. Immediately, I felt I'd hit on something. The bigger vehicle didn't seem able to follow my snaking path. It even dropped back—for all of twenty seconds. As Summing roared back into close contact I realized he had only been checking if my steering had gone haywire. Since I had only been showing off he was determined to hit me harder than ever.

'Aaaaagh!'

The shock wave got me right at the base of the spine. The mental after-shock threw up an image of the best I could hope for out of all this—the rest of my life in a wheelchair. All because of my failure to read between the lines of this weird man's rambling conversations, to sense how much he wanted to recruit me into his evil world.

'Hang on!'

This time I hadn't been bumped. We were coming up fast to the gateway which led to Summing's boathouse, and the police must have been checking if he had made his escape by river. A patrol car was nosing outwards through the gate as I was chased by. And suddenly our hectic convoy got longer, though the flashing light and the whirring siren behind him had no effect on Summing's bad habits.

I was hit twice more before I saw the road block ahead.

Stopping at a road block might be possible if you haven't got a murderous farmer/smuggler driving tight on your rear end. Otherwise you have to crash and probably die, or in this case, execute a screeching corner in through the nearest open gate. The gate in question led me into an all too familiar field, and my van was suddenly bouncing along in the rough direction of a set of outbuildings I wished I had never designed. Summing's vehicle clumsily followed, having ricocheted off a metal gatepost. Possibly there were police vehicles immediately on his tail, but I didn't have time to check. I was too busy coping with the realization that my van was stuck. The front wheels had gone down into a drainage channel whose presence I might have remembered in the light of an unflustered day.

All the witnesses in the world weren't going to stop Gordon Summing. I jumped clear by way of the passenger door and ran in the direction of the outbuildings. My hope was that his concentration would be totally on the van, that he wouldn't spot me in the dark, at least until I was climbing to safety up one of the exterior ladders. Instead, he swerved away from a final vehicle-on-vehicle collision at the very last second, and his headlamps caught my fleeing figure full in the back. I still ran on, chasing my shortening shadow as Summing continued to drive after me. And then came a series of wrenches and clatters which had me turn my head, miss my footing and crash to the ground. The Range-Rover's nudge bars, loosened by too many impacts, had slipped and then skewed into a tangle with the front right wheel. As the tyre became shredded and the four-wheel drive was reduced to three, Summing found himself veering almost at full tilt into a corner of the outbuildings.

Within seconds I found myself being half carried away from the crash area. At the same time a couple of officers moved slowly in with extinguishers at the ready. But the Range-Rover didn't burst into flames. There was just a certain amount of hissing from the mangled engine, while no sound at all came from Gordon Summing. A gesture from the first policeman to go close suggested that this silence wasn't that of a man waiting for his solicitor.

CHAPTER 27

Day of Rest

In the small hours of Sunday morning, Francis Wyatt gave me a lift to the bungalow. We found Janine and Josie in a state of half-dozing neurosis. It was good to be welcomed like a returning warrior, but since everyone was exhausted, the de-briefing was kept short. Subject to official requirements we all agreed to meet for lunch at the pub. As Wyatt drove away after dropping us home, Josie asked, 'D'you reckon that futon's just for show?'

'No. We saw him lying on it earlier.'

'You know what I mean.'

'Yeah, I know, but I don't know. Come on.' Eddie ran ahead while I helped Josie to limp up the path. Once we were through the front door I was hardly aware of how we got up to and into bed. I'd never been so tired in my life. And I had no dreams—at least, none that I could remember.

The phone started to ring at around 8.50 and when it didn't stop for over a minute I guessed that it might be my ex-wife.

'How could you, after all this time?' Rosemary yelled down the line.

'How could I what?'

'You know damn well. He's got an ulcer. And chronic indigestion. Heartburn, he calls it. Means he's always having to nip off to the bathroom. Leaves a nasty smell, even when what he brings up has been flushed away.'

'Do I have to have these details?'

'Serves you right!' And she let her outrage flow until it merged with a lecture on the gratitude I owed her for persuading her lover not to publish his story about 'The Vicar's Wife and her Secret Admirer'. As it happened, I'd already felt an occasional twinge of guilt about hitting the guy, and when she finally shut up I made a peace offering. 'If Clive's still hanging around down this end I'll fill him in on last night's excitement.'

'What sort of night's excitement? *Are* you up to something with this Mrs Vicar?'

'Forget all that. I'm talking about my first-hand experiences as a temporary private eye. Clive will be able to write under the headline: "Tycoon Arrested in Midnight Child Prostitution Swoop".'

'Thanks for reminding me!' Rosemary said sharply.

'Eh?'

'Just now and then I forget the main reason I had to leave you. You always despised my profession. Never lost a chance to send journalism up!'

'But . . .' But she had already hung up, on the sort of misunderstanding that had been quite common between us.

I let Eddie out into the garden and crept back up the stairs. On this occasion it was unlikely Josie had been listening in. When I got into bed she rolled over and gave me a nuzzling kiss before curling up again in comfortable sleep. No such luck for me. After ten minutes of failing to conquer a vague restlessness I decided to get dressed. I would go and buy one of those newspapers whose writers I apparently despised.

'Thought I might as well check my "reviews",' Steve Philpot murmured sheepishly. He was before me in the queue at the Miston Stores, buying several papers. When we were outside I sat with him on the rustic bench while he read through various versions of his release. He pointed out a few misquotes and omissions in the reported statements from himself and Chief Inspector Niles, who was in charge of the murder inquiry. In the end, he gave a great sigh. 'Oh well, more or less what I expected. I come across as a typical, batty Anglican cleric, searching for some sort of martyrdom.'

'So what were you up to, confessing to a crime you didn't commit?'

'Will you walk up to the church with me?' he asked, standing. He didn't wait for an answer, but I decided to catch up with him.

'You weren't wet or muddy enough to have just drowned someone when you came to my house that night.'

'Wasn't I? I got pretty close to the edge when I threw what was left of that stupid skeleton in. But you're quite right, and the police came to the same conclusion quite early in their questioning. They decided I had confessed because I was afraid my wife was involved in the murder. And they kept hammering away to get me to admit it. It wasn't until quite late on that they got their way.'

'But they haven't arrested Dora yet!' And how could he speak calmly of a possibility which I'd stubbornly refused to entertain?

'That's because the police don't think she did it, either. I was questioned over several sessions and eventually the Chief Inspector kicked one off by saying he'd just received information which officially placed Dora away from the scene of the crime.'

'Could have been a trick.'

'I know, my dear friend, especially as they wouldn't tell me where she had been, or who she might have been with. But I broke down and admitted to making a false confession. After that, all they were interested in was as much detail as I could remember of what I saw down by the river. I was allowed some hours of sleep, in the hope my memory would be refreshed. I doubt if I gave them much further help.'

'It must have been a hellish experience,' I said tritely. We had reached the gate to the churchyard and I didn't follow him through.

He turned with a cheery grin. 'But the future will be better. There'll be difficulties, of course, but I'm determined to make a fresh start. So before I begin acting as though the past few months never happened, I want to thank you from the bottom of my heart. Dora told me how kind and helpful you and young Josie were.' At this point Mr Ainsly came out of the church and gave a wave. The old boy's loyal affection for his vicar seemed unshakeable. Steve, switching fully into his priestly mode said, 'Must go and get ready. There'll probably be a bigger congregation than usual. But perhaps a few who come for the gossip "will stay to pray".' Then he passed his newspapers over the gate, asking, 'Would you do me one more favour and drop these off at the vicarage? Dora's up and about. Get her to give you coffee and some cake.' And he strode off to talk with his caretaker. The previous night's events would probably push him off the front page by Monday morning, but I was glad he hadn't given me a chance to mention them. His manner suggested that he was enjoying his notoriety just a little.

Before I could carry out my duties as paper-boy, Eddie made a lolloping emergence from the alley just across from the churchyard. It was unusual for him to run loose like this. Since my garden was separated only by a narrow footpath from the rear spread of one of the grander houses in Church Lane, it was possible my voice had carried through. Certainly he was pleased to reach me. As I leaned over to stroke him, I remembered that he would have started off on the same route the night he didn't quite come to our rescue. Cutting through into Church Lane after coming down the side of the old Manor House he would have turned right and run past Janine's bungalow, past the vicarage and on almost as far as the village green before rounding the Miston Stores corner into our street.

On an earlier night still, I had watched as Dora set off from my garden on the same first stage, except that—since she didn't want to go straight home—she must have turned left into Church Lane and headed towards the Downs. That way she would have avoided the risk of Steve seeing her as she passed her own front door. She wasn't to know he had already set out in the direction of the river.

In her letter Dora wrote that she had walked for miles and miles. Viewed generously this had to be an exaggeration. Soon after she set out, perhaps in the small wooded area beyond the top of Church Lane, she would have met up with the person who, even back then, was under surveillance from one of Francis Wyatt's team. A person who, for reasons of discretion, had left his car in the next street, not far from my house.

The doorbell had been reconnected and Dora, having checked from an upper window, came down and let me and Eddie in. She showed no interest at all in the newspapers and tossed them on to the hall table. I realized my own paper was mixed up among them, but when I mentioned this, she said, 'You can pick it up on the way out. Come on through.' We followed her into the kitchen where she filled a bowl with water and put it down for the dog. I wasn't offered a coffee. Or cake.

'At least the Press have pushed off,' I said.

'Yes, they all went by late afternoon, but it's been ridiculously hectic in the lane this morning. The police were outside next door first thing, loading a motorbike into the back of a van.

'Ah.'

'Obviously something you know about.'

'Josie and I rode up this way on it last night. After Gordon Summing took a few pot shots at us.' She said nothing. 'It's Darren's bike. We found it hidden near your old meeting place. Whoever killed him stuffed it in the nettles behind the rusted car.'

She gave a dry laugh. 'Well, it wasn't me. For some reason the police know I was somewhere else.'

'They know where you were because they were keeping tabs on Summing. Who had decided to take over from his errand-boy as your pill supplier. Which is the real reason you made it to his party. You haven't given them up. Right?'

She shook her head. 'Right and wrong! You see, I was greedy in those days. I wanted the pills and I wanted you. Now I'll just have to settle for the pills, won't I? There's damn-all else in my life.'

'I'm sorry, Dora . . .' But I couldn't get the rest of the words out. She would have to learn from someone else that Summing was dead, that she would have to find herself a new supplier. In the depths of her misery, Dora's face took on an extraordinary, unearthly beauty which, because it was fuelled by her addiction, I could hardly bear to look at. I shifted my gaze to the window. Over the back garden wall Mrs Leigh-Harcourt was pottering about near the trellis I'd put up for her.

'I expect you'll be wanting to get on,' Dora said, and she walked back through to the front door, though she didn't open it immediately. When I caught up with her she slipped her arms around me and murmured, 'Just one more for the road?' The rosebud lips pouted, and then curved in a genuine, warm smile, and then opened slightly. As we locked into the deepest, most passionate goodbye kiss I had ever experienced, Eddie started to make a grim noise, a cross between a whine and a growl. We ignored him for a full minute, but his persistence finally caused the embrace to end in strained laughter. 'Obviously Josie's been training him when your back was turned.'

'I wish I'd left him out in the drive.'

'But you didn't, so I want you to leave quickly, while I can still imagine we were that close to making love again.' And she opened the door and gently pushed us on our way.

I walked back to my house feeling depressed and guilty in several directions. After running up to the bathroom and quickly washing my face, I joined Josie in the kitchen, and she did offer to make coffee. 'I thought you must have gone to get a paper,' she said.

'I did. I've left it at the vicarage.' And I gave her a skeletal version of my meeting with Steve Philpot and having to drop his newspapers off. If I hadn't been starting a summer cold I might have anticipated Josie's eventual response.

'If you're determined to keep seeing her, you ought to tell Dora that posh perfume's a dead giveaway.' I bent my head forward and sniffed. The scent came faintly through. 'And talking of your other women, someone claiming to be your ex-wife rang.'

'Again? She called earlier to yell at me for hitting her bloke.'

'Well, this time the message is—"Clive will be round to see you as soon as possible"—and another bit which I didn't understand—why didn't you tell her you *weren't* pulling her leg?'

Both bars at the One-in-the-Eye were like a madhouse. The pub was busy on any normal weekend, but extra visitors had come because of our famous vicar, and the Press brigade were back in full. To Clive Buxton's annoyance, I wouldn't let myself be spirited away to a secret hotel until my story had been published. But I did speak to him in detail before going to the pub, and I promised not to give too much away to any other newshounds. Even on these terms, my financial situation would be comfortable for the near future. Josie had refused to stay around and talk about her part in any of it. Clive lost his chance the moment he had revealed his interest in her as Darren's ex-girlfriend. I also refused to talk about that angle, but I knew there was no chance of it being totally suppressed.

Ralph the fisherman and ex-forecourt attendant had got the gossip machine going strong before I arrived in the public bar, but not all the talk was about 'the Special Branch shoot-out at Woodhouse's Garage'. Albert and Alfred had been to church and revealed that, facing a huge congregation, our vicar had cheated expectations and not lapsed into any pulpit revelations.

'He played a straight bat right through the innings,' Albert said glumly.

'The sermon might as well have been delivered by horse and cart,' Alfred added more obscurely.

'But did you stay to pray?' I asked.

'What? And risk losing our seats if we weren't down here the moment Tony Koerner opened up?' It was Alfred who spoke, but both of them turned their sightless gaze on me in pity. I decided I had better re-establish my sanity by buying them a drink. Our landlord was looking harassed, but he brushed aside several angry customers to serve me quickly.

'Is Josie in the next bar?' I asked him, having failed to find her in the public mob.

'She's saving my life in the next bar,' Tony said. 'Marianne's not well again. She only lasted ten minutes down in this chaos. And the latest girl's so slow I could brew a pint in the time she takes to pull one.' As I brought out a note he added, 'Those are on the house. But please don't drink them too quickly!'

The illnesses of Marianne Koerner were something I thought about as I slowly levelled my beer. Could it be that this latest one was genuine, triggered by the news that her friend Gordon Summing was dead? That true fact was circulating amid Ralph's exaggerations and miss-hits. Also, some of the journalists had cottoned on to the discovery of Darren's bike. Would that detail have shaken up Marianne, proven frequenter of the riverbank? If Darren had, say, been blackmailing her, might she have gone and poisoned the Vicar's ear with tales of the dirt lane meetings in the hope that Steve would sort the lad out? And when that tactic didn't bear fruit, was our landlady moved to act for herself?

Just as I finished my first drink, Janine and Wyatt arrived and the three of us transferred to the restaurant bar. On the way I said to Wyatt, 'Can we talk shop a bit —after lunch?'

'Definitely after lunch, please,' Janine said. 'He's been on the phone all bloody morning, and he's off away this afternoon.'

By now we were surveying the unlikelihood of getting a table. 'I thought you would have been around for a while, wrapping up details.'

'Unfortunately, I have people to do that for me.'

'Like whoever tailed Dora and Summing the night of Darren's murder?'

'Stop it! Or I walk out!' And in no way was Janine joking.

I apologized and asked what they would like to drink. The clamour for service was worse than next door and Josie didn't give me preferential treatment. While I was waiting, Tony Koerner came through and asked his slow barmaid to take over in the public bar for a couple of minutes. He was holding a hand tight against his abdomen and seemed to be in quite some pain. Moments after he had gone through the inner door a loud clatter could be heard. For the first time, Josie looked at me directly. 'Will you go and see what's up?'

I ducked under the bar flap and went through to find Koerner slumped on the stairs. He let me help him to his feet and we progressed slowly up the stairs. 'I've never gone on about it,' he groaned. 'But this bloody stomach of mine's been giving me hell for months.'

'Haven't you seen a doctor?'

'Haven't I just! Take it easy, he says. Cut down on the stress and you'll be right as rain.' Once we were at the bathroom door, he lurched through, fell to his knees and belched into the lavatory bowl. Even the constraints of my cold couldn't keep at bay acrid fumes exactly like those I had first smelled weeks ago in a Brighton bathroom.

'Pathetic, isn't it?' I almost jumped out of my skin as Marianne Koerner brushed by me and shouted at her husband, 'If they don't find your prints on the bike I've decided to tell them anyway.' And she brushed by me again. On the landing she came face to face with Josie and said, 'Darren was a lying, cheating, petty criminal, but he still made me feel more loved than that prissy thing in there ever did.'

Tony Koerner pulled himself to his feet at the same time

as he flushed the toilet. When he grimly looked at me, I said, 'You were sick like that at Darren's flat, weren't you? And then you hid away when I turned up. Why on earth did you go there?'

'Because I suspected that romantic hardcase out there had written love-letters to him! And I was right.' He wiped his face on a towel which he then folded carefully and draped over the side of the bath. 'Now I must ask you to take yourself back downstairs and on to the other side of the bar, Sam. This part of my public house is private.'

On the one hand, I felt inclined to let Darren's killer have what would be his last minute or two of chosen privacy. On the other hand, I worried about what he might try to do. Turning towards the landing, I found no guidance. Marianne and Josie were clinging to each other—presumably in belated, shared love and grief for Darren—and for a split second I felt utterly alone. Then an impatient Tony Koerner pushed me out of the bathroom and bolted the door. Rational bargaining was out of the question. I stood back, took aim and drove the base of my foot at a point just under the door handle. It almost gave, but before I could try again, Francis Wyatt shifted me to one side while Chief Inspector Niles shouldered the door open.

As soon as I could see that Tony Koerner was in comparatively good health I left them to it. I felt no desire to witness a formal arrest, though a few of the words followed me down the stairs. Back in the bar, I looked around for Janine Quibbley. I suddenly shared her craving for a break from crime and all its side-shows. But she had gone.

CHAPTER 28

Tail End

From the top of the church tower the graveyard seemed like the lay-out for some mysterious board game. Even the stones which lay flat were too far away for my eyes to make out their writing, so they looked merely like safe areas on to which one's counter might move if the dice rolled favourably. Only three graves stood out against this idle fantasy. That of my aunt whose house I was back to sharing only with Eddie the Puritan, and those of Ron and Darren.

My companion on the tower was also getting used to living alone in these late summer days, but desertion by his wife had had one extraordinary effect on the Revd Steve Philpot. He no longer suffered from vertigo. Though it was only when he had done 'test heights', first by climbing a stepladder and then by walking with me up a particularly steep slope in the Downs, that I agreed to return to the scene of our near disaster.

'Do you hear from Dora at all?' I asked.

'The occasional postcard. She and her sister are in Geneva at the moment.'

'I thought they'd fallen out.'

'Only because of me. Now they're happily back to being poor little rich girls together.' An edge of bitterness made me wish I hadn't opened my mouth, but he went on, 'The amount I miss her decreases significantly by the day, Sam. And when I move to the college it will be easier still.' He was about to leave what he called 'active ministry' and take a teaching job abroad. 'It must be much harder for you, with young Josie still here in the village.'

I smiled. 'Her being "young" Josie was one of the problems. And in a way we only got together through force of circumstance. We were both still . . .'

'In love with someone else?'

'That sort of thing. But it isn't so bad as all that. At least neither of us has started up with a new partner yet.'

'And she's actually living at the pub now?'

'Yep. Which meant I had to make a crucial decision—either to give up drinking, or to suffer seeing Josie every day. So it's just as well we've stayed friends.'

Josie, as my good pal, was sometimes a nuisance. While she herself had gladly retired from sleuthing to become Marianne Koerner's business partner at the pub, she refused to believe I had also finished with detective work. Now and then she would advise customers who mentioned a problem well outside the normal scope of odd-jobbery to come to me. She had even convinced Laurel Glover that I was the one who had really identified her son's murderer. In truth, Wyatt and Co. had already been 99% sure, but wanted to keep it to themselves until their complex operation was wrapped up. Chief Inspector Niles and his boys were apparently not pleased to learn weeks after the event that Gordon Summing's tail had spotted a dishevelled Tony Koerner coming out of the dirt lane. Poor old Tony, who wished for a whole world as neat and tidy as his normal self, had also been seen by the man being tailed. And, after Darren's body had been found, the mourning Marianne had sought comfort from one of the few people who could more or less confirm her own suspicions.

When Steve Philpot and I were back on solid ground he said, 'Thank you, Sam, for your patience and friendship. And your courage. After what happened up the tower before, I wouldn't have blamed you for keeping well clear of me.'

'You were under stress back then.'

'I was in a living hell,' he said grimly, and left it at that. Some weeks earlier, just after Dora had gone off, he had given me a fuller account of his life on the rack, torn by sexual jealousy and by the dread he hadn't been able to admit when he came to me for help, that his wife's drug cure had lapsed. No wonder he was driven out of his wits.

I now followed him into the churchyard where he gazed at the nearest gravestones. Softly he quoted:

> 'The boast of heraldry , the pomp of power,
> And all that beauty, all that wealth e'er gave,
> Awaits alike th'inevitable hour:
> The paths of glory lead but to the grave.'

Since it didn't sound exactly biblical I made the other standard guess. 'Shakespeare?'

'Thomas Gray. From his *Elegy Written in a Country Churchyard*. I suppose we both have reason to be in an elegiac mood.'

If elegiac meant gloomy, that's certainly how I felt as we parted company. I left him going back into the church and headed home. Work was slack, but by the time I'd collected Eddie it would be opening time. I did have a fitness regime in mind, but the starting date kept being moved back a week.

'D'yous want a job, mister?'

The soft Scottish accent was one I hadn't heard for five weeks. Dr Quibbley had been away to the North to see her mother, and then she had flown direct to Portugal for a history conference, or so she claimed on the back of a picture of an Algarve beach.

'Are you serious?'

'Am I ever! I get back ten minutes ago and what do I find outside my kitchen door?'

'Tell me, Janine.'

'Two tea-chests full of books, with the feeblest of weatherproofing over their tops. Just as well there's been less rain here than I suffered in the Iberian Peninsula.'

I walked around the bungalow with her and saw what she meant. 'The illegal Heatherstone shipment was in smaller boxes than that.'

'These are my own books, dumped here by that bloody dentist it was my misfortune to co-habit with. Help me into the house with them and I'll buy you lunch.'

'Let me treat you. I've lots of ill-gotten newspaper money left.'

'OK. As a matter of fact, I'm completely broke. But you still have to lend me your muscles.'

Half an hour later, with Eddie in the back seat, Janine was aiming her Metro out of the village. We had decided on a pub lunch in Woolfield, the other side of the river. We had also decided that there should be no conversation about Francis Wyatt, Josie Fletcher, Dora Philpot, Rudolph Wescott, Gordon Summing, the Heatherstone Library, or anything generally to do with love or crime.

'It'll be an interesting test of our friendship, to see if, under these rules, we lapse into total silence.' Janine said this while moving up to fifty m.p.h. still in a built-up area. Suddenly there was a wrenching and clattering which gave me a shuddering reminder of a recent car chase. She brought the Metro to a screeching halt and we both looked behind us. Once Eddie had been made to duck down, we could see the car's rust-ridden exhaust pipe lying fifty yards back.

'Whoops!' I said.

'Och, well!' was her response, and she fetched up her bag which had been stuffed under the dashboard on my side of the car. From the bag she pulled a neat, black portable telephone.

'That's new,' I said.

'Newish. I got it before I went away.'

'How much did it cost?'

'What's it with all these questions? I thought you were Sam Bevan, ex-detective?' I shrugged, and she half smiled. 'If you must know, it was a present. From someone who's always on the move.'

I stopped myself suggesting it should be the man-on-the-move who had the mobile phone. Instead I asked, 'Are you calling the AA?'

'Bugger the AA. Since you're so rich, I'm calling a taxi. I want my lunch!'

THE END